SALOME BOOK 2

The GOOD WIFE

JACK A. TAYLOR

 FriesenPress

One Printers Way
Altona, MB R0G 0B0
Canada

www.friesenpress.com

Copyright © 2023 by Jack A Taylor, PhD
First Edition — 2023

Scripture texts are from the NIV 2011

ISBN
978-1-03-915080-5 (Hardcover)
978-1-03-915079-9 (Paperback)
978-1-03-915081-2 (eBook)

1.Fiction, Christian

Distributed to the trade by The Ingram Book Company

❧ FAMILY TREE ๑

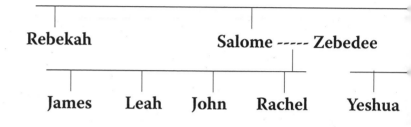

SALOME'S FAMILY

Heli (Joachim) ------- Anna

Rebekah   Salome ----- Zebedee

James   Leah   John   Rachel   Yeshua

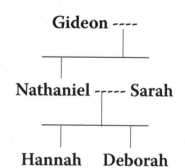

NATHANIEL'S FAMILY

Gideon ----

Nathaniel ----- Sarah

Hannah   Deborah

ZEBEDEE'S FAMILY

Hadassah   Judith   Zebedee -----Salome

James   Leah   John   Rachel

Mariam -----Yuseph

Assia   James   Joseph   Elizabeth   Simon   Judas

Diana   Dinah   Donna

MAIN CHARACTERS

Residents of Nazareth

Heli and Ana—parents of Rebekah, Salome and Mariam

Gideon—gatekeeper and father of Nathaniel the shepherd

Hosea and Shoshanna—butcher and village gossip

Lydia—potter's sister and Zealot messenger

Roman centurions based in Sepphoris

Marcus Valerius Suetonius

Anthony Brutus Vassilius

Zealots

David (Ox)—self-proclaimed local leader, based out of Nazareth

Hiram (Leopard)

Jonathan (Wolf)

Thomas (Stag)

Judas the Galilean—Messianic-type regional leader

Parthians

Pacorus—soldier and messenger

Darius—Leah's love interest

Table of Contents

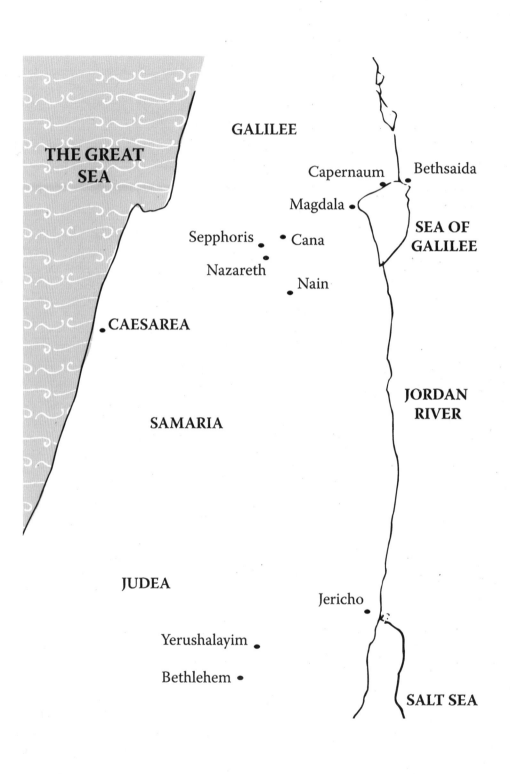

CHAPTER ONE

Capernaum / Nazareth – Unwelcome Intruders

Being good might get her loved but could it keep her alive? Right now, staying alive seemed a distant hope for Salome. "Wait! I mean no harm," she called out. The quivering arrow three feet above her head pierced the illusion of peace. "Good wife, daughter, mother, and freedom fighter," was a poor epitaph on a tombstone. Especially when love wasn't a guarantee from the person that really mattered.

The arrow, now embedded in the oak tree, vibrated alone as she raised her face out of the dirt. Her red scarf, skewered by the missile, flapped violently in the wind. Death never sends invitations. At least not in the Galil. Her instincts, from years of Zealot training, had saved her this time. In the past two years she had lived discreetly. Did the arrow mean she had been found out? Invisibility had vanished as an option.

A moment before, she'd been jabbering to her black dog as it sat, tongue lolling out, head cocked as if in rapt attention. "Being good isn't an option for me," she'd said. "If your older sister was raped by Romans, your younger sister was unwed, pregnant and still insisting she was a virgin because some angel talked with her, and if your parents forced you to marry a fisherman to save you, you know goodness is a duty. Honor demands it." She had plucked a handful of berries and put them in her basket. "I just hope my Zealot friends understand. A dozen children have gone missing and they think I can help them. I'm too old for those kinds of adventures." She had then attempted to step over the hound but it jumped up and sent her stumbling into the bush.

Annoyed, she had snarled, "Be good and go home!" She'd dusted herself off as the arrow hit the tree. Now, her face was in the dust again.

Tumbling storm clouds charged over the hills like hungry dragons. Her heart thumped in her temples as she held her breath. Fingernails dug into the palms of her clenched fists. She eyed the arrow, listened as the dog raced off, exhaled, rolled, and rose to stand behind the tree. "Just breathe," she coached herself. Humidity wrapped its cloak around her and the earthy, oily scent of coming rain sprouted. A trickle of sweat snaked down her spine. She'd tolerated the dog racing around her feet long enough and the burrs from thistles clung to her tunic like locusts on a wheat field. Her husband, Zebedee, would be waiting for his fish stew and the boys would be driving him crazy. If only she didn't have to go home. Not like this.

Death was here. Like a hand groping forward in the darkness toward its prey. Salome trembled. Silence vibrated through the trees, interrupted only by her gasp. A bark to her right stopped short with a yelp. She waited several minutes then examined the arrow embedded in the tree. Was it Parthian? The feathering appeared that way. Who was out there? There was no movement visible. She ripped her scarf away from the shaft of the razor-edged projectile. Three deep breaths shook off the fear.

She crouched, crawled toward the basket she had dropped earlier, gathered the scattered jasmine and tubers, then regulated her breathing. She bent low and raced toward the direction of the last yelp.

Her sprint along the deer trail was halted by the body of the dog. A half-buried arrow lodged in the soggy mane. The heartbeat pounding in her ears quickened as a tremor passed through her hand. She yanked the arrow free. It matched the one in the tree. What was going on?

The bony ribs protruding from matted fur lay still. Amazingly thin and fragile when no longer part of a bouncing, barking, slobbering guardian. A bent yellow camphor-weed flower quivered under the animal's front paw. "So much for being good," she muttered.

James, now ten and the eldest among her sons, loved the dog. He had no idea of the risks she took to protect him and to rescue other children who had been snatched from their families but he would not easily forgive this loss. The boy bucked her authority like a penned wild stallion and needed a firmer hand than her husband Zebedee's to gentle him. Their limestone-block house lay hidden beyond the sprawling market buildings near the water. It seemed an unbridgeable distance with an invisible archer at work.

The boy and his siblings played for the afternoon at their aunt Diana's, knowing only that their mother hunted for mushrooms, tubers, and berries. Her eight-year-old daughter, Leah was no doubt bossing her younger brother John around. Innocence flourished despite danger.

"Stay away from the lake and don't fight," Salome had warned. In truth, she needed space. Her slingshot had proved to be a helpful distraction as she targeted the young locusts alighting on the new growth. Would she need it now? It wouldn't do much against a skilled archer.

Rain drops pattered on the leaves. Dark spots dotted her olive tunic. An indigo sheet of liquid spent itself across the lake and unleashed its fury on the basalt hills beyond. Disposing of the dog would have to wait. She turned toward the outskirts of Capernaum below. Smoke tendrils drifted up the hill from the lakeshore to mark the fishing community. Boats were beached and the nets stretched out on drying racks in preparation for the evening ahead. The shower didn't last long and the sun burst forth. Breathing deep, she slowed her pace. The citrus and jasmine fragrances gave the illusion of peace and freedom despite the chaos surging from Herod's reign.

~ ~ ~

Nathaniel ben Gideon glanced briefly toward Capernaum as the dark clouds spent their feeble fury over the lake. "Why can't you drop a little moisture over here?" he muttered. His sheep crowded each other for the tender shoots of grass pushing up through the gray sandy loam and the reddish-brown clay. He could use some of that rain closer to Nazareth. He nudged an ewe with his shepherd's crook and limped quickly toward a curious lamb straying into a crevice in the cliff rising up toward his village. A dozen sheaves of straw rested there among a scattering of boulders.

The Romans had been busy today. First had come the legionnaires questioning his townspeople about the sabotage of the aqueduct providing fresh water to Sepphoris. The burgeoning metropolis being resurrected on the adjacent hill to Nazareth was Herod Antipas's crown jewel to provide protection against potential Parthian invaders. The Parthians from ancient Persia had recently controlled the land until ousted by the Romans. Anticipation was high that they would try to reclaim the land to provide a way for their silk trade.

A great paddlewheel near Sepphoris, designed to elevate the water from a spring up to the wooden troughs sloping into the city reservoirs, had been damaged when thick logs had been jammed into the spokes. None of the local guards had seen anything and the Romans had no doubt the Zealots were responsible. The dust from a cohort of galloping cavalrymen had only just settled.

Bedouin caravans featuring dozens of camels loaded with spices and other cravings desired by the empire eased through his herd without pause but hardly disturbed the dust. The desert nomads strolled alongside their beasts of burden in sleeveless woolen cloaks, white tunics, and colorful head coverings. Their rhythmic stride and proud stature drew attention from pilgrims, traders, and businessmen who pulled aside their own donkey and ox carts to let the newcomers pass.

A shepherd boy, Nahum, perched on a rocky outcropping part way up the cliff, watched the cavalry disappear over the crest of a hill and then scampered down and approached Nathaniel. He bowed to the shepherd and waited for the return nod giving him permission to speak. It was given.

"Thank you for guarding the freedom fighters through your silence," he said. "You will not be forgotten." The boy pulled out a small wooden sword and flashed it back and forth at an imaginary foe. "One day I will face the Roman champion and free our people. Never will we have to hide away again."

"I only seek peace," Nathaniel said. "The greatest foe you will ever face is the one inside you where a sword cannot reach."

The boy frowned then knelt to run his fingers through the wool of a lamb. "You have the best job. We will call you again if we need a distraction." He stood and stared toward Sepphoris. "The occupiers have taken my uncle Abraham and we had to make a statement. They force our men to work and they steal our girls for their pleasures. Those who resist are taken in the night."

Nathaniel unstopped a small gourd, poured water into his cupped hand, and lowered it for the lamb to suck up. "I'm afraid that the Romans may make the final statement with their crosses if you continue."

The boy shrugged and let out a low whistle.

THE GOOD WIFE

As Nathaniel turned toward home a bearded head emerged from the straw sheaves by the crevice in the cliff. The full figure emerged and soon half a dozen others followed, brushing off the debris clinging to their tan tunics. Within minutes the group retrieved a variety of tradesmen's clothing from behind the boulders, donned the outfits, and dispersed along the roadway.

Nathaniel prodded the lead sheep toward home. His wife, Sarah, and curly haired daughter, Hannah, stood at the gates waiting as he made his way up the steep incline. The little one hopped several times, clapping her hands in anticipation of her dad's arrival. He smiled. Life was good. One last glance toward Capernaum confirmed that the rain cloud had spent its nourishing treasure. If only some things had been different.

~ ~ ~

The hills vibrated with shimmering waves of red, purple, blue, yellow, and white as anemones, cyclamen, lupine, and marigolds fought for space and sunlight. The abundance of new growth on cedar, olive, oak, and brush added to the artist's palette. Nearby, poppies, buttercups, tulips, sage, and thyme made their presence known. In the crook of Salome's arm nestled a handful of jasmine freshly regathered. A blue gossamer-winged dragonfly darted close.

Salome set down the half-filled reed basket, arranged the jasmine on top of the mushrooms and tubers, tucked her red scarf inside, then flipped her waist-length auburn braid back over her shoulder. The whitecaps cresting on the lake below warned that sheltering soon would be wise. A sparrow somersaulted past as wind whistled through the forest around her.

What was going on? The Romans and Parthians wrestled like raging bulls over territory while the Zealots quietly tried to reclaim freedom for the land and the people. Being a good wife had failed to secure love just as being a good daughter and good sister had failed before. Fulfilling a youthful promise seemed the only door left.

The slightest movement of shade against shadow flitted at the periphery of Salome's vision. He was there! A Parthian warrior lurked near the sheep pens before blending into the forest. The oily, dirty odor of wool and dung raised the memory of her birthplace in Nazareth. Love had been such a dream then. But this wasn't Nazareth. What was a Parthian doing this far into Roman territory?

The leather-vested man, wearing the underdress of a horse archer and sporting a full red beard, stepped out from a grove of trees, his horse in tow. A girl, not much older than James, walked behind him. Who was she? His daughter? A slave? Certainly not his comforter. She held the bow like an experienced huntress. Perhaps the girl had unleashed the arrows but why would the girl shoot at her? Why would she kill the dog? Nothing was making sense but there seemed nothing much to fear. She huddled in place.

"Wait!" the warrior ordered. His Parthian was clear and urgent.

The horse halted like a trained dog. Ears flickered as flies buzzed nearby. It looked in her direction.

The Parthian showed no sign that he had seen Salome. He watched the town below. The four-foot-long sword in his hand appeared heavy but he held it parallel to the ground as if weightless. The warrior tied his mount, motioned for the young girl to stay and then crouched, watching a group of tradesmen debating under a canopy around a small campfire below. Salome retreated into the bush and waited. The warrior crept down the hillside.

A twig snapped to her right, and the sound cracked like a whip. She ducked lower. Moments later, the centurion from Sepphoris, Anthony Vasillius, appeared and hunched—twenty-five feet behind the Parthian.

The centurion had removed his helmet and breastplate but that muscular frame and that grip on his dagger were all too familiar. Why was he so far from home? A scene from Sepphoris flooded Salome's mind. The soldier gasping for breath. *So, you've recovered from your poisoning and you haven't changed your appetites.*

The centurion moved toward the tied-up mount. The young girl hadn't noticed him. Was she about to become a stolen girl? Stolen girls comforted the Roman officers in the fortress.

Salome wrapped her arms around her knees, hunching tighter. What did this incident have to do with her? Why should she care about Parthian girls when she had a hard enough time protecting Galilean youngsters? Sheltering in the bush made sense. But is that what a good mother, a good person, a good freedom fighter would do? Why should the Romans steal any child? Especially this Roman who had taken so much from her.

What did she have to prove to anyone, anymore? It would be over in a moment and she could go back to her family. Would The Almighty count this as goodness? The world had become darker and more dangerous. It was a playground for the powerful, not for the weak.

The centurion crept closer to the girl and raised his sword toward the Parthian.

She'd made a difference before. Why not again?

Salome pried a jagged pebble from the ground at her feet and fit it into her sling. Her right hand trembled. She stood and hurled the pebble at the Parthian. The missile hit him in the elbow and he pivoted—spotting Anthony. Without hesitation, the warrior whistled. The horse reared as Anthony drew close, slashing at the air with its hooves. The Parthian drew his bow as Anthony rolled away into the bush. The young girl faded from sight.

Run? Scream? Thoughts sprang up like wild flowers after the rain. Fear coursed through her veins. What had she done? She had poked the beast. *Was the girl safe now? Courage! Breathe!* Anthony's gone for now. Three deep breaths. Again. She stepped forward and moved toward the warrior.

How will I communicate that his girl killed my son's dog? With one hand she held up the arrow.

The man turned in her direction, raised his sword and scanned the bushes as if expecting an ambush. There was no sign of Anthony or anyone else.

"Hello, friend, Shalom," Salome called out. "You've come a long way on a beautiful day to our peaceful town."

The warrior took a defensive posture with his sword extended but she marched forward holding out the arrow. The girl appeared behind him. When Salome stood ten paces away, he grunted and gestured to the ground.

"Your daughter tried to kill me and she killed my dog."

The Parthian stepped forward and pointed toward her scarf. "Red like Roman. Dog, black like leopard."

The girl rushed forward and claimed the arrow. Nodding, the warrior turned, mounted his horse, lifted the girl to ride behind him and trotted away into the trees. He left the basket untouched.

What is it about these mysterious warriors who probe the tender underbelly of the Roman beast?

Instead of asking her husband Zebedee about the Parthian presence, she hiked down the hill, past the traders at their campfire, and sought wisdom about the warriors through the women emerging from their homes. The women hauled baskets of laundry to wash and pound out the stains from their men's clothing on the rocks by the shore on the sea of Kinnereth. "What do you know about Parthians?" she asked.

A jeweler's wife named Tamar had the most interesting news. "Thousands I tell you," she said. "There were thousands of Parthians on camels and horses." She held up a tunic for examination. "The whole of Yerushalayim was filled with the sound of their animals. They sang as they rode—an eerie chanting kind of song. King Herod was terrified—at least that's what my Haime said when he got home."

"Why was the king so frightened?" Salome asked. He'd murdered his wife and sons. Paranoid, yes, but frightened? It seemed unlikely.

Tamar threw the tunic into a woven basket. "These Parthian Magi were king-makers looking for a new sovereign. Haime said they had seen a prophesy and something in the stars to show them that a new king of the Jews was born." She tossed another tunic into the water near the scrubbing rocks.

"Sounds crazy to me," Salome said, looking back at her own empty wash line. Why was this always women's work? "You'd think we would have been told if there was a new king in our land."

"The way Haime explained it to me, Rome and Parthia now have a peace agreement and the border between them is somewhere near here." The woman bent over the tunic on the rocks, scrubbing at a stain. "That's why Rome is building Sepphoris and other fortresses. In the last battle between them the Parthians slaughtered 40,000 Romans and took over this whole land." She stood and stretched her back. "Your father can tell you what it was like to live with Parthians in control of this land. They even installed their own high priest in the temple at Yerushalayim."

"You've already told me more than I care to hear." Salome skipped a stone across the lake surface. "What these nations do can't really affect a fishermen's wife like me. The Parthians look like young men dressed up in warrior's garb—nothing more." She turned to leave. Talking about a young Parthian girl who had shot an arrow no longer seemed significant. Even if it had almost skewered her. "I hardly know what to believe about events so long ago," she said. "Maybe I should worry about the Parthians more than I am."

"It's not the Parthians I'm worried about," Tamar said. "When Herod sent his men to kill off those babies, mine was one of them. Only one child got away and to this day I believe he's the one Herod was after. Now, Herod's son is on the throne and all our children are at risk."

Her sister, Mariam's words stormed back to grapple with Salome's thoughts. "Ha'Shem—God—warned Yuseph in a dream that the king would come for my son. The Parthian Magi left and we went down to Egypt." She shook her head vigorously and strolled away along the lakeshore.

Why would Ha'Shem take the legitimate child of one woman while sparing the illegitimate child of another? How could he call on people to trust him?

The rush of wind across her cheek lingered like the touch of a passing feather and she caressed the place with her fingers. The clouds skittered across the hills. Did Ha'Shem know? Did he hear the unspoken prayers and questions of his own people? Even women?

~ ~ ~

The sheep crowded into their pen in Nazareth. Several flocks mixed into the guarded enclosure but a simple whistle brought Nathaniel's own flock streaming through the open doorway in the morning. A shepherd boy reclined again across the opening and became the doorway to restrain any wandering lambs. He raised his staff and bid farewell. "Shalom."

Swinging Hannah up onto his shoulders, Nathaniel sang a Davidic Psalm about the shepherd who cared for his lambs. His daughter giggled with joy as he squeezed her knee and smiled at Sarah. "There is no better place to live than the Galil," he said.

Sarah reached over and playfully tugged on his beard. "We won't always have to stay poor shepherds you know. With my family's olive business in Cana and our new grapevines here, we will soon be trading internationally. My father may yet be proud of you."

Nathaniel swung Hannah down off of his shoulders and onto her feet. "Our great ancestor, king David was a shepherd and saw Ha'Shem—God— as a shepherd for his people." He opened the gate to their compound and followed his wife and daughter through before securing it shut again. "We don't want to get into businesses that will create tension between our people and the Romans. I'm just as happy to wander the hills and stay safe."

Sarah sat on a wooden bench outside their humble limestone home and drew Hannah's attention to a hawk flying high overhead. "See that bird, Hannah? One day, we will fly free and see the world like your grandfather. Only for now are we penned like chickens."

"It's not that bad," Nathaniel said. "We have what we need here."

"Maybe that's the problem," Sarah said. "You don't understand what we need."

~ ~ ~

Salome turned the last corner toward home and saw him. She ducked behind a bush, rage filling her mother's heart. The centurion stood a few strides from her son, James. If he dared lay a hand on the boy there would be fury to pay. But what could she do? She maneuvered through the bush and unleashed her sling. She had used it once with effect. She could do it again.

The soldier scanned the beach and then called to his mount. The horse obeyed without hesitation and came to him. It was a magnificent black stallion, a war horse to make any combatant proud. Anthony hoisted himself up and rode off.

A few moments after James retreated into the house, Salome ran across the clearing and lunged through the door. She ran fully into James coming out.

"Mom! What are you doing?" he yelled.

"Shhhh!" she said, hanging onto his arm. "What did that soldier want?"

James pulled his arm away. "He wanted to know how old I was and whether my mother knew where I was. He also asked if I had ever thought of going to Rome as a soldier."

"I don't want you ever talking to him again," Salome said. "Is that clear?"

"What's going on?" It was Zebedee, coming in from the fishing boats.

"Ima is paranoid about some soldier that stopped to talk with me," James answered. "It was nothing, but she's telling me never to talk with him again."

The intensity escaped with her words. "That man is dangerous. He steals kids and I don't want my kids taken."

"So, you know this soldier?" Zebedee asked. "Every man has to learn to stand up for himself. It seems like James did fine. Don't put your womanly fears onto your sons. Now, be a good wife, stop your imaginations, and get us some fish stew!"

CHAPTER TWO

Capernaum / Nazareth – Unwanted Opportunity

Within a week after her third missed cycle Salome knew for sure. She sensed the fluttering. Of course, her husband was away. The sardines were at their prime and Zebedee was out early with the men catching fish, repairing nets, and then trying to sell off the abundance when everyone else had their share. This meant traveling farther inland to find new markets. *When the next full moon comes, I'll make a special meal and congratulate him.*

The first spotting on her undergarments took her by surprise but she still persisted on her foray into the bush for mushrooms. The cramping started slow and then took her breath away. *Ha'Shem, please!* A gull swooshed by and it was as if that bird took the life within her as it passed. Tears streamed as she wrapped her arms around her abdomen and rocked herself toward comfort. *Ha'Shem, not now. No, no, no!* A song, a moan. Nothing helped.

Mariam drops children like a rabbit, even after all she did, and now this. What did I ever do?

On her hands and knees, she crawled through the bush toward home but the cramping paralyzed her movement. In the end, she succumbed to the loss and lay like a wilted flower, unseen and uncared for. The birth pangs eased only when she'd released something hardly bigger than a passionfruit. She held it, gasping for air and sobbing for what would never be. When sufficient time passed, Salome dug in the dirt with a stick and her fingers, buried the tiny form and the bloody issue without ceremony, then set a rock over the small grave. *Ha'Shem ... Did you see this little one? Did this one count?*

A heavy weight drizzled into her limbs and settled over her heart. Taking the steps home was like walking through deep mounds of clay. She passed her sister-in-law, Diana, without a word and wilted onto her bed for a nap.

James, her son, stopped at the outside door to yell, "Ima, I'm going to my friend's house for supper. Don't wait up for me." She heard him tiptoe into his room sometime after sunset. It was the longest night she had ever known.

~ ~ ~

Nathaniel cuddled the lamb and held its nose to the small pool of water in the palm of his hand. "Lick it up little one," he urged. "Yeshua thinks you're nothing more than a sacrifice but you're more than that aren't you?"

"Why do you talk with the lambs?" the shepherd boy, Nahum asked. "They can't talk back with you."

"I talk to the lambs so they will know the voice of their shepherd," Nathaniel answered. "When they are older they never even have to hesitate on who to follow. They know their shepherd's voice and they will follow him. They know I'm the one who will protect them and who will provide them with green pastures."

"I guess they're not as dumb as some people think," Nahum said. "It sure would be good if someone would come and shepherd our nation. These Romans are like wolves and it doesn't seem like we have a chance."

"Be patient," Nathaniel urged. "Your shepherd may be closer than you think."

~ ~ ~

Days later, when Zebedee returned and expressed his desires, Salome feigned weariness and turned away. "The children . . . it's late . . . not tonight."

"You unfaithful wench!" He grabbed her shoulders roughly and turned her on her back. Being suffocated by a bear soaked in fish oil would have been less terrifying and revolting. Zebedee's voice was a roar in her ears. "My sisters keep reminding me I got dumped with the trash of Nazareth. So be it! You're my wife, now learn your place." She fought back her gag.

He would not be denied and when he had spent his passion, she curled in place, tears streaming. Is this what her sister, Rebekah, had endured? A boiling pit of lava bubbled in her soul. While Zebedee snored, she regained her dignity and started to pack. Where would she go?

Things had started so well with the arranged marriage until Zebedee's elder sisters latched onto the news that Salome's older sister had been raped by Romans and her younger sister had become pregnant before the marriage ceremony. They had turned their brother's heart against her. Nothing she did or said was good enough for the family by the sea. One whispered phrase had become common place. "Everyone knows that nothing good comes from Nazareth!"

Dragging herself from bed in the morning she stumbled out to feed the chickens. The boys should have been doing this if Zebedee hadn't coddled them. Leah had other chores. She picked up a broom to sweep. A feather, stuck in the interwoven branches of the chicken pen, fluttered in the breeze. "A dove!"

She set the broom against the wall and pivoted to survey the bush. One Zealot above all others used dove feathers to signal messages. It had been two years since the last feather and she had tossed that one aside. No one in sight seemed suspicious. Two stonemasons walked alongside their ox cart filled with tiles. A carpenter loaded a donkey cart with fresh-cut logs. Fishmongers, carvers, and vegetable salesmen flogged their wares while a gaggle of young boys, including James, wrestled in a game as the rabbi nearby looked too long at one of the comfort women who lured soldiers, strangers and husbands alike. All of them were a normal part of the landscape.

A hawk circled above. When it glided into a dive for a mouse or other rodent, she said out loud, "I know what that mouse is feeling."

Without hesitation, she set off up the pathway into the forest behind the butcher's shop. Two hundred paces in she veered on a branch of the trail toward a large oak. At the base of the trunk, she set her foot on a large rock and forced it aside. Sure enough, underneath was a piece of vellum—tanned sheepskin. It contained two words. *Sepphoris. Baker.* She snatched the piece of leather and moved the rock back into place.

David ben Hinnom had been the first young man to hand her the dove feather. Ruddy faced, red-haired, and fearless, he reminded her of what King David might have been like. He took on the nickname "Ox" to portray his strength. His family had moved into Nazareth when he was sixteen and

Salome was eleven. David had quickly taken charge of the young men in the village and was the first to allow her to tag along on the group's adventures. He had taught her how to use a sling and attempted to teach her how to hunt with a bow. He had been her first crush until the fateful night when a Roman legion had killed David's father in an ambush on a caravan of traders along the road to Caesarea—insisting they were smugglers. David—now Ox—had vanished to join up with a new freedom fighter named Barabbas.

A high-pitched wail from the forest got her attention. She looked toward the cave and remembered Diana's words upon her first arrival in Capernaum. "Come, let's go explore the caves," she had said. "If you ever need to hide from Zebedee, I can show you the best places."

Behind the butcher's holding pen, three cows and four sheep had munched ignorantly on the feed provided. "Look at them," Diana had said. "They don't even know what's coming."

"I know how they feel," Salome had responded.

"Zebedee's not that bad," Diana had said. "You just have to watch his temper."

The clench in Salome's gut only increased after that but Diana hardly seemed to notice.

As they rounded a corner that day, Diana had pointed toward the cave sitting on a prominent hill. "Whatever you do, don't go up there. That's Bartholomew's haunt. He's a demoniac. Little children have disappeared near here and never been seen again. Zebedee says that dragons, sorcerers, and demons live there."

"I may be new but I'm not naïve," Salome had said. "The forest is my friend."

"I'm glad you think that now." Diana had then pointed up the hill. "The good cave is up around the corner. Compared to Bartholomew, Zebedee is a prince and you may never need to come here."

But Salome had been there far too many times.

A plan to protect her own children and to save others hatched in her mind. Holding the feather and the vellum she looked upward and said aloud. "Ox, I'm coming."

~ ~ ~

Nathaniel brushed aside the shaving from the carving he worked on. He held the figure closer to the light of the clay lamp and rubbed it with his thumb. The contour of a young woman danced in harmony with the wood grain. Fine detail marked the mantle and tunic but no facial features had been attempted.

His wife sat down nearby, folded clothing and placed it on a wooden shelf. "Is that her?" she asked. "What was her name? Salome."

He held his work up for her inspection. "How do you know it isn't you?" He set the figurine to stand on the table. "We've been married eight years now. Why do you still question my commitment?"

Sarah slid off her mantle and examined it. "Only last week you called her name in your sleep. Do you expect me to forget your first choice for betrothal? No woman wants to be second in her husband's world."

Nathaniel pocketed the carving and rose. "My parents chose you and your parents chose me. That is all that matters." He shirked his outer tunic and hung it on a wooden peg in the wall. "Who knows why I dreamed about her. We were childhood friends. Maybe she's in trouble." He sat on the reed mat. "When she was ten, she fell into that pool below the shepherd's field. I knew she was afraid of water so I was watching. I happened to save her that day and maybe I was remembering that moment in my dream."

"I don't care what happened when you were children," Sarah snapped. "You need to get her face out of your dreams and her body out of your carvings. I can't imagine her being a fisher's wife if she's so afraid of water."

Husband and wife readied for bed and lay on their sheepskin-covered reed mats. Nathaniel led the prayer. "Blessed be you, King of the Universe, who blesses us with sleep and with peace. Amen." He blew out the flickering lamp.

Sarah turned on her side. "I just wish you didn't have to go." She rested her hand on his shoulder. "How do I know you're really going to hunt for animals you can stuff? I thought you were happy here in the Galil."

"You know we've been trapped in this battle between the Zealots and the Romans," Nathaniel said. "Now that Judas is dead and the hope of a Messiah is gone, we have to get on with life. We are in a time of tension and peace and I need to do something different."

"I heard that Judas's sons, James and Simon are taking up the cause," Sarah said. "My father told me to keep you close and to not let you go chasing after another warmonger. I just want you to stay here and be happy. How does hunting poor animals make you happy?"

Nathaniel sighed. "Sarah, you know I am happy wherever you are and you know that with my crippled foot I can't hunt for anything. I'm going to visit my brother who will catch what I want and then teach me how to preserve the animals. You'll be fine at your mother's with Hannah."

Sarah lurched out of the blankets and grabbed his arm. "Just promise me you won't find an excuse to spend time with that Zealot queen."

The grip tightening now around his wrist felt like a noose around his neck. What could he say? "You're the mother of my children. I will not be anywhere close to Salome. I don't understand why you're jealous of her."

She released her hold. He could feel the ice freezing him out. "You spend your days carving her body out of wood and I'm sure you're sitting up on that cliff dreaming about her and watching for her. I share my dreams and visions for our life and our business and you ignore me as if I'm nothing. Yes, you do your duty as a husband but I'm not ignorant." She rose and stood over him. "I feel like I was deceived into this marriage. I can do this business by myself but the least you could do is to be a father to our children. I don't know what hold she has over you but one day we are going to have to break it."

~ ~ ~

An hour after dawn the next morning Salome wrestled her children over to Diana in the adjoining limestone block home. Her sister-in-law bulged with a second child and grimaced as she waddled toward the entrance. "Another bad night?" Salome asked.

Diana nodded. "Can't believe I asked for this. What's happening in your world?"

"I need another favor," Salome pleaded. "I need you to watch these three." She dragged James through the door and set the three in front of her. "Leah can help around the house. The boys will probably go off fishing with their dad. I'm going up to Nazareth for a week or two."

Diana shrugged. "That bad? You've already been up there twice this year."

"My parents need me." Salome fidgeted with the ties on her leather bag.

Diana scooped up John, rocking him on her hip. "They have your sisters to look after them. If you see my husband, Simon, tell him I need him to get home for a while. You warned me about marrying a freedom fighter but I really thought things might change."

Salome stepped outside and motioned to her sister-in-law. "Listen, I'm trying to be good here but I'm not doing so well with your brother. There's something I have to do and he wouldn't understand. When I get back you can ask for whatever you need."

James poked his head out the door, listening. "Hurry back."

Diana nodded. "The longer you take the bigger my favor."

"You'll have to make my excuses to Zebedee," Salome said. "My mother, my sister—some friends—they needed me and I didn't have time to wait."

"He's not going to be happy."

Salome gave a hug to James and Leah and patted John's head. "That's the biggest thing I'm afraid of."

Diana set John down. "I can hear you two, you know."

"Please!"

"Go."

~ ~ ~

Some days there was no winning. Nathaniel corralled a lamb at the field above the pond and cradled it in his arm. "She wonders why I spend so much time with you lot," he mumbled. "There's nothing I'd like better than to be the perfect father and the perfect husband. The problem is the rules and expectations keep changing. When I don't respond quickly enough to some statement of hers then I'm being too introspective or not paying attention." He ran his fingers through the wool, checking for ticks. "If I do try to answer back then I'm either trying to fix something that doesn't need fixing or I'm not listening well enough to understand. If I'm not thinking about anything and she asks me what I'm thinking I get accused of thinking about Salome. She can't believe that sometimes I'm just not thinking about anything much at all." He set the lamb down and watched it skip back to its mother. "How do I not think of Salome if she keeps accusing me of doing just that?"

"What's this I'm hearing?" a voice behind him said.

Spinning around, he nearly tumbled off balance. "David! Ox! What are you doing sneaking up behind me?"

"I was wondering if you'd be open for a chance to help an old friend?" Ox said.

"And who might that be?" Nathaniel asked. "I'm not in a good place to be away from home right now."

"Salome's on her way up to help us out with something that is bigger than her. She could use someone she knows to provide support. Would you be willing? It won't take long."

Nathaniel slouched onto a stump. "The last thing I need right now is some reason to get closer to Salome. Why don't you get someone else?"

Ox glanced across the valley floor toward Sepphoris. "She'll be coming soon and I haven't got anyone else. She trusts you. You sit here and do what you need to do. I better get to Sepphoris before things get too complicated for her."

~ ~ ~

A half hour from Sepphoris, Salome cut through a back trail to save time. A whiff of smoke drifted by in the breeze. She was familiar with the area from her childhood days and enjoyed the isolation of the forest canopy and the birdsong all around. There was something peaceful here that the unpredictable sea by Capernaum never offered.

Rounding a corner onto an open section she heard a moan. A man lay sprawled on the path. A spear protruded from his abdomen. Hurrying closer, she recognized him as a carpenter from Nazareth. A friend of her father.

Salome bent over the dying man and compelled her courage through the plea in his last breaths. "I tried to stop him. Save my daughters—the centurion took them."

"I'm no one's savior," she said. The empty pathway mocked her plight. Where was help when you needed it?

"They're all I have," he gasped. The patch of blood spread into a small pool.

The rolling hills of the Galilean countryside displayed a splash of wildflowers undulating in the breeze. The Beit Netofa Valley below vibrated with waves of wheat and the Via Maris streamed with ant-sized caravans of international traders leading camels, donkeys, horses, and ox carts. The white sails of Roman galleys shone bright on the Great Sea in the distance. The slightest tang of salt hung in the breeze.

"Benjamin!" she called. No response. "Benjamin!" She shook him. No breath. No pulse. *Why me?*

No one else traipsed this isolated path overlooking the fortress of Sepphoris. *Ha'Shem, are even the fathers in our nation of no value to you?* She glanced back along the trail she had taken, then grasped the spear protruding from her former neighbor's side and yanked it out.

"Sparrow!" a voice called.

She pivoted and tossed the spear into the tall grasses nearby. Blood! On her hand. She wiped it along the grass.

"Sparrow!"

A lean warrior, bronzed by the sun, stepped out from the forest. Ox? One hand stroked his close-cropped beard and the other grasped a dagger tucked into the leather belt around his tunic. "There are more stolen girls to rescue." He pointed toward Sepphoris. "Are you with us or not?"

"I'm not supposed to be here," she responded, adjusting her mantle over her mouth. "Why are you following me?" The forest behind the warrior lay still and dark. He had grown muscular since she'd seen him last.

The man glanced toward the fortress. "We know you're a woman on the run, looking for love." He held out his hand and took a step toward her. "It's been years since you played messenger for the warriors of the homeland but we need you now. The girls need help. And you've answered the call of the feather."

She held out a sling, extracted from her simple beige tunic. "I'm here for my sister. This is the only weapon I know how to use." A red streak between her fingers needed attention. She rubbed it off on the grass until she was satisfied.

The Zealot warrior crouched over the still form on the path. The scent of wood, smoke and sweat hung in the air. "Who was he?"

Salome wiped the corner of her eye with her mantle. "A neighbor when I was young. A carpenter. You would have seen him if you'd stayed home a little more." The twisted mouth framed by a salt and pepper beard betrayed the legacy of a community pillar known for his laughter and generosity. "A friend of my father."

The Zealot squinted at her. "I am sorry for your loss but we need to act now. We know you played chef to the centurion a dozen years ago. We know that his desires were not only for your food. You have other weapons." A gentle finger closed the dead man's eyelids.

The scar on the carpenter's wrist turned more gray. "I have children now," Salome said. She wiped away blood from curled fingers. "The centurion's thirst is for untouched maidens."

Grasping the dead man's ankles, the Zealot nodded toward the stiff hands and Salome took hold of the cooling flesh. Together, they dragged the hefty tradesman into the forest. "You have kept your youth and your beauty. I'll alert the gatekeeper in Nazareth to claim this carpenter," he said. "And I'll tell your father to meet you tonight. You need a reason to be here."

"What do you expect me to do?" She wiped away the last of the blood stuck on her fingernail.

"Find out where the centurion keeps the girls," the Zealot replied. He broke off two sections from a cedar branch and laid them over the body. "If you're not going back to Capernaum soon, perhaps you can find work in the fortress and renew his acquaintance."

The intensity of the shudder surprised her. If she didn't step up to help stop these abductions then her own children might be next.

The warrior laid his hand gently on her shoulder. "Leave us messages in the usual places," he said. "The girls need you. We need you. The one on the cross is Abraham."

The Zealot vanished into a crevice in the hills and Salome scanned the fortress again. A dozen years. So much had gone wrong since that first day she had chosen to pass on the message for her friend Thaddeus. She had walked into the city and gasped at the sight of the cross raised in the center of the plaza inside the main gate. The putrid stench of an unwashed sewer hovered. Birds pecked at the eyes of the naked man hanging there while tradesmen, craftsmen, shoppers, citizens, and soldiers flowed like a river around the spectacle.

Had she really lived and loved on these streets during those heady days?

CHAPTER THREE

Sepphoris / Caesarea – Hidden Message

The donkey cart hauling Nathaniel to the coast was well on its way before sunrise. The repeated pleas of the Zealot leader the evening before had not been easy to ignore. Benjamin, the murdered carpenter, had been his neighbor from the time he was young. His blood called for vindication. He had watched the carpenter's two stolen daughters grow from birth and often let them feed his lambs. The two needed rescuing.

What confused him was the third reason given for his involvement in the latest Zealot ploy. Ox had informed him that Salome had re-engaged in the effort to rescue the two girls. "She needs you more than ever right now. She's been away from the freedom effort for years and her senses will not be sharp."

Images of a young Salome flashed through his mind. Those deep hazel eyes smiling with life; the long silky auburn hair tempting him to touch; the lilting laughter that penetrated to his soul. The same person who resisted him when it really mattered.

Nathaniel winced and turned to watch the sky transform into flaming orange scattered amidst a brilliant blue and pink. The faint scent of jasmine fought to overcome the strong odor of sheep and oxen in their pens. The chatter of villagers settling around fires in their courtyards and the distant bark of a dog mixed with the rising chorus of crickets, bullfrogs and the swishing of branches in the breeze.

"We know how you feel about her," Ox had said. "For her sake, stay one more week."

His calloused thumb stroked the figurine nestled in his tunic. Sarah's accusations rose again like burning arrows in his soul. He shook his head. "Not this time," he said. "Someone else will have to take the risks. I have a commitment to keep."

~ ~ ~

While Ox spread the news about the death of Benjamin and recruited help for the new mission, Salome took a few moments to rest on bales of hay in a warehouse. The cosmopolitan flow of an international center of trade washed over her like a river as dozens of languages, scents and costumes floated by. There had to be a way to stop this traffic in children.

After being satisfied that no unhealthy interest in her presence was obvious, she stepped out into the flow and wandered to the plaza. Some self-preservation habits had become instinctive. Anthony's promiscuous ways in her early days with him had tuned her senses. Somehow, this whole plan had to do with thwarting his efforts in the community.

Twelve years. Who could believe it had been so long? But who could forget that day?

On the day that changed everything, Thaddeus had writhed on a cross in this same place until the last gasp of sunrays faded. Apart from her infatuation with David, the Ox, Thaddeus had first claimed her heart through his flattery and flirting in the kitchen at the fortress. He had also recruited her for her first efforts with the Zealot cause.

As if in answer to his final desperate breath, a chilled airstream had flowed from the heavens, wafted by his still form, and glided over Salome as she inched her way toward him. Too late. Back then, love had died. Now, she pulled the mantle tighter. The same earthy aroma of damp soil hovered in place, but it was Abraham who hung here.

As shadows lengthened across the plaza and the stone alcove took on the heat of an oven, Salome moved to cooler quarters under the canopy of the baker. She placed the feather casually on the corner of a table and waited for the merchant to notice her. When he did, she looked down and said, "Our bird has lost another feather."

The man retrieved a bag from under his table and placed it in front of her. There were five small buns inside. "These things happen," he said. "As long as she doesn't lose anymore, it will be okay."

Behind a water fountain, she slowly tore apart the buns. Inside the second was a message scrawled on parchment. *Come again tomorrow.* She ate the bun, left the rest in her bag, and strolled through an alley. A legionnaire kept pace about a dozen people behind her, walking when she walked, stopping when she stopped. She stepped into a women's bathhouse, walked through the flurry of undressing women and exited out the back.

As the sun ceased its relentless touch on the crucified Jew, Salome crouched out of sight from the two Roman sentries standing ten feet from the cross and hurled a pebble to the far side of the clearing. They might as well have been marble statues fastened to the cobblestoned plaza. Not even a turn of the head. A dog, curled up at the base of the cross, lifted its head for a moment and then laid its snout back on its paws.

To her left, a large tile mosaic of a woman adorned the side of the theater. The face was young, starry-eyed, and Hebrew but the pose and expression were alluring like a Greek goddess. If she'd known the purpose of the centurion's request so many years ago, she never would have agreed to let the artist use her face as a model.

The last of the market vendors closed their stalls and pushed their beasts of burden toward the city gates. Salome bent low and sprinted in beside the ox cart. Thick odors of musk and dung clung together in the space. A small rock dislodged as the toe of her sandal sent it rattling across the cobblestones. She tensed in place. There had been enough trouble for one day.

The image of Thaddeus making a breakfast of sizzling beef sausages for the centurion a dozen years before still danced with life. Now he was gone. But did the centurion, Anthony, know about her role in the plot? Were his spies still watching?

On the other side of the gate, Salome stepped away from the ox cart and walked quickly down the path. No one stepped out to stop her. The last shadows of day blended with the encroaching fingers of night.

Was that really a footstep? She looked for a stick or stone along the path. A girl needed to defend herself where necessary.

"Sparrow!"

Her shaking fingers stopped inches from the stick.

"We're going to take Abraham down." The deep whisper rumbled like thunder in the stillness of night. "Come with us!"

Salome straightened up, straining to glimpse the one who called. Could this be a trap? "It's too late. He's gone."

"Sepphoris looks magical in the moonlight." The Zealot's code phrase reversed.

"It's better in the sunshine," she replied.

"It's only 400 paces up the back ridge to conquer Herod's crown jewel," another said. "Abraham deserves a decent burial. There's enough moonlight to help without betraying us."

"Enough men have died today," she said. "There are sentries."

"Our daggers are quick and sharp." The slightest swish of a branch betrayed the presence.

Nothing was visible. She took a step forward. "Keep them sharp to protect the living."

"Thaddeus cared for you." The voice had moved away.

She called over her shoulder as she turned away. "That didn't help him, did it?"

No response.

"Ox!" she called softly. A dog bark, several hundred paces away, erupted for a few seconds. A harsh voice stilled it.

After a dozen steps toward Nazareth, she turned back. If the Zealots were going to successfully take down the body, someone needed to distract the sentries. That dog at the cross would betray the men's presence when they arrived to take Abraham down. Duty called.

Hiking back to Sepphoris winded her. Hunched over at the top, she gulped for air. She wasn't so young anymore. The main gate's one guard leaned against the pedestrian doorway by the shuttered entrance, watching. A single torch flickered in the breeze. If Anthony, the centurion, discovered her involvement Abraham might have company on another cross. The mantle shielded her face and she tugged it tighter.

The guard stepped toward her. "Unless the centurion is calling in a favor from you, go home."

There was a gap in the wall near the butcher's sheep pen. She hung her head and left. The guard slumped on a stone and rested his head back against the wall. No one would get through the main entrance.

Within five minutes after leaving the guard's sightline, Salome skittered through the trees, breeched the fortress a stone's throw from the butcher's shop and crept in the shadows toward the square. A lamb bleated. A beggar coughed. She froze in place.

"Who goes there?" a voice called. "In the name of Rome, present yourself."

Wild yapping from the dog beside the cross erupted into the darkness. Sentries bellowed for assistance and footsteps scurried in response. Salome retreated toward the gap in the wall and hurried through the trees toward Nazareth. Too late for a distraction. The Zealots would need another plan.

~ ~ ~

Half-way to Caesarea on the coast, Nathaniel huddled by a fire at the edge of a caravansary. The caravansary was a large, open courtyard walled to keep animals safe for the night. The dazzling sunset stepped off the stage of men and gave way to a curtain of twinkling lights. Mars stood boldly in place and Venus added its light. The camels from an Arabian convoy voiced their displeasure and discomfort with their lot. Oxen moaned, a lamb bawled and an energetic band of Phoenicians drank and danced and sang the night away. He tossed three more chunks of wood on the sizzling pile and watched the consumption of dry cedar begin.

The figurine grew like a weight in his pocket and he withdrew it for examination one more time. His leg tingled with pins and needles so he rose to limp around the fire, continually rubbing his thumb over the face of the figurine. Sarah's voice was strong. "Is that her?"

He straightened his arm over the leaping flames, dangling the carving by the feet, wiggling it, as if tempting the flames to jump up like a hungry dog and snatch it from him. The light of the flames exposed even the fine details he had finally added to the face.

"What have you got there?"

The interruption jolted him into almost dropping the treasure. An Arab tradesman confronted him across the fire and examined his effort. "Is it your goddess?" he asked.

Nathaniel shook his head strongly. "No. I serve only one God. Adonai."

"So, you are one of the people of the book?" he asked. "What use do you have for such a fine piece of work?" The man held out his hand. "May I see it?"

Nathaniel released the figure to the Arab and stepped away from the fire. "It is a fine piece, is it not?" He waited, watching. "For a price it can be yours."

"She has the bearing of a queen, if not a goddess—wouldn't you say?" The man moved his hand slowly up and down as if attempting to assess its weight. "A beautiful olive grain and just the right size for transport." His opening offer of a shekel set off an intense round of bartering. When the Arab finally walked away smiling, he guarded five shekels less in his money pouch.

Nathaniel raised the coins in the direction of Nazareth and said aloud, "I hope you're happy."

~ ~ ~

Ice seeped into her bones as Salome crouched in the bushes waiting for the footsteps. Crickets and bullfrogs made it hard to hear anything—even the heartbeat pounding through her skull. Other sounds filled the void. The echoes of nails pounded into wrist after wrist as she hid in the shadows, reverberating in her mind and the piercing, jagged pain seemed to sear through her own wrists.

Dozens of huddles of seething Zealots had generated plan after plan to stop the insanity but the Roman juggernaut rolled on and on sapping the land of its most passionate devotees. And now the next generation was being scooped up to feed the insatiable lusts of the degenerates who worshipped only power and strength. And the worst of them all had held her heart in his control without mercy.

She was the Sparrow, the Shadow no one noticed. That had to change. But how? Family honor needed to be regained. Everyone, from rabbi to shepherd boy, knew the disgrace of how the legionnaires had ravaged her older sister. They tittered and mocked at how her younger sister had claimed to be a virgin despite her pregnancy. They knew her previous work for the centurion at the fortress and the gossip was cruel and unrelenting. All that had stolen her own chance of love. If dying didn't hurt so much she would have grabbed a Zealot dagger and plunged it into that Roman heart.

What was she thinking—believing that she still had what it took to thwart the Romans and help the freedom fighters? She had her own children to protect in Capernaum and that was perhaps her true incentive. She was past the prime in both beauty and strength. What was she doing hiding in the damp bush while another plan came to nought?

~ ~ ~

The extra coins in his pocket brought a gurgle to his stomach. It was an easy thing to search out what delicacies might be available throughout the camp. Indian sweets, Persian stew, and Roman raisin bread filled his belly. He refrained from the sweet white wine and beer flowing freely around the fires and took time to walk the perimeter where covered carts and carriages had been stored while the animals rested in the center of the enclosure. The night was young and he was restless after giving up his favorite figurine.

Gentle breezes teased his hearing. It seemed a whimper from a Roman carriage had aligned itself to imitate the wind whistling through the foliage. Checking over his shoulder, he shuffled into the shadows of the carriage and moved closer. Definitely a child's soft cry. Perhaps a family bedding down for the night in a secluded space.

"I'm hungry!" a girl's voice called out in Greek.

"Shhhh! Do you want to get us all whipped?" another girl responded.

A thick tarp lying over the carriage bed was easy to move aside and so Nathaniel eased under and added his own *shhhh!* to the group. "I've got some sweet bread and some dried fruit for the two of you. I'm sure your parents will be here soon." He held out the food in his fingers and felt it grabbed by numerous hands as the carriage began to bounce. "Whoa!" he said. "How many are there?"

"Twelve." The voice was tentative and uncertain.

"Where are you going?"

"We don't know."

"Where did you come from?"

"They took us from our fields and gardens."

"Who did?"

A blow to his kidneys brought him to his knees. An elbow to the side of his head sent him sprawling. "Get away from my property," a gruff voice demanded in Latin. Nathaniel tried to roll away and managed to elude all but the heel of a kick aimed at his back.

If the sentry hadn't been drunk, he probably would have finished the job. Instead, he slumped down next to the carriage cursing and shouting into the darkness. Nathaniel slunk off and returned to his own fire.

The Arab who had purchased the figurine warmed his hands over the flames. "Did you get your fill from the others," he asked. "I could have fed you the finest of fare if you had only asked."

Nathaniel extended his hands. "I got beaten for being too curious," he admitted. "There's a carriage with twelve girls on the far side and I tried to feed them. The owner wasn't too happy."

"Serves you right," the Arab said. "The girls are for the pleasure of the Romans and they don't want anyone spoiling them."

"All those girls were stolen from their families," Nathaniel said. "What if they were your daughters? I know I couldn't stand by and watch my daughter being ravished by some hungry legionnaire."

The Arab snorted. "How do you know that the girls weren't purchased fairly? They're being sent for service in the temples. It's a noble cause."

"So, if your daughters were taken to be used as priestesses or harlots in the Temple of Jupiter you wouldn't say anything or do anything?"

"Of course! If they were my daughters, I'd draw my sword and decapitate every one of those pagans. Maybe we should do that just to liven things up around here."

"I think we'd need more of us," Nathaniel said. "Those men are drunk enough that I think you could draw them away with a challenge and I could let the girls out."

"Then what would you do?" the Arab asked. "How will you get them away from here?"

"That's where we'll need someone else to help us," Nathaniel conceded.

"I saw an Egyptian with a larger cart near the start of this camp," the Arab said. "I'll try to recruit him and you find out how many men I'll have to challenge."

Nathaniel scouted out the carriage and counted three men lounging in the area. As he sauntered back toward his own fire a scuffle broke out nearby. "It's the Hebrew!" the Arab yelled. "He's the one who wants to steal the girls. Get your hands off of me or I'll slice you to pieces and feed you to the flames."

Slinking back into the bushes, he watched three men force march the Arab into the light of the fire. "There's no Hebrew here," one of the men said. "Until we see the twenty shekels per child, we aren't doing a thing. You can rescue those girls yourself. Now, don't bother us again."

The Arab drew his sword. "Hebrew!" he yelled. "Come out and prove yourself a man." He swung the weapon in skilled circles until he wearied and sheathed it again. In moments, he was snoring.

CHAPTER FOUR

Nazareth / Caesarea – Dark Tensions

A single star twinkled in the heavens as Salome left Sepphoris. The acrid smoke of evening fires settled like a winter quilt on all who dared to pass, leaving a taste of ash in her throat. One glance back. The silhouette of the crucified Abraham, framed by the moon, produced an involuntary shudder.

A figure stepped out from behind a bush as she turned to the path. She inhaled quickly, clenched her jaws and stifled a scream. Her mother, Ana. *What if I'd had a club?*

"Hurry, Salome," Ana said. "Your father sent me for you."

"Yes, Ima." She grasped her mother's arm. "You're a good mother for risking the journey to bring me to him at this time of night."

"Watch your step. I almost slipped on my way to get you."

"No wonder! It's so steep and muddy." She skirted a puddle. "I don't understand why Abba didn't come to see me."

Ana stepped on two rocks to get across a rivulet. "He couldn't take the chance of being caught by the guards."

Salome followed. "I hope he's not going to lecture me on being a good wife again."

Ana reached out and grabbed hold of her daughter's hand. "Your father only wants to keep you from regrets."

Salome pulled her mother behind a bush. "Hoofbeats! Crouch low." A pair of mounted legionnaires raced by.

"Hurry! She can't have gotten far," the lead horseman called.

The hoofbeats faded.

"How did you hear that?" her mother hissed. "Why are we hiding?"

"Shhh!" Salome straightened and stepped out onto the roadway. "They're looking for Zealots and it might be wise for us to take the back-way home." She rose on tiptoe and craned her neck. "Okay, they're gone."

"Surely, you're not mixed up in this?"

"Hurry, Abba awaits." A soft breeze, scented heavily with jasmine, brushed her cheeks like the gossamer strands of a spider's web. The damp grass underfoot carried the chill of the last rain. The tang of smoky cooking fires infiltrated the luxurious aroma of nature. An orchestra of crickets and bull frogs tuned for the full symphony ahead.

The crest of the hill approaching the village of Nazareth provided a great place to pause and to look across the Beit Netopha Valley. Sepphoris seemed a mere sling shot away. So close. The fortress glowed in a moat of torchlight. The centurion in his quarters must surely be busy inspecting the meal by now. If tradition continued, it would be grilled tilapia fresh from the lake, coated with a special mix of honey, garlic, spices, oil, and vinegar. Whatever did he think about the one who made his meals? Or the one he had ordered crucified?

"Come, Salome," her mother urged. "Watch your step. What brings you to this godless place? I can't imagine what you find so captivating about that center of pagan depravity."

Salome held out a small cloth bag, ignoring the statement. "Ima, these are for you."

Ana accepted the pouch, stuffing it into her tunic. "What bribe is this to distract me?"

"Walnuts, almonds, chestnuts, hazelnuts, and sesame seeds."

Her mother pulled out the pouch and examined it in the moonlight. Pocketing the nuts, she marched on, chin up. "Hurry now! We have work to do."

Salome planted her sandals firmly on the muddy path. "After such a day can you only think of work? Don't you ever wish for something else to do?"

Ana waved dismissively. "Welcome to womanhood! Someone has to do it and Ha'Shem—God—has chosen us. If you aren't at home serving your husband then you are welcome here to serve your Abba."

Salome touched Ana's arm. "Ima, do you ever wonder about Rebekah? Do you think she's happy?"

This time Ana halted and pivoted toward her daughter. "Hush, child." She pulled her arm away. "Your Abba has forbidden us to mention the things that happened to her. If you forget you had an older sister then it will be easier for all of us."

"Ima, those soldiers stole her virginity." She reached out to her mother again. "Surely, women have the right to have their say in the guarding of their treasure."

"No more!" Ana ignored her reach and resumed the march. "There are some things that should not be put into words. Our shame is our own to bear."

Salome hesitated at the village gate. The scent of roasted lamb hung in the air. She breathed deeply and feasted on the pleasure. Probably the rabbi or one of the other families fortunate enough to afford such luxury.

Home. The chorus of crickets and other night creatures escalated their praise to Adonai, the Lord. A dog barked and a donkey brayed. Old Samuel, the village night watchman, hailed a shepherd boy hurrying his sheep into the corral. If only it was possible to forget an older sister then all would be right with the world—apart from one thing: the condition of the younger sister.

"Ima, did you really think Mariam was pregnant before she rushed off to Cousin Elizabeth?"

"Hush! This isn't the time to bring more shame on our family. You never know who is listening. We know she said that an angel talked with her."

"I heard you and Abba talk that first night when she returned; wondering whether she was shamed by the neighbor who escorted her or if it was a soldier or even Yuseph."

"There's no hope to hide anything within the walls of a carpenter's shack." Her mother swung the family compound gate wide and motioned her through. "That was so long ago. Whose ears did you inherit? Sometimes I think you can hear the whispers on the far side of the village."

"Ima, I only hear what I need to hear and our house is small."

Ana nodded. "Some days, I long for the comfort of my own Abba's vineyard mansion." Her outstretched foot prevented the village dog from scurrying into the compound. "In my Abba's home we had room to grow. Being the last to marry was not a benefit to me."

Salome retrieved a leather water pouch lying on its side next to the front door of a cousin's hut. "Everyone in town knew that Rebekah was violated by the soldiers before I did." She swung the water pouch around, emptying the last drops on her sandaled feet. "One day she's sweeping after the chickens and the next day she's gone. Why did you take her to Cana?"

"Speak no more." Ana clamped her hands over her ears. "The past is the past and nothing can be changed."

Salome tossed the pouch across the small gap toward the stable. "When are you going to make Mariam tell you the truth? She's not a child anymore. Her children are old enough that they're going to hear the village gossips."

Ana turned. "We must protect your younger sister while we still can."

"Ima, she's a grown woman with children of her own. Why pretend she's any different than the rest of us?" A half-buried stone caught her off guard and she stumbled into her mother.

"Watch your step!"

Salome crossed her arms and looked away. Some sister! How could she get away with lying about her pregnancy?

Minutes passed before Ana reached out for her daughter. "Salome!" she whispered. "Stop staring at that moon. It's not going to rise any faster with you fawning at it. Your Abba is waiting."

"I don't think I'm in the mood for a lecture anymore," Salome declared. "I won't be afraid to stand up for myself. I tried to be a good sister and I've tried to be a good wife. It wasn't me who arranged this marriage."

Salome stopped outside a crudely built shelter slaked in limestone. Her mother sighed. "It looked much bigger when your father built it for only the two of us."

"The three of us girls loved this home," Salome said. "Perhaps if your two boys had lived Abba would have built us a new one."

"They are in the Almighty's hands. Bless His name. Look!" Ima pointed to the far side of the yard. "The washing is still draped all over the hedge. It should be dry. Bring it in and I'll set out Abba's dinner."

~ ~ ~

THE GOOD WIFE

The moon shone full and bright, floating in a sea of stars. The animals in the caravansary were restless as Bedouins and Arabs settled down. The flickering coals of the fire faded as Nathaniel nodded off. A howl changed everything.

The dog had started the cacophony but the travelers escalated the chaos. The reason lay overhead. The moon had slipped on a deep orange coat and a monster was devouring it whole. Traders, soldiers, and pilgrims from every religion cried out to their gods, begging for mercy. Ice crept up Nathaniel's spine as more and more of the celestial light disappeared.

The longer the orb lay dark the greater the intensity of terror erupted from the void around. One piercing shriek sounded nearby. "You cursed carver. Where are you? You deceived me with this abomination." It was the voice of the Arab trader. "This goddess doesn't hear my prayers for light. She devours my soul."

Another voice added to the tumult. "We need greater sacrifices. Bring the children. The moon goddess has cloaked herself in blood. She needs the sacrifice of innocents to appease her wrath."

Never before had Nathaniel realized how sheltered he was. On his knees, he turned to the Creator and mumbled his own heartfelt prayer. "Lord, Almighty, Creator of heaven and earth. Lay not my sins against me. Restore to us the joy of your light and restore to us the peace of your life. Save the children from the ignorance of men terrified by this event."

Bonfires lit up in various areas of the caravansary and dancers circled screaming and calling out to the heavens. Again, the Arab shouted out nearby. "The carver who sold me this goddess has brought a curse on us all. Find him. His blood will satisfy the goddess above."

Nathaniel hobbled away from the writhing mob into the bush across the way. Not until the moon emerged from the belly of the beast above did he stop running.

~ ~ ~

Salome hugged the carefully folded laundry to her chest and stared at the moon again. It appeared to take on a deep shade of orange. What a child she had been. Desperate for love. Trying so hard to restore a family reputation on her own. So careful to protect her reputation as a good girl with everyone beyond her mother. And yet, so desperate to make a difference in her world. What good did it do?

"Salome!" Her mother called. "Hurry up with that washing."

Reluctantly, she ferried the laundry into the house, washed her feet and then set the clothing in the nooks where they belonged. Her Abba sat at the table where the clay lamps flickered brightly enough to convey the look of disappointment on his face.

She stood in place, looking down on him. "What?"

He motioned for her to sit and waited until she had. "I have heard things," he said.

"Clearly about me," she responded. "Just tell me who said things so that I know how to respond."

"Salome, show respect to your Abba!" Ana interjected.

Eyes lowered, she focused on the grain of the table top her father had made. He reached across to take her hand. She let him and waited.

"One of the stonemasons I work with told me that when he was younger he created the mosaic on the wall at Sepphoris." He stroked the back of her hand with his thumb and then moved away. "He told me that the Zealot who was crucified was killed because he tried to take that mosaic off. He told me that the mosaic had been fashioned after you."

The small house grew even smaller. "That was over twelve years ago," she said.

The silence was deafening.

"It was while I worked for the centurion," she blurted out. "I didn't know what he was going to do. I was working in his kitchen and he asked me to let someone paint my picture. What did you expect me to do?"

"A man is dead trying to defend your honor," Heli said. "For years people have been saying that the mosaic looked so much like you and I told them that it must be a coincidence. Every morning I walk through those gates in the city and I tell myself that it must be an image of a Roman goddess or a Greek harlot or a priestess from one of the temples. All I asked of you is that you be good while you worked over there."

The hammer on her heart almost set a chain on her mouth, but not quite. "I did everything I could to be good for you. When Rebekah was raped by those soldiers, I stayed brave and put myself at risk every time I left home.

The centurion wanted Mariam to work for him but I volunteered to go in order to protect her." She wiped at the tears flowing down her cheeks and tried to control the intensity in her voice. "When Mariam told us she was pregnant, that she was still a virgin, and that some angel had spoken to her, I worked harder to restore our family honor and not once did you see how hard I was trying to be good for you."

Ana sat beside Salome and put her arm around her. "That time was hard for all of us," she said. "Even for your father."

"What have I been hearing about your possible involvement with the Zealots?" Heli said.

"That's what you care about?" Salome asked. She wiped her cheeks with the back of her hand and took a few short breaths. "I have friends who are trying to restore this land to its rightful owners. They're trying to stop our children from being taken. I have tried my hardest to be good for you but I also want to be good for them."

"Maybe we need to talk about this another time," Ana said. "Let me put out the dinner."

"You need to be home with your own husband and your own children," Heli said.

"Sometimes, that's the last place I want to be," she answered. "If you want me to be good then please give me some space when I need it."

The truth of the mosaic adorning the theater at the fortress weighed on Salome. The centurion had commissioned it and had personally overseen that Salome's face was enshrined for all to see. She chafed at Mariam's indiscretion but she hadn't been so innocent herself. She had modeled a month for the artist. Few would recognize her now, after years of struggle with Zebedee in a fisherman's camp at Capernaum. What had happened to love? The mosaic was an image from a long time ago when innocence was still a possibility.

Abba finished his dinner in silence, said his prayers and waited. Salome bowed, "Abba, can we wait until tomorrow?"

Her father rose without a word and left for a walk. He returned when the moon faded into darkness.

~ ~ ~

The deep guttural snarl erupted from the depth of darkness among the bushes to Nathaniel's left. A leopard. Despite the full moon flooding the land with light, the midnight coat of the cat blended with the shadows of the forest around it. Nathaniel stood tall and walked backwards toward an oak tree on the opposite side. It was a mistake. Two gargantuan warthogs charged out of the bush goring at a cheetah that raced right for him.

Springing back, he avoided the flashing fangs and claws of the cat but was broadsided by the backend of one of the hogs. His legs buckled under him as he landed on a knee and found himself face first in the dust. Searing fire shot through his nose and back as he flopped out on the roadway. The pounding of hooves thundered in his ears.

"Whoa!" a voice called. "Someone is down."

A hand turned him over and slapped his cheeks firmly. "Are you drunk or are you okay? We saw the cat and the hogs take you out. What are you doing out here on your own?"

The words were Aramaic but the accent was Parthian. He scrambled for words but groaned instead.

"Ignore him," another voice said. "The Romans will be here any moment."

The first rider gripped under Nathaniel's armpits, dragged him to the edge of the road, then dropped him. "You better wake up before the cats come hunting," he said. In a few beats of a heart his rescuer was gone.

He was on his hands and knees gasping for breath when the next contingent of riders arrived. "Whoa!" yelled a voice. "The smugglers must have run him down. See if he knows anything."

A strong arm grabbed him by the collar of his tunic and hoisted him to his feet. A foul-breathed face spit out words in Latin. "How many riders did you see? How far ahead are they?" Nathaniel turned his head to get fresh air. "Six riders. They just passed."

"Take him to the next camp," an authoritative voice commanded. The rest of the legionnaires charged away while his interrogator threw him onto the back of a horse. "Figures I would get stuck with the drunk," he growled. "I'll take you to the camp but I'm not slowing down when we pass so you better know how to land on your feet."

He clung hard to the arms of the soldier as the horse pounded through the moonlit night. "Let me off before the camp," he pleaded.

The soldier was true to his word. He grabbed Nathaniel like a rag doll and tossed him into the bush as they neared the flickering of fires from the camp. Without slowing, he galloped after the rest of his cohort.

The pain in his back, from a protruding stick, eased as he rolled out of the bush and onto his side. Sarah had been right. He should have stayed home.

CHAPTER FIVE

Sepphoris / Nazareth – Failed Excursions

"Salome? Is that you?"

The grin on the face of the baker's wife near the theater in Sepphoris sported three missing teeth. She drew back her mantle and engulfed Salome in a bear hug that endured far longer than comfort dictated. "I still see the resemblance," the woman said as she jutted her chin at the mosaic.

"Shoshanna!" Salome wriggled out of the arm cocoon, creating distance with her hands on the woman's shoulders. "What a surprise? I see you are married to a baker now instead of a butcher."

"My Hosea is with the Almighty," she said grimly before smiling broadly. "Sometimes we women can't be choosey. Motherhood looks good on you, little dove," Shoshanna cooed. "Who could believe people mocked you as 'the Virgin's sister.' How quickly time passes and how quickly people forget the past."

"We all grow up and try to move on," Salome said. "You, apparently, are one of the few who doesn't forget."

"Hard to keep up with that sister of yours, isn't it?" the baker's wife said. She looked toward Nazareth perched on the adjacent hilltop. "She would love to see you as I'm sure Nathaniel would. I still say it's too bad you didn't marry him. He's such a successful businessman."

Salome released the woman's shoulders and stepped away. "I'll see them soon enough. Right now, I have business in the city. May Ha'Shem bless your bakery and your family."

THE GOOD WIFE

The woman hurried on her way home. Salome slipped behind a Roman shrine outside the city wall and wept. She had given up so much that one night when she had rejected her Abba's choice. It had been a dozen years, yet it seemed like yesterday.

~ ~ ~

The blistering Mediterranean sun stretched the shadows of a dozen Roman galley warships anchored along the new dock in Caesarea. Phoenician sailors scrambled over the decks while legionnaires oversaw slaves loading heavy sacks of grain and other supplies. Sailors gambled with knucklebones while vendors hawked their wares to passengers, onlookers, and anyone who would give them a second glance. The cacophony was deafening for Nathaniel after the quiet trip through the countryside.

As he leaned on a guardrail watching the organized chaos a hand clamped on his shoulder. "There you are—you son of a lost sheep. I couldn't believe your message after all these years. I thought you'd forgotten your Uncle Zeke."

The two men shared a strong embrace. Uncle Zeke, though Hebrew, was dressed in the higher-class garments of the Phoenicians with a close-fitting patterned shenti wrapped around his waist and a sleeveless short tunic over his shoulders. A red mantle draped over his left shoulder. Three rings adorned his left hand and a conical hat rested on his braided hair.

"Are you sure you're ready for hunting?" Nathaniel asked. "Last time I saw you, you were hauling bricks for the Romans at Sepphoris."

Uncle Zeke smiled. "Yes, that was over ten years ago. The last time I saw you, you were panting after that little stonemason's daughter. Did you ever marry her?"

Nathaniel shrugged. "What can I say? Abba chose someone different. I've got two daughters and another on the way."

"Well, don't you worry. A few weeks chasing down wild animals in Egypt will get your blood boiling again." He turned and motioned toward an Iburnian-class sailing ship bobbing alongside a dilapidated section of wharf. "That's our ticket to Alexandria. This thing can outrun almost any pirate ship. I hope you've got a good stomach. It's rough out there today."

~ ~ ~

That long-ago night, when Thaddeus died, her father had finished up his prayers as Salome stepped into the house. She knew her father wanted to discuss a possible betrothal with Nathaniel, the gatekeeper's son. "Abba," she had said. "I've got too much to do. Maybe we can talk tomorrow."

Missed conversations were hard to make up. She had been taken to Zebedee in Capernaum and Nathaniel had been betrothed to another. Those days as a girl had been filled with thoughts of Ha'Shem—God—and with adventure. Love was an uncertain dream confused by the rape of her older sister and the unexplained pregnancy of her younger sister. It certainly had nothing to do with choice.

Belief in Ha'Shem was so easy when one was a child. Salome had bathed in the truth of the immensity of the Creator and his character as seen in the majesty of mountains, the design and beauty of flowers, the love and compassion of people for newborns. Hiking in the hills and through the forests had been enriching and soul filling. Now, even the songs of her sister pushed her to the limits of tolerance.

During the days of innocence, she hadn't realized what she could tolerate. Now, marching thunder reverberated off the stone walls that Salome huddled by in Sepphoris. The problems she once had with Ha'Shem would have to wait. The Roman squadron guarded a small caravan of carts holding covered cages. The double-headed Roman eagle crest on the front of the wagon clearly marked the ownership of the contents. Dust, mixed with the stench of urine and more, swirled around her, choking her. She snugged the shawl tighter over her nose and squeezed her eyelids tight.

The shadow of the carts washed over her body and a chill, as tangible as a sniffing dog, moved around her. A shout from the commander halted the group.

A whimper drew her attention and she stole a glance toward the nearby cage. There, between the bars, a small hand pushed away the covering. Mournful hazel eyes framed by long dark lashes begged for help. Dark curls, twisted like tangled ropes, hung in Medusa-like chaos. Earthy smudges flowed across nose, cheeks, and chin. A collar and a chain held her fast. One hand penetrated the bars and reached out, fingers waving frantically. In a moment, a soldier lashed the canvas covering with a whip and the child shrieked and withdrew. Other cries joined in an eerie choir of terror.

Images of another child, a Persian boy named Behrouz, flashed by. A boy Nathaniel had helped to rescue. A boy as innocent as the little girl reaching out to her. The Romans had beaten that Persian boy mercilessly and two Zealots had died trying to rescue him. Somewhere, he was now training with other freedom fighters.

An archer's bow, a dozen paces away, hung on a peg fastened to a nobleman's stable. Careless fool. Anyone could snatch it up and use it on these legionnaires. Intentionally, Salome unclenched her fists and flexed her fingers. Chilled fingers were marked with wrinkles as if her hands had been submerged in icy water for hours. *They're fortunate I took up the sling instead of the bow.*

When the wagons lurched forward again, Salome willed her limbs to unbend and follow. One leg had fallen asleep and the pins and needles demanded her to stop and rest. There wasn't time. The crowd was already swallowing up the space behind the legion. It was disappearing in the warren of streets around the fortress. The one task she had for today was to find out where these girls were kept.

As she pushed through the bodies, accepting the abuse of elbows and fists, she burst into a space surrounding a figure with long dark robes. A rabbi. His beard was more speckled than she remembered but the fiery eyes under bushy brows were unmistakable. She ducked under the cane he swung.

The religious figure was one she would not forget. That day so long ago hit her powerfully. The rabbi had come to visit her father and Salome assumed it was the main reason everything changed for her. The villagers were no doubt concerned that a sixteen-year-old maid like herself lay unclaimed by any man. The longer a woman waited, the greater chance the family would be shamed into marrying her off to someone with no significant family connections.

She'd overheard a little of the conversation when she'd returned from the butcher shop. The rabbi had been speaking to her father. "Heli, you know that your daughter is not getting any younger. You have turned down the only three suitors in the village. Surely, you can reconsider Nathaniel."

Her Abba was patient but firm. "Rabbi, Salome knows the kind of man she looks for. We'll look elsewhere. We have family in Capernaum."

"Please, my friend. Honor your family and arrange something soon. There are strange rumors about what happens between that centurion and the women who work for him."

It had been weeks later when her father took her to Capernaum where he left her with Zebedee's family. Forgiveness for his betrayal had stretched the limits of her love.

Now, in Sepphoris, as a responsible adult trying to rescue other children from their own terrors, she vowed her own vengeance. The hours of exploring, since ducking under the rabbi's cane, finally paid off. A half-opened door to a stable revealed a familiar cart, cage now empty. A quick scan of the surrounding buildings settled her orientation so she could find the spot again.

As she turned to go, a centurion backed out of a room screaming, "She's mine until I say differently." His fist was closed around the scruffy hair of the urchin Salome had seen in the cart. Without mercy he threw her into the middle of the courtyard where she sprawled, screeching. The centurion raised his whip and snapped it hard on the cobblestones right beside her ear. The child went deathly still.

The centurion stood over the child. It was Anthony. For a second, he looked toward the opening and locked eyes with Salome. An eternity passed. Salome lowered her eyes and walked away as the gate slammed behind her.

As she slid into a doorway, the gate lurched open. "Hey, woman!" Anthony yelled. "I know you and I'll find you."

The shadows of evening swallowed up the streets before she found shelter in a stable. Leaving Zebedee this time might have been arrogant. Facing abuse at home or death at the hands of the centurion brought life into perspective. How had things gotten so dire?

~ ~ ~

The pair of Friesians galloping away from Caesarea forced Nathaniel to keep a stranglehold on the sides of the heavy Roman chariot bouncing along behind them. The white-knuckle ride was orchestrated by a young Persian thrashing the reins above the coal-black stallions. The powerful, sloping shoulders on the compact, muscular bodies featured a long, thick mane and a silky tail flying in the wind. The schooner outracing pirates might have been a safer choice.

THE GOOD WIFE

The trip to Egypt had been abandoned ten minutes after standing on the pitching deck of the sailing ship. Nathaniel determined that hunting was no longer his priority. Before the anchor was raised, he crawled onto the dock and firmer ground. He was too queasy to leave Uncle Zeke with a proper farewell and negotiated a ride with the first available vehicle on the road back to Nazareth. He was sure every bone in his body would be displaced before he arrived. The two-day walk would be a half-day chariot dash. The balance of the five shekels gained from the sale of the figurine now covered his ride. The caravansary where the Arab had bought his treasure was a blur as they passed.

Horses were changed at the half-way point. Nathaniel took the time to relieve himself at the rest stop and to purchase small pouches of walnuts, almonds, pistachios, and hazelnuts for Hannah and Sarah. He also bargained for a roast pigeon covered in pulverized sesame seeds mixed with a sweet wine sauce as a glaze to fortify his own strength. Too soon, the shaking ride resumed.

His first step off the chariot lurched him sideways and he fell onto his hip. The Persian waved farewell and left him choking in a cloud of dust. In a moment, a shepherd boy stood over him flashing his wooden sword. "So, you have returned to help us. You're too late. Uncle Abraham died on the cross and was burned in the Roman fires." The youngster bent close as if in conspiracy. "Our revenge is coming soon."

Nathaniel accepted the extended hand and managed to stumble onto his feet. His ankle burned with pain as he limped up the steep incline toward home. No one stood at the gate to welcome him back.

~ ~ ~

Uncle Avraham was almost as round as he was tall. He waddled like a pregnant donkey and had a long, bearded face to complete the picture. He didn't look at all like his tall and slender sister, which led Heli to frequently joke that his brother-in-law must have been mixed up in the barn by the midwives. He arrived at the door of his sister's, huffing as if he'd run all the way.

Ana welcomed him in.

"I can't stay," Uncle Avraham said. "My gardener told me that the centurion is sending his men here to pick up Salome."

"What? Why would he do that?" Ana replied. "You could have sent a messenger."

Regardless of his looks, Uncle Avraham was a successful money lender, trader, and ship builder. The ship building had come through inheritance from his grandfather who had created huge fleets for the Phoenicians in Tyre and Sidon. The Romans had taken over the shipyards and the contracts without consideration of who built and who took all their coin. They did know that he was a man of distinction and not someone to be bothered.

"I came to take her to safety," Uncle Avraham said. "They won't think to look at my place."

"But what has my Salome done?" Ana protested. "She finished working there years ago."

"Hurry! It won't be long," the big man urged. "We can send her back here once they're gone."

Uncle Avraham kept a fair-sized home in Nazareth, plus others in Cana, Caesarea, and Yerushalayim. Salome's mother secreted her daughter into her brother's fine carriage before dusk and sent Salome on her way. Uncle Avraham squeezed into all the remaining space and settled in to catch his breath.

Salome kept her silence until her uncle's gasping settled to a pant. The horses moved slowly down the uneven roadway but the carriage continued to rock like a boat swamped in the waves.

"So, I hear you tried to poison the centurion in Sepphoris." A distinct guttural giggle created a new quaking in the cart. "That won't go over well with the Romans."

Salome gulped. "You don't think I'd really do anything like that, do you Uncle Avraham? I try so hard to be good and things like this seem to keep happening."

The big man chortled and his shaking body compressed Salome against the sides of the carriage. "I heard they crucified one of those Zealots over there. It wouldn't take much to hang a few more bodies on those wretched posts."

"I used to be the chef for the centurion but that was a long time ago and I don't control everything people choose to do," Salome said.

"I could use a new chef. What did you make over there that us common folk aren't eating?"

Salome, suffocating under the strong body odor of her uncle, raised her nose for air. "Probably nothing Jewish people should eat. Items like pig's feet and pigeon tongues."

"I shouldn't have asked," he rumbled. "Your mother says I only have you for one or two days so you can look around in my pantry and make up something special. Who knows what these slaves hide in there?"

The carriage rocked to a stop and two large Greeks reached in to extract Uncle Avraham. The fresh air and sense of space invigorated Salome and she gratefully followed a Syrian maid into the room prepared for her. Her uncle left the next morning for destinations unknown and, before she thought to ask, the same carriage took her back to her home three evenings later.

"The soldiers are gone," the gardener told her.

Salome persuaded the driver to drop her off near the synagogue in Nazareth. She slipped out of the enclosed carriage and huddled behind a hedge, watching for observers. The rabbi's ten-year-old daughter giggled and stood near the weaver's son. Surely, they were too young for thoughts of love. The two didn't even look her way as she skittered across the pathway and rested, panting, behind the butcher's donkey.

Michal, the leather worker's wife, labored under the weight of a bucket of water she hauled from the village well. She was clearly pregnant but still determined to do her tasks. She passed by the young couple and stopped long enough to share a tongue lashing. The two split and ran in opposite directions toward their homes.

Old Shamri, a cane in each hand, swayed unevenly on bowed legs as he moved toward his beggar's spot near the synagogue. An eager pup, tail wagging, ran in and around the beggar's canes, barking and threatening to trip him up. The rabbi appeared from a pathway leading to Salome's home. "Shamri," he called. "Have you seen Heli's daughter? I'm afraid something terrible has happened to her. No one has seen her lately."

The old man wobbled to a stop and shook his head. "No, rabbi. I haven't seen her anywhere. She's the one the soldiers were after, right?"

"Yes. Shalom to you," the rabbi said and headed off in the opposite direction.

Joel, the pigeon catcher, pulled a cart filled with snares and small bird cages toward the village gate where he would set up for the day in the nearby forest. His mother, single and sickly, would spend the daylight hours in their small kiosk hoping that someone would purchase what her son had caught.

No one noticed Salome as she squeezed through the hedge near her childhood home. Her mother took the bread out of the oven when she slipped into the house. "Goodness, child!" Ana said. "Why don't you warn me before you surprise your mother?"

"Ima, I'm home. It looks like the rabbi was looking for me."

Her mother set the bread on a plate and looked toward the front door. "He was just here. He thinks the centurion will send another group of soldiers to search through the whole village. He wondered what you could have done."

"Ima, I'm scared." Salome peered out the window and then went to her mother for a hug. "I haven't been this scared since that night the man killed grandfather in front of me."

Salome's mother embraced her daughter and rubbed her back. "Easy, child. Your Abba took care of that trouble then and he'll take care of this trouble now."

CHAPTER SIX

Nazareth – Surprise Encounter

Nathaniel scooped up a gourd of water at the village well as the rabbi rushed up. "Praise Adonai—you've returned," he said. "Your wife told me of the pagan figurines you were carving of Heli's daughter and we both thought you had abandoned the faith. Where is that wench? Has she led you astray?"

One look into the rabbi's eyes said it all. He was serious. Nathaniel chortled, then bent over in a belly laugh. "What foolishness has Sarah been telling you now," he finally said. "Heli's daughter threw me away over ten years ago. Why would you imagine that she had anything to do with me leaving to go hunting?"

"Hunting!" the rabbi said. "You hardly hobble. How would you hunt?"

Nathaniel set the gourd back in the bucket by the well. "It seems I have a lot to speak to my wife about. I trust services at the synagogue are going well."

The rabbi nodded. "It seems the young ones are learning to debate well. We've been exploring the Torah to understand whether the commands of Ha'Shem to our people under Joshua still apply to our conflict with the current occupiers."

"You mean the Romans," Nathaniel said.

Glancing over his shoulder quickly, the rabbi put a hand to his mouth. "They've sent strangers to our village disguised in an attempt to stop us from supporting the freedom fighters," he said. "For now, we are telling all our men to be cautious and to continue in their prayers."

"What about the women?" Nathaniel asked.

The synagogue leader smirked. "The women? There isn't a woman I know who would endanger her family by getting involved in some pointless struggle. Your wife, Sarah, is a good example for all our women in the way she does business and cares for her family." He rested a hand on Nathaniel's shoulder. "Perhaps you should go home and encourage her on what a good wife she is."

When he did hobble into his own home, his daughter Hannah ran to him open-armed. Sarah stood in the background drying a dish. "That was a quick trip," she said. "Was the tigress not up to being hunted?"

He lifted Hannah into his arms and swung her around and around as she giggled with glee. "A few minutes on Uncle Zeke's boat was all I could tolerate. I don't have the stomach or the balance to even get to the hunting grounds." He set his daughter down and watched her wobble across the grass before tumbling. "Perhaps you and I should talk about such things before the rabbi, the baker's wife, and everyone else in the village comes up with their own version of whose children really live with us."

Sarah set the dish and towel down. "What are you trying to say? I am not the unfaithful one in this relationship." She marched over to Hannah and set her daughter upright. "Please go check on the baby," she instructed. "I'll be with you shortly." When Hannah skipped into the house Sarah turned back to her husband. "You come home looking a mess after running away despite my pleas. You flaunt your passions openly by carving your old love in intimate detail. You come and go without explanation and without any attempt to help me in the business I am trying to set up so we can be prosperous, and then you accuse me?"

"I'm not trying to accuse you of anything," Nathaniel said. "I don't appreciate being told by the rabbi that you are telling everyone that I am being unfaithful when there is no truth in any of it. I want you to talk with me if you have troubles instead of sharing with everyone else."

Sarah crossed her arms and glared. "I'm tired of living with a man whose heart is clearly divided. If you're going to live here then I expect your heart, your mind, and your body to be here when you're needed. I'm tired of the whispers that come my way from the women in this village." She turned away. "Our child needs me. Perhaps you can fetch some water from the well so we can wash our feet when we get home. Maybe if you were here to talk with, I wouldn't have to talk with the rabbi."

~ ~ ~

If only her Abba could help her now. As a child, she had run from her doorway into the street to welcome her grandfather. Just before she reached him, an assassin had stepped out of the shadows and knifed the man she loved. The open mouth and shocked eyes of her grandfather's death mask still haunted her dreams at times.

Her father had taken up his hunting bow and chased down the man to mete out his own justice. Salome had knelt, cradling her gasping grandfather's head in her lap until he was still.

Now, Salome determined on her fifth day to lay low in Nazareth and avoid Sepphoris. A special meal would ease the strain with her Abba. Her sister Mariam was stopping by. The butcher had exactly what she needed. As she doffed her sandals and washed her feet outside the door, raised voices filtered from the inside. Her Abba and the rabbi!

Salome backed away from the door and tripped over the village dog who had followed her home. The lamb shank she carried flew back and hardly hit the ground before the dog was on it, dragging it out of the yard. Not wanting to alert the rabbi to her presence, she stumbled back to her feet and raced after the dog.

A chunk of meat broke off as the pup dragged the lamb shank around the donkey at the olive press. The dog snatched a quick swallow, a new bite, and the race was on again. A young teen stomping on grapes in the wine press laughed so hard at the dog's antics that he fell to his knees in the mix. Salome pressed on. When she caught up to the thief, the mutt stood over the meaty bone and snarled at her. Three girls nearby stood open-mouthed as they watched.

A large olive twig lay by the chickens, so she grabbed it and prepared to strike the pup. As she raised the branch Nathaniel stepped into view with his hands held high. "Wait!"

Mid-swing, Salome stopped and watched Nathaniel hobble closer. He knelt down a few feet from the pup and spoke to it. The dog cocked its ears and watched him. Pulling a small rope from his pocket he formed a noose, hovering it near the pup's nose as the dog sniffed at it. He dangled it in front of the pup and laid it over its head. In a moment, he cinched it tight and tugged the whining pup away from the bone. He tied the resistant canine to a post in the chicken pen.

Salome latched onto the lamb shank and raised the muddy trophy over her head while the dog strained at his new leash. "Thank you."

"Glad I could help." His dimpled smile added depth to his strong jawline and dark eyes. His broad chest and thick shoulders strained the limits of his garments. His deep dark eyes seemed to penetrate her.

She lowered her eyes. "Perhaps I've misjudged you." She picked out bits of rock and brushed away a layer of dirt. The three young girls peeked around the chicken pen and giggled.

Nathaniel took a step toward her. "Perhaps you have." The dog whined.

Her lungs hesitated to breathe. *What's happening?* Gentleness bathed those eyes. Vitality filled those full lips. "Perhaps we should talk some time." She clamped her jaw shut. A frown at the three girls did nothing to dissuade them from their eaves dropping.

Nathaniel stopped in place. "Perhaps it's too late."

She turned fully toward him. "What do you mean?"

He held out his hands, open and empty. "We are both happily married and the village has enough gossip to keep it busy."

"So, I am too late." More neighbors gathered.

Nathaniel smiled as he hugged the dog's neck gently. "Only if you don't get that bone cleaned up and to your mother before dinner. Perhaps one day we will see the best in each other and understand the plans the Almighty has for each of us."

"Thank you."

Salome endured the looks of villagers as she carried her muddy shank bone to the well and did her best to wash it off. Significant chunks of meat were missing but once it was roasted it would still provide enough for her Abba.

The roasted meat worked well in a stew with extra carrots, onions, peppers, and cabbage. Her Abba patted his stomach, let out a small belch, and leaned back into his pillow. He shared his stories from the day but didn't mention his conversation with the rabbi. Ima shared her stories of gossip from the marketplace regarding the lamp maker's new baby, a donkey colt born to the plow maker, and a new visitor who had warned the rabbi that the Messiah would soon come. Her dad nodded and scratched his chin through his thick beard.

Mariam shared stories about feeding the chickens, about creating a new song of praise to Ha'Shem, and about her new baby's first kicks. Salome noted that she had seen Nathaniel on her way home from the butcher.

"Shouldn't you be getting back to Zebedee?" Mariam asked. "You should bring your children. Abba and Ima aren't getting any younger."

Abba furrowed his eyebrows and rubbed his chin again. "Grandchildren are a delight, indeed. Perhaps not all children are as easy going as Yeshua. Perhaps, I can take you home and see them while I'm there."

"I can find my own way home," Salome said. "I will come again."

"Make sure you stop by and see my children first," Mariam said. "After all, you are still their aunt even if you live so far away."

Clean up was quick and when night had settled on the land the lamps were extinguished and everyone settled onto their cushioned reed mats. Mariam decided to stay overnight with her sister but fell asleep quickly. It was annoying to hear her sister breathing so peacefully.

As Salome unfolded her blankets her father stopped by the doorway. "Salome. Come walk with me."

The icy wind ripped at her shawl and crawled inside her tunic. Dark clouds drifted across the face of the moon and the howl of a wolf sent shivers down her spine. Father seemed oblivious to the elements.

Her Abba interlocked fingers behind his head and waggled his neck. "Salome, do you know why we named you Salome?"

"No, Abba."

"Salome Alexandra was the last of the great Maccabean rulers and the only Queen—her husband was the first to take on the title of king since the destruction of the first temple." Her Abba pointed toward the synagogue. "She was the sister of Rabbi Shetach who was the famous leader of the Sanhedrin."

Hands on hips, she took her stand at the compound gate. "So, you think I could be a queen?"

"Perhaps if you live out your role as a wife well." Her Abba swung the gate open. "When Salome's husband died, she released her husband's brother from prison and married him—because she was childless and our Jewish law instructs us in this way to raise up the next generations." The pair walked on through the open gate.

"I don't understand what this has to do with me."

Abba held up a hand. "Her husband was busy with his military campaigns so let her rule over the land. She removed the Sadducees and installed her brother as the leader of the Sanhedrin. Schools teaching Torah were installed all over the land and people were happy."

Salome swung the gate closed behind them. "So, if I had a brother who lived, and I put him in charge of the schools, and I had a husband who ruled this country, then I could live up to my name."

"Hush, my child." Abba put an arm around her and pulled her close. "Salome's husband betrayed her and the righteous sages by returning from his battles and killing eight hundred of them. He restored the Sadducees to power."

"So, I need to be careful in case my husband betrays me?"

"No, child." A stronger shoulder squeeze. "Salome's husband grew sick, he repented, and in his last will he restored the rule back to Salome."

"So, I should make my husband important but do something to make sure he doesn't live too long."

"Salome, you miss my point." A release as they U-turned around the village well. "Queen Salome ruled for nine of the happiest years our people have ever known and it is to this memory we gave you your name. You made us happy."

"I shall do what I must to keep you happy." She sighed. "If only you hadn't married me to someone I could never love."

"Be at peace, child. We all do what we must."

"Abba, do what you must but spare me from an unrighteous man whom I could never love."

Her father walked quietly for a long time before speaking again. "Salome, you have been so good to me in every way apart from this one way of not exalting your husband."

Salome gripped his arm with both hands and pulled close to her father as they strolled through a small apple orchard. "Abba, I would do almost anything to please you. Only now, my heart is breaking."

Her father stopped and took her face in his hands. "What is it child?"

"The Romans are capturing children to comfort their soldiers. It breaks my heart to think that these children could be my own."

Heli frowned and held her gently by the shoulders. "Return to Capernaum, to your husband. Let others struggle with such issues." He released her and led her through their compound gate. "You are now a fisherman's wife. Be who you are, not some dreamer who is out to save the world."

Salome nodded. "I can only be who Ha'Shem has made me to be. I will return to my husband after the Sabbath. I have more to do in Sepphoris tomorrow."

~ ~ ~

Only when Salome was out of sight did Nathaniel release the mutt. It looked longingly in the direction she had gone. The three girls, who had watched the escapade from their shelter near the chicken pen, stepped forward to pat the dog and test their girlish charms on the handsome hero. "You like her, don't you?" one of the girls said. "We can tell by the way you look at her."

"Do you think you should be out here without a protector?" Nathaniel asked. "I hear that some parents are being extra careful with their children with so much trouble around."

The oldest of the three crouched beside the dog, patting its head. "My Abba says not to talk with strangers but you're not a stranger. We see you with the sheep and my brother, Nahum, works with you. He's a Zealot but he doesn't want my parents to know."

"Do you think it's a bad thing, to be a Zealot?" Nathaniel asked.

"Nahum says we need to get our land back." She stood, looking toward the village gate. "He wants to learn to fight the Romans. He says he's not afraid of them but sometimes I overhear him talking to my dad about children that the Romans are taking far away from home. Why don't the Romans like us?"

Nathaniel scratched his beard thoughtfully. "Your brother may not be the only one who is afraid," he said. "Even grown men get afraid of what they don't understand. These soldiers don't understand our faith or our way of life. They're already far away from their own homes and sometimes they do things that no one likes."

~ ~ ~

The conversation about Queen Salome with her Abba had been intriguing and revealing but it was her brief interaction with Nathaniel that filled her thoughts as Salome walked down the steep hill from Nazareth on the following morning. Especially as she bid farewell to the gatekeeper, Gideon.

The gatekeeper's son's broad shoulders and strong chest were easy on the eyes. His scruffy beard and tanned face had a rustic charm different from Zebedee's leather-like skin and graying features. He had proven himself as a faithful pillar in the community and the respect others had for him was evident. Even the titter of the three little girls by the chicken pen revealed how easy it was to trust him.

If only he might team up with her and Ox to put a stop to the trade in children. His limp made it clear he was limited. Plans swirled in her head to counteract what she had witnessed but she was a woman, a mother, someone isolated from the group at the center of all the action. If the Romans found out she was active again then her parents, her sisters and even her husband and children might be at risk.

Her thoughts drifted to consider the mosaic and the centurion who had commissioned it. Anthony had been a charmer when she was young and working for him in his kitchen. She'd seen his temper with others but witnessing his intensity against the girl from the cage tapped into an unrealized rage. The fear on the face of the waif both pulled her toward getting involved and frightened her to stay away.

Besides, there were too many children involved. What could she do against Anthony and warriors like him? It was going to take something special to make a difference that mattered.

CHAPTER SEVEN

Nazareth / Sepphoris – The Rescue

Because his ankle was swollen, Nathaniel fashioned a crutch and eased himself out of the village with his sheep. Hannah had been pleased by his return but when the sun rose the sheep needed his attention. His late departure and slow gait enabled him to see Salome hurry down a pathway toward Sepphoris. From his perch atop the hill, he watched a Zealot warrior shadow her across the valley. She would be safe.

Seeing her face to face as he rescued the lamb shank from the dog had shaken him to the core. Being near her again had taken his breath and filled his dreams again. Her hazel eyes seemed to look right through him. Her long auburn hair invited him to reach for its shimmering softness. Self-discipline was needed even more now. Sarah was more right than she realized.

The shepherd boy, Nahum, stood in place as Nathaniel balanced himself among the sheep nosing their way along the precipice toward the ridged plateau. The sparse tufts of grass sprouting from the edges of the path classified this area of the valley as a green meadow. "You are late, shepherd!" the boy called. "We are already here." Three other youngsters his age hurled rocks at a large boulder in the ravine below. "We have learned the psalm you taught us and now we need to learn another."

"Your minds are quicker than mine, Nahum," Nathaniel responded. "Sing it for me so that I make sure I taught it well."

The quartet of boys continued to improve their aim at the boulder below as they harmonized a psalm that echoed through the ravine. None of them even noticed the wolf slinking toward a wandering lamb on the periphery of the flock.

The alarmed bleat of the ram raised Nathaniel's attention. In seconds, he crouched, withdrew his sling and released a missile that caught the predator on its snout. The sharp yelp sparked the boys who turned and pelted the startled wolf. One of the boys raced for the lamb with a fist-sized weapon as the wolf made its lunge. Nathaniel unleashed his sling and caught it in the ear. The wolf dropped, rolled and faced its attackers. The ram charged. The boy hurled his rock and broadsided the predator. In minutes, the attack was over and the wolf skittered away, watching from a nearby hillock.

The shepherds stood between predator and prey. "Here is your psalm for today," Nathaniel said. "Praise the Lord, who is my rock. He trains my hands for war and gives my fingers skill for battle. Sing it after me, men."[1] And so, the ravine echoed with the unified chorus of five voices praising the one who saves.

Salome climbed to the top tier of the amphitheater in Sepphoris. It nestled into the eastern side of the hill and could seat four thousand spectators without strain. A handful of snow-white clouds hung across the backdrop of powder blue. A dozen or more crows cawed and flitted in and out of the marketplace while sparrows watched for seeds and gulls circled overhead. A small boy, perched on a fountain rim, targeted the big black birds with a handful of pebbles.

A cohort of nine thespians donned masks on the platform below and rehearsed their lines as two armored gladiators crossed wooden swords on the main floor. A noblewoman, dressed in the finery of Rome, escorted seven young girls from diverse nationalities along the top row of seating, pointing out the scenery far beyond the city walls. The girls were dressed with too much finery to be local farm girls. *Could these be some of the stolen girls?*

Salome moved to stand near the group, focusing her attention on the actors below.

"Notice the two roadways bringing life to Rome and to all of us who depend on her," the woman with the girls crooned. "The Via Maris is where those camel caravans are taking the treasures of the East to the Great Sea and on to Rome." She turned to her charges with a smile. "Some of the finest silks, perfumes, and delicacies your men could ever dream of will pass this way." She faced inland toward the lake that Salome now called home. "Beyond the hills, winds the Acre-Tiberius and the new city built to honor our great emperor. From here and from there, all the wonders of this land are collected to satisfy the taste of the one we worship."

Two of the young girls looked down and the oldest nearby reached over and gently slapped the back of their heads. "Respect. Power. Life," she said.

The older woman glared at the girls until she was satisfied with the stiff backs, lifted jaws, and expressionless faces. "Respect. Power. Life. These truths will carry you through all you will face. Listen and learn the art of being a flower in the emperor's garden."

Salome leaned on the wall and scanned the Beit Netofa Valley below. Nazareth and Cana seemed so close that a slung stone might reach them. Fields of golden wheat shimmered all around. The Great Sea sat calmly to the west, awaiting another flotilla of trading ships escorted by the Roman warships.

Beauty was everywhere. Within the city limits dozens of mosaics decorated the sides of bathhouses, aqueducts, Herod's palace, and the exterior of a massive reservoir. Residences were larger and more ornate than she remembered. The fortress hadn't changed.

The woman and girls meandered their way down the rows of seats until they reached an exit near the main marketplace. Salome watched the girls from above. Shrines to Hercules, Pan, Dionysus, Venus, and Mars provided a protective ring around the vendors and the goods they sold. Masterpieces of revelry and paganism.

Somewhere in this center of pagan wonder, Yuseph worked. Could she count on her brother-in-law if needed?

The horse's hooves alerted her first. Before her eyes located the centurion Anthony riding in through the city gate, her ears picked out the distinct staccato of the stallion despite the cacophony of the market, the fortress, the builders and the shrines. The burnished bronze breastplate and helmet glistened on the warrior who carried the stature and confidence of a monarch.

The guardian of the girls appeared outside the Temple of Venus where Anthony waited on his steed. She bowed low before the centurion. It made sense that these girls were being prepared to serve the love goddess. Hamurti, the Egyptian slave who worked for Anthony, had specialized in reproducing the goddess within.

The first note for her Zealot contact was simple. "Seven girls prepared for the Temple of Venus." The small scrap of papyrus tucked easily into the niche behind the loose stone in the wall behind the bakery. She withdrew the two scraps already there. The first must have been new. "Nazareth carpenter's girls taken into bathhouse." The second made no sense. "The nest is empty."

The first note tucked in beside her sling. The second returned to the wall. By taking a message she committed to act on it. *How do I get the girls out of a bathhouse? I've never made use of one before. At least Anthony won't see me in there.* For two days she hovered around the outside of different bathhouses attempting to catch a glimpse of the carpenter's daughters. Dozens of girls came and went but none of them were Jewish.

The thought of having to strip down and expose herself to get into the bathhouse kept her wandering the city, considering any other option. How would she know what the carpenter's daughters looked like? *Who would know? Mariam, my sister? Shoshanna, the baker's wife? Who else could do this? Am I in or am I out?*

A trip to Nazareth was unavoidable. The hour-and-a-half walk left her thirsty as she approached Gideon, who was on guard at the gate. "Salome? Is that you?" he welcomed. "How do our young girls stay so beautiful even after they are mothers of a tribe of their own?"

Salome chuckled. "So, the rumors are true. The goats have eaten your eyes."

Gideon nodded as she passed and then picked up his cane for the trek to the baker's wife. Soon, the whole village would know she was home.

Mariam sat calmly bathing a small boy as three other children marched around the yard silently. Yeshua was absent. "We're replaying the battle of Jericho," Mariam informed her sister as if Salome's arrival was an everyday happening. "This is the best part—silence."

The children raced in for a hug, then continued to march as the sisters exchanged news. When home news was done Salome spoke of her encounter on the road with the dying carpenter. "He asked me to find his lost daughters in Sepphoris," she summarized. "Before I find them, I need to know what they look like."

Mariam glanced at her own little ones. "I can't imagine the pain of their mother. We heard the father and daughters had disappeared and wondered if there was trouble we didn't understand. But what can you do?"

Salome smirked at the middle child, James, who was poking the back of the oldest, Assia as they marched. "Stop it!" Assia finally commanded.

"You talked first," James responded. "Ima, Assia talked first. She has to clean up after the chickens."

"That's not fair!" Assia protested. "He wouldn't stop poking me. The children of Israel didn't march around Jericho poking each other."

Mariam nodded for Salome to take over bathing the baby. "Trouble in paradise," she smiled. "Okay, I'm Joshua," she told the children, "and here are the next commands. Each of you stand in a corner of the yard and quote the Shepherd's Psalm to yourself ten times. When you're finished, we'll decide on what happens next before the walls fall down around here."

Mariam took the baby and dried it off while trying to describe the carpenter's two girls. "The oldest daughter is Huldah and the youngest is Abigail." She swaddled the baby and then handed him to her sister. "Huldah is a hand taller than my Assia and Abigail is about the same size as Assia. They're about a year apart. If you call them by name they'll respond."

Salome rocked the child as it stared up at her. I wonder what these little ones think when a stranger takes them? I wonder what Huldah and Abigail thought when a stranger took them?

It was easy to postpone getting back to Sepphoris so she could enjoy familiar hospitality. Her nephews and niece took advantage of her presence once their penance was complete. Salome walked the two older ones around the neighborhood to give Mariam space as she prepared dinner. Soon after their return, Yuseph arrived and shared the meal of lamb stew, bread, cheese, olives, and dates.

Once the children were in bed, Salome questioned her brother-in-law regarding Sepphoris. "What do you know about the young girls brought in to comfort the Romans?"

Yuseph grimaced. "Do you really need to talk about this?" he asked, looking at Mariam.

Salome ignored the dodge. "Your neighbor was murdered by a Roman who stole his two daughters. You know Huldah and Abigail better than I do.

I would expect that if your daughters were taken you would want someone to do something to save them."

"You know I'm just a tradesman trying to do my job," Yuseph said. Before Salome could respond he held up his hand. "I'm a tradesman, but I'm not blind. The Romans bring in girls and train them through the baths. Once they get used to the baths they are moved to the temples for further training." He rubbed his hair. "I can only imagine what that means."

Enough had been said. Shortly after dawn, Salome walked through the gates of the city with Yuseph and headed for the baths. "If the carpenter's girls are still new then I'll probably find them there." *What am I getting myself into?*

The direct approach seemed to make the most sense and the public baths near the fortress were a logical place to start. Salome met the matron at the door and stated plainly, "I'm Jewish and I've never been to the baths before. I'm looking for help from Jewish girls. Maybe ones that are new."

The matron looked over her shoulder. "Go away!" she said. "This is not the place for your first bath. We don't take new girls here."

Treatment was the same at the baths by the Temple of Venus and the Temple of Aphrodite. The face of the pleading carpenter, etched into her memory, urged her on when she wavered in her courage or succumbed to fears of humiliation. *Would I do this even for my own daughters? Why would I even think of this for strangers? If Zebedee finds out, or the Romans find out, there is no way to explain this.*

Sitting by a fountain praying for guidance brought peace of mind. As she sat surveying the crowd, a middle-aged woman stepped out of the stream of humanity and sighed as she sat. Her pale-blue mantle and tan tunic were fashionable but not expensive. A dozen bangles on her wrist displayed familiarity with fashion from different countries. Turning to Salome she smiled. "Everyone should take a rest, don't you think?"

Salome nodded.

"I love this place," the woman continued. "Sepphoris looks magical in the moonlight, don't you agree?"

A sword in the belly couldn't have surprised her more. The old Zealot code word. She scrambled for the right response. "It's even better in the sunshine." It was hard not to stare.

The woman removed two of her jade bangles and held them out to Salome. "The next street over by the taxation center. Say nothing but hand these to the matron at the door. She will take you where you need to go."

The baths weren't hard to find and the matron at the door seemed to be expecting her. Salome held out the bangles and the woman motioned her inside to a side room. "Leave your clothes here," she said. "You can wrap in a towel if you'd like. The two you desire will be together in the last room." The matron looked around. "Take your time in the waters and act like you are enjoying the experience. There are watchers who will stop you if you act suspicious. Behind this basket there are tunics for your friends."

Her monthly mikvah cleansing in the pool at her home in Nazareth had been a pleasurable time of privacy and renewal. Stepping into a room with dozens of unclothed women and girls sitting, chatting, laughing as if it was the most normal thing in the world numbed the mind. Women would walk into the room, toss their towels to the side and plunge into the pools. It took a moment to catch the routine of the regulars.

"Looking for someone?" a broad-shouldered Persian asked from her place at the edge of the warming pool.

Salome swallowed, tossed her towel to the side and plunged into the pool feet first. Surfacing, she faced the Persian. "Just looking for a familiar face."

"Pretty quick with that towel," the Persian said. "First time?"

Heat flushed her face but she nodded. "I guess we all have to learn to live sometime."

The Persian laughed. "Well said. I won't ask you to sit up here and talk. It takes time to get past worrying what everyone else is thinking." She pointed toward the other two pools in the room. "In here, we are all the same. Without clothes, we don't know who is rich or poor, master or slave, fashionable or not."

When the Persian moved on, Salome waited a few minutes and followed into the cool pool. It was a shock to the system and she emerged quickly to reclaim her towel. A young girl held it as she struggled to modestly climb out of the water. There was no easy way to exit without drawing attention.

Safely wrapped again in the towel, Salome skipped the steam room, where dozens of women sprawled, and headed for the last room. There were ten tables with women laying on each one, stretched out as masseurs worked on them. Five women stood waiting for treatment, including the Persian.

Salome prepared to bypass the massage room for the changing room when she saw the two girls. They huddled self-consciously behind armloads of towels near one of the changing tables. Meandering toward them she smiled. The two girls bowed and waited.

"You two look like friends of mine," she said. "Huldah and Abigail are two of the best friends anyone could ever have." The girls stiffened. "I would love to show you a home in Nazareth if you can think of a way to come with me. I'm going to slip and fall and I need you to help me to the changing room."

The slip wasn't worthy of a thespian but it drew attention. Silence filled the space at the tables. The masseurs stood dripping in oil, the strigils used for scraping off lotion stuck in their hands. They looked at the young girls hopefully. The girls dropped their towels and worked to assist Salome to her feet. Once the unclothed trio moved toward the changing room, the conversations returned to its previous din.

Salome pulled out the basket indicated earlier by the matron, retrieved the tunics and tossed them to the girls. She then dried off and donned her own clothing.

"Follow me," she said. "Say nothing. For now, act like I'm your mother."

The matron stood with her back to the door of the baths and ten steps past her the middle-aged Zealot who had given Salome the bangles fell into step. At an alley she motioned the others into an alcove where another woman threw additional tunics over the trio and added different colored mantles.

The jade-bangled wearer nodded to Salome. "You've done your part. Go back home and wait until someone calls you again. Watch for the messengers and the messages. You are highly favored."

The two women moved down the alley where they met with a man leading a donkey cart. The group piled on and Salome was left to find her way back to Capernaum. The lake had a glorious sheen on it as she crested the hill. The sun was brilliant and soothing, the wheat fields waving, the gulls gliding, and dozens of fishing boats bobbed peacefully off shore. It was good to be back in a place where people could be counted on.

CHAPTER EIGHT

Nazareth / Capernaum – Nightmare Relived

The shriek from below surprised Nathaniel. His shepherd's staff had flipped the cobra over the edge into the ravine to clear the path for his flock. There was nothing below except an abandoned cave and a small underground spring forming a pool. He dropped to his belly and inched forward to peer over the edge. Five hooded figures circumnavigated the pool and moved toward the trail leading to the back entrance of Nazareth.

"Shalom, my friends," he called. "There's an easier way if you want it."

The lead figure held out his hand in a motion to stop and looked up. "Shalom to you, friend. We are passing the way we must and I encourage you to hold your peace."

The voice and form seemed familiar. "Ox! Is that you?" he called.

"It is, Nathaniel." The Zealot warrior removed his hood. "We have rescued the carpenter's girls and need to remove them to Cana before the Romans respond. If you can tell Benjamin's wife to join us near the village dump, I would be grateful. She already knows we are coming."

He motioned for one of the shepherd boys to come closer. "Nahum, watch the flock and especially that old ram. He's been more aggressive with that young ram over there. Keep them separate while I pass on a message."

The crutch provided support but not comfort as he moved quicker over the rough ground. As he neared the village gate, Heli, Salome's father, emerged from the bush pulling a large branch. His face brightened when he saw Nathaniel. "Shalom, my almost son-in-law," he said. "How are you changing the world today?"

Nathaniel lifted his crutch. "I'm afraid this has slowed me down. Maybe I'll change the world tomorrow. The sheep seem to like sticking to the same old routine."

Heli motioned to precede him and followed dragging the limb. "This cedar is perfect for making the cradle for my next grandchild. You can't start too early."

Nathaniel stopped. "Is Salome expecting again?"

Heli laughed. "Maybe if she stayed in Capernaum long enough there might be a chance. No, it's my daughter Rebekah in Cana." He pulled the branch through the village gate and turned toward his shop. "Oh, I'm sure Salome would want me to pass on her goodbyes. Praise Ha'Shem that she's gone home."

~ ~ ~

Diana met Salome still a mile from home, walking along the beach. "What happened?" she asked.

"I visited my sister," Salome answered. That was enough.

"I think the children better stay another night with me," Diana said.

"What do you know that I don't want to know?" Salome asked.

"Just go home and stay there for a while."

Over the next weeks, Zebedee appeared attentive and respectful when he was home. A decade earlier, life in the community, huddled on the northwest shore of the lake in Galilee, had taken on its routine. Zebedee had declared that most of the local families had given birth to boys who farmed and fished and he'd been right. Girls were brought from elsewhere and trained by women who had adjusted to the fishermen's life. The women were up before dawn to provide hot tea for the men and boys who plied the lake with their trade. They cleaned and gutted sardines and bass and tilapia for soups and stews. They offered hospitality to all who stopped by for whatever reason. Every woman lived for news from travelers with reports of what happened with her family.

And always the lake stood like a menacing terror ready to devour her.

A month after her return home from Sepphoris, Zebedee took Salome's hand and walked her to the beach. The wind whistled through the trees and churned up the lake into whitecaps. "Come, sail with me!" Zebedee urged. "It's been a long time. You need to try this again."

Salome pulled back. "The water still frightens me."

"Trust me," the fisherman urged. "I know this lake like the nose on my face. I won't let anything hurt you. I won't laugh this time."

Stomach churning, she clutched on tight to her husband as he guided her to a small wooden craft pushed up onto the shore. It rocked wildly as each wave hit it broadside. "This little one is especially quick across the surface. The joy you feel can't compare with anything else in the world. Trust me."

Zebedee straightened the craft and forced its bow first into the water. She doffed her sandals and followed him into the lake. The rolling waves seemed to delight in spurting spouts of chilly water onto her legs and torso as she valiantly attempted to step into the rocking tub.

As soon as she stepped into the craft and reached for the mast, a rogue wave crashed against the boat and sent her flying into the stern. The pain in her back was intense but the shock took both her breath and her voice.

Zebedee pushed the boat forward and then unleashed a small sail. The vessel hurtled across the choppy water, bobbed up and down, crashing and crushing her spine against the wooden frame. Zebedee howled with delight as Salome hung on in terror.

Several hundred yards from shore, another rogue wave slammed against the boat and tossed it sideways. Zebedee lost his hold on the rudder and sail long enough to send them in a spin so that the bow dipped into the waves and filled the bottom of the boat with lake water. Salome opened her mouth to scream as a full rolling wave hit her in the face. She released her hold, fell overboard and lashed out her arms at the endless churning of black, green, and blue that swallowed her. The hideous death mask of Thaddeus loomed into her mind and her soul begged the Almighty for one more chance to be good.

Zebedee jerked her to the surface and held her head above the waves as she choked, sputtered, and tried to scream. He pulled her, kicking and punching, toward the shore. As she fought for breath, she repented for every selfish act. *Ha'Shem, I'm sorry for refusing Nathaniel's betrothal, for losing the meat to the dog and for despising Mariam for her lapse of judgement in having a child before marriage.* Even when her feet first touched the bottom, she was sure her life was over.

Crawling onto the shore, she pushed Zebedee's hands away as she retched and retched. When she had nothing more to give, she dragged herself up and stumbled toward home. When Diana rushed out the door to embrace her, Salome clutched the girl and sobbed harder than she had ever done before.

Trust was too precious a treasure to give away to someone who would put your life at risk. Her husband had saved her but he had also first put her in the place where she nearly died.

Zebedee did his best to explain away the mishap but all he said only seemed to evoke other family stories of near fatality on the lake. For weeks, she woke in terrors clutching at her throat, screaming all the screams she couldn't get out as she went under the water. Zebedee didn't try to take her out again.

~ ~ ~

Five weeks after the rescue of the carpenter's daughters, Ox appeared near the ravine where Nathaniel watched the sheep. Nahum had vacated his post to join a band of young Zealots eager to try their skills with weapons training. The other boys had been called by the rabbi for a day of studies.

The muscular crusader settled himself on a stump overlooking the valley view of Sepphoris. "Have the Romans ever suspected you for being the eyes and ears of our little band of freedom fighters?" he asked. "It might be easier for us if you could get closer to the traffic on the main road below. Perhaps taking your daughter might prove beneficial to suspicious minds. The shepherd boy, Nahum, seems capable of managing the flock on his own."

A camel caravan paraded by on the road below, followed by a small band of horsemen. "Idumeans," noted Nathaniel. "Bound for Caesarea to trade dates, figs, and olives for oranges or something fresh."

"What about the donkey carts coming by the edge of the cliffs?" Ox asked.

The donkeys strained at their yokes, plodding deliberately and slowly. "Bricks, tiles, lumber for construction," Nathaniel answered. "Probably from this side of Damascus."

"Good eye," Ox said. "The one thing you don't see is the dozen crates of apricots for the Sicarii at the coast. Barabbas is testing the Roman security through here to see what other possibilities might get through. Having someone managing a station along the way would help out the cause."

The donkeys slowed to a stop as the drivers consulted and looked up toward the overhang where Ox and Nathaniel sat. One of the drivers moved his arms in a wide circle and then returned to his conversation.

"Did you notice that?" Ox said. "He's saying they have had no trouble being stopped along the way. Think about it."

"Give me time," Nathaniel said. "How are the carpenter's daughters you moved to Cana? That must have been a daring rescue."

Ox smiled. "Yes, all thanks to Salome. She had to expose herself in the bathhouses to find them and bring them out. She's become as valuable to us now as she was in her teens."

Nathaniel rose and walked closer to the Zealot. "Our Salome? In a bathhouse? How did you persuade her to do that?"

"I had little to do with it," Ox said. "She's got more courage than most of us. She's passionate about these children. If I can get her back into action, we may stop this thing yet."

"I saw a carriage of twelve children near Caesarea," Nathaniel said. "They were guarded well so I couldn't do much. You people are taking big risks trying to stop this flow to satisfy the cravings of the Roman Empire. Sarah just wants to make sure I guard our daughter Hannah." He used his sling to get the attention of a ram that was wondering on the fringe of the flock. The animal turned back to the group. "Nahum could probably watch the flock but Sarah wants me harvesting grapes soon. I'm not sure if I can make much difference with this limp."

Ox stepped away from the stump and into the bushes. "Look! Roman cavalry scouts are moving fast from Sepphoris. There's a spy around here somewhere. I've got work to do."

~ ~ ~

The nightmares continued for Salome but Zebedee stopped pressuring her to enter his fisherman's world any further than she was able. She focused her energies on the family garden, on beating out the clothes with the other wives, and on keeping her men well fed with the fish stew they loved.

One morning, when the boys had occupied themselves elsewhere, she headed off to search for tubers and berries in her favorite haunts up the hill. Her feet discovered the trail where the Parthian girl had shot at her and killed the dog. The clouds tumbled ominously as they had on that day.

She came to the tree where the arrow had burrowed itself. Had it all been a dream? She stepped off the path and examined the bark. Sure enough, the head of an arrow was still embedded. The shaft had been broken off. What had happened to that girl? Had her archery landed her in trouble elsewhere? Had Anthony ever added her to his list of stolen children?

Sinking down to the ground, she sat with her back to the oak and pondered the heavens. "Creator of the heavens and earth," she began out loud. "I only want peace for my family. Raise up someone else to save these children. Preserve me from pride and arrogance." No more words came.

Later, with her basket filled, she passed by the market and a strange thing happened. It was as if every child in the village appeared in the crowd and every one of them watched her go by. A sensation like spiders crawling up her legs and spine took over. She shuddered and walked away, her face focused on the ground.

Half way home her path was blocked by two little girls. She hesitated, to let them move aside, but they held their ground. Not recognizing the pair, she spoke politely. "Hello, I'm Salome, and I live just ahead. Are you new here?"

The older one, barely seven, nodded. "Our Abba says we're safe here because you know how to protect us. Is that true?"

"Who's your Abba?"

The girls giggled. "He's just Abba. We used to live with Uncle Benjamin but he died. Our cousins had to move somewhere else so we came to be with you."

The Almighty had a sense of humor. The nieces of the dead carpenter, whose daughters Salome had rescued, had come in answer to her prayers to be relieved of her mission to save the children. She smiled. "Your Abba is right. You are safe with me. Now, do you want to see where I live in case you need help?"

~ ~ ~

THE GOOD WIFE

The squadron of cavalry militiamen charged across the valley floor below as Nathaniel watched. Their target was clear. The drivers of the donkey carts sensed that too. The men stopped the carts and dismounted, pretending to adjust their load. They were soon surrounded.

The lead militiaman got down from his mount and shouted at the men who cowered under his whip. The other legionnaires joined in the activity by throwing lumber, bricks and stones off the carts. It wasn't long before the crates of apricots were hoisted into the air as evidence.

Barabbas and his men had taken their chances and lost. Unless another daring rescue materialized from the Zealots there would be two more bodies on the crosses at Sepphoris by nightfall. Roman justice was swift and decisive. Nathaniel shuddered and turned back toward his sheep.

~ ~ ~

The two girls, Zilpah and Tikah, giggled as Salome tossed the salad for the Passover meal. Her own children were off playing with their aunt Diana. "Now, remember this song," she chanted. "We plough and we grow after summers heat. We suck on the olives then for a treat. Before rains come, we seed for the wheat. We rest in the winter and then back on our feet. First flax, then barley, and then back to wheat. During summer we have figs, then grapes and dates sweet." The girls swirled in dance to her tune, smiling and thriving in the joy of learning without fear.

"Teach about the foods of Passover," Zilpah, the older girl urged.

Salome beckoned them to the table where various bowls were arranged around a larger bowl. "Watch and listen carefully as I reach into each bowl. For the salad, we use a bit of mint, rue, coriander, parsley, and of course olives. We add green onions, lettuce, coleroot, thyme, carmint, green fleabane, and celery." She rearranged the bowls and then chuckled. "All right, girls. Who can tell me which ingredient is in which bowl?" The game made the time pass quickly.

Leah wandered in and crossed her arms. "Why do they get all the Ima time? You should send them back where they belong!"

Whose daughter was this? She marched around and gripped the girl's shoulder firmly. "Zilpah and Tikah don't have an Ima to call their own so they are sharing. If you want to come and learn how to be an Ima with them then you are welcome but you are not welcome to chase them away."

The chastised girl jutted out her lip and dipped her chin, furrowing her brows to demonstrate her unhappiness. "If they have to share how come they get all your time?"

Salome crouched and looked her daughter in the eye. "I know that sharing is hard. Why don't you come and help us prepare the lamb? We've only done the salad so far."

"Do I get to put the mint sauce on?" Leah asked.

"After we roast the meat," Salome answered. "Your father should be here soon from the market. I'll show you how to make bread and then we'll finish the other dishes."

The shadows grew longer as the sun slid for the hills and Zebedee delayed still. The chard had been made into a dish with lentils and beans, mustard greens, and artichokes. Dried pears had been boiled in wine, water, and honey. Apples were mixed with toasted sesame and still no husband in sight. The smell of freshly baked bread began to wane. The girls worked well together but as evening approached Salome gathered samples of the salads, desserts, and bread, sending the girls on their way. "We will have lamb another day," she promised.

"Why isn't Abba home yet?" Leah asked. "I'm going to get the others for dinner."

The children were fed and fast asleep by the time Zebedee stumbled in. He righted himself against the door frame and stared at the food still on the table. "You're spoiling the food, leaving it untouched like that," he growled. "Wash my feet." He half-missed the stool but caught himself with one hand, pushing himself up again. Salome undid his sandals and carefully washed his feet, drying them with a towel. "What have you been doing all day?" he asked. "Chasing more of those Zealot fools?"

"I was teaching the girls how to make dinner," she answered softly. "They were sad you weren't here to enjoy what they made for you."

"You worthless liar," he snarled. "Trying to blame me for your own problems."

"We were waiting for the lamb you were supposed to bring home to roast," she said, rising and backing away from him. "This is Passover and we need to celebrate as a family. The children need to ask their questions and learn their history."

"All I care is if they know how to fish," Zebedee retorted. "You can teach them all that other information when they're doing nothing important. Teach them to honor their Abba and to run fast enough so I don't beat them to death." He chuckled at himself and fell off the stool. "Help me up, woman!" he shouted. "Can't you see I need help?"

"Abba?" It was James. "Abba, we waited for you for Passover."

Zebedee struggled to his feet. "You can learn all those stories when you're older. I listened to that stuff year after year and look what's happened. We've moved from being slaves to the Egyptians to being slaves to the Romans." He staggered to the table and picked up a loaf of bread, breaking it in two. "See!" he said, triumphantly. "We're a broken people living in a broken land. Learn everything you can to take care of yourself before you lose everything you have." He stuffed his mouth and staggered out the door.

"Ima, where's the lamb?" James asked.

Salome hung her head. "Your Abba found other ways to spend the money we had for the lamb. Try not to remember him like this."

CHAPTER NINE

Capernaum / Nazareth – Troubled Paradise

The vines bulged with their clusters during the season of heat and Nathaniel watched the workers gathering the ripe fruit into the reed baskets resting on their hips. He had walked the fields with Sarah's father, Abel, and brother, Eli, testing the grapes and deciding which part of the crop would flourish in fields near Nazareth. Sarah would be pleased with the volume of vines that would soon be growing.

Asaph, the chief vinedresser, stopped to sample the soil and lectured on about the best varieties for the soil in the area, the best time for planting and harvesting, the spacing of vines, the exposure of sun to ensure sweetness, plus the composting, pruning, and weeding needed. Nathaniel's mind was overloaded and he was grateful when his father-in-law motioned for him to step aside and drink some water.

A young girl, following along behind Asaph, shrieked and jumped back flailing her arms. "Get it off! Get it off!" she yelled.

Asaph calmly walked to her and plucked a large locust from out of her hair. Without hesitation he pulled off the legs and wings, put it into his mouth and crunched on it. Once he had swallowed, he crouched down before her. "My little deer," he said. "Ha'Shem has given us locusts to sustain us in our famines. There are eight hundred different kinds of locusts we can eat." He rose and patted his daughter's head. "Usually we boil them in salted water so they taste like shrimp or we fry them. There are some who see these creatures as enemies to destroy us. I see them as friends to sustain us."

"That is quite the lesson," Abel said. "However, if you see locusts in my fields you are instructed to destroy them before they destroy me. You can eat them, beat them, or burn them, but don't let them feel welcome anywhere near my home or fields."

"May your fields and crops always increase," Asaph said with a nod.

"Speaking of increasing, we are pleased to see you expanding the family holdings," Abel said to Nathaniel. "I don't mind telling you that Sarah has been quite concerned about living with the smell of sheep all her life. She dreams about the two of you marketing your olives and wine to places as far as Rome." He hesitated when he saw Asaph moving toward him. Holding up his hand to stop his chief vinedresser from coming closer, he whispered to Nathaniel. "We are also hoping to work out a deal with the Parthians to bring the best of silk from the Orient. We just have to navigate the fury of the Zealots and the paranoia of the Romans. We need you to work with us if wealth is to come our way."

Nathaniel's twisted gut grew nauseous as Abel left to consult with Asaph. What had he got himself into?

~ ~ ~

Within the year Salome gave birth to a daughter, Rachel. This time she spent a month in Nazareth with all four children convincing everyone that all was well in Capernaum. Walking through the terraced hills with their variegated red earth and green vegetation eased her heart and settled her mind. One afternoon she walked by the sheep pens and was surprised to hear that Nathaniel had given the primary care of the flock over to two of the young men who had tutored under him.

Upon her return to the fishing village, she circulated through Zebedee's family members, shared the briefest news of Nazareth, then opened doors and shutters in her own home while sweeping out the dusty interior. A dead rat in a corner had to be tossed before her mother-in-law might decree her to be an unfit wife. Zebedee's mother and two younger sisters had returned from Persia for a brief surprise visit. *Who knows what she thinks after I leave her son for a few weeks?* A candle and bowl of incense helped refresh the interior environment.

It was unfathomable how her husband could have been living on his own in this place for weeks and not have noticed the mess. She borrowed ingredients from her neighbors and set out a feast to welcome Zebedee home after his day selling fish in the market. It was well after dark before she gave up, blew out the candles and crawled into a cold, lonely bed.

Morning arrived with no news of Zebedee. James returned from his aunt's and asked, "Where's Abba?" but she had no answers. She didn't dare ask her mother-in-law, so she sought out Diana.

She watched as her sister-in-law wrestled dough into submission before baking it. "Good morning, Diana. I've missed you while I was away."

"You look happy to be back." Diana sprinkled a few herbs into the mix. "How was your sister?"

Salome collected dishes and set them in a bucket for washing. "She was still my sister."

Diana flattened the bread mix onto the side of the purni oven. "How's her oldest?"

"Yeshua is a young man now." Salome washed the wooden bowls. "She has six children. Her second youngest is James, just like my James."

Diana picked up a broom and swept the floor. "We didn't expect you for another week."

"I guess I should have sent a message." *Something wasn't right. Does even Diana resent me for leaving?* "Do you know where your brother is?"

The sweeping continued toward the door. "He could be anywhere."

Salome shook off the water from her hands and then wiped them on her tunic. "When was he here last?"

"He's been in and out." Diana swept the last bits out the door and set the broom against the wall. "Maybe a week."

Salome moved quickly to stand in front of her sister-in-law. "He hasn't been here for a week? Where's he staying?"

Diana looked away. "Not sure. I don't keep track of him anymore."

Salome persisted. "Is he at the market?"

"Could be."

Salome stared hard at Diana then grabbed her by the shoulders. "What aren't you telling me?"

Diana hung her head. "It probably would be a good idea if you didn't go to the market today."

She handed baby Rachel to her sister-in-law. Without another word, Salome pivoted and headed straight for the market.

Her set jaw, gritted teeth, pounding heart, and racing imagination didn't prepare her for the reality. Zebedee lounged in an alcove, sprawled in a drunken stupor on the lap of an Egyptian brothel girl who dropped grapes into his gaping mouth. The unbridled laughter emanating from the two of them drew stares from all who passed by.

Salome marched into the alcove and slapped the Egyptian. She grabbed Zebedee by his scrawny beard and yanked him onto the ground. As he blinked in confusion, she reached down and slapped him before turning toward home. A Roman centurion leaned against an archway grinning. Now, the whole town knew what a fool she was—thinking that she could trust her husband to be different. This was one story her family was never going to hear.

She marched from the market and straight up the path into the forest. She hesitated as the shadows seemed to increase the size of the demoniac's cave entrance. Diana had warned her not to go to the market but it had been midday and what could happen?

She passed the opening to Bartholomew's cave and spent the rest of the day in her own cave until her breasts let her know that baby Rachel needed feeding. The acid stench from the bat guano in the cave was far worse than the first time she had visited. As the sunlight faded, the bats dropped and flapped around her. Visions of being devoured by the demons of the night filled her mind and she crawled toward the entrance as quickly as she could. She ripped her tunic in the process but didn't stop.

As she rose to her feet a bat bounced off her shoulder. Her own unearthly scream frightened her as much as the bat. Before her feet found the trail among the shadows of dusk another screech reverberated off the rocks and trees. It wasn't hers. A great crashing through the underbrush paralyzed her and she fell to her knees, gasping for breath. There was no doubt. Bartholomew, the demoniac, lurked nearby.

Head between her knees, she prayed to Ha'Shem in desperation. A leopard's snarl sounded and she cried out louder. And then, a great crashing of snarling beasts entrenched in combat swallowed the forest.

Looking up toward the rising moon, she set her feet to the path and raced home. She crashed through the last bushes, slid down the hill, stumbled past the butcher's dozing sheep, and pushed into her own compound. Out of breath, she leaned against the wall, peered into the dark shadows of the forest, and waited for the screeching to stop. A hand closed around her wrist and she screeched as she fought off the attacker.

"What is wrong with you?" Diana yelled. "It's me."

Salome slumped onto a stool, gasping for breath. "It almost had me."

"What almost had you?"

"The demoniac, the leopard . . ."

Diana put a hand on her shoulder. "I don't know what you saw out there but I can tell you that I saw my brother come home from the market and he was not happy. I told you not to go." She held out baby Rachel. "Here, your baby needs feeding."

Salome took the child and set to letting it suckle. At last, something safe and warm. It's good to be needed.

Salome hid out at Diana's overnight and waited until the fishermen had vacated the place before she went home. It was mid-morning before the dreaded encounter happened.

The little one suckled contentedly on Salome's second breast until Zebedee rounded the corner. He kicked a bucket into the wall of the chicken pen as if it was a ball. The little one started. "You disrespectful wench!" he yelled. "How dare you humiliate me in public." He grabbed a handful of her hair and twisted. A pitiful cry sounded from her arms.

"The baby!" she cried out. "Don't hurt the baby."

He released his grip and marched back into the house, muttering.

Diana appeared and held out her hands for the baby. "You probably need to go for a walk," she said. "I'll try to calm the seas here before you get back."

Salome meandered toward the shoreline, watching the gulls glide above her. How good it would be to glide away from it all. Two small boats bobbed gently at anchor as the waters lapped against the beach. So peaceful. Her scalp burned with pain. A lazy swirling column of smoke drifted heavenward on the far side of the lake. The fluffy white clouds napped in place. James's sail boat sat perfectly still on the lake surface. With a good wind on quiet waters the trip might take a few hours. Doffing her sandals, she waded calf-deep, adjusting to the icy water and the shifting rocks underfoot.

Face your fears!" she commanded. "Show that fool you aren't afraid of a little boat ride."

She walked purposefully toward the smaller family boats anchored in the shallows nearby. Zebedee taught the boys to sail on these so how hard could it be? She grasped the bow of James's craft and pulled it closer until it ground on the bottom. "It's the last place he'd expect you to be. If I'm smart, I'll keep on going."

Before stepping into the boat, she glimpsed Diana standing and staring from the roof. The baby rocked gently in her arms. *That's all I need is for something to go wrong so my children end up without a mother. Diana would never forgive me.* Shoving the boat hard, she sighed. "Maybe next time."

~ ~ ~

The carvings continued to grow in number as Nathaniel perfected his art. He varied the size and shape to avoid having Sarah ask him her question, "Is that her?" Once a month he set out his display on a table along the Via Mara where traders and travelers scooped them up. It wasn't long before he was getting advance orders.

The morning after the Sabbath he set up his table with Hannah at his side. She marched the figures around his display table in a pantomime and customers laughed at her antics. It helped add to the sales. Just before noon, Anthony, the centurion from Sepphoris, stopped on his black stallion to examine why the crowd gathered. His bronze armor glistened like gold and gave the impression of invincibility. His red cape showed wealth and status. His ostrich feather-topped helmet conveyed authority. His unsheathed sword threatened without a word. The people parted and stood back as they waited his next move. Six of his legionnaires rode with him. "Carver," he called, "what is the meaning of this mob?"

Nathaniel picked up two figurines and hobbled toward the horseman. "Greetings, your excellency, on this fine day. My daughter and I are sharing our craft with those who are interested. There is nothing here to cause concern."

Anthony alighted and walked past Nathaniel to the table. "Is it your daughter who you use to fashion these beautiful pieces? She is quite the work of art for someone disabled like yourself."

"Our God has been gracious to his servant, my lord. My daughter is another gift given to me."

The centurion rotated slowly as he examined the faces in the crowd. "How can I know that you're not harboring Zealots in this crowd? Perhaps if I took your daughter, you might be more eager to expose those who rebel against me."

"None of us here seek to trouble you or the emperor," Nathaniel assured. "I will put my business away if you consider it a problem, my lord."

"Listen, shepherd," Anthony said. "I realize your people hate us Romans being here. I don't like being here either." He crossed his arms looking toward the Great Sea. "My family has an estate outside Rome with vineyards and beautiful gardens. My older brother is set to inherit it all. Because I am second-born my only chance for glory and status is to serve in the emperor's army." Sighing, he scanned the crowd again. "You're not the only one forced to live a life he wouldn't choose. Those of us far from home may have values and dreams different than yours but we are also men with needs and desires. If you could help me out a little, I'm sure we wouldn't have to be so hard on everyone."

Nathaniel nodded briefly. "I will do what I can do. Would you like me to pack up my business?"

Anthony returned to his horse and once astride he nodded. "No need. If I suspect you are undermining my rule I know where to find you."

Nathaniel would never forget the leering look the soldier directed toward Hannah. He determined never to expose her to the public like this again.

When he wasn't carving, he focused on nurturing the grape clippings and caring for his small plot. The more he focused on enlarging the vineyard, and the more he delegated shepherding to the younger men, the more Sarah expressed her happiness and the less he expressed his. The friction with his own father also grew as it became apparent that Sarah's family considered their work superior. Sarah clearly didn't understand her own father's involvement in the illegal silk trade or the pressure Nathaniel was under.

As he watched over his display table, he noticed an increasing number of covered carts being hauled straight through to Caesarea. One of the young Zealots standing near him nodded and said, "Children! Those perverse Romans are sucking the children from the lands nearby and shipping them into brothels and bathhouses. The warriors of the homeland are not going to turn a blind eye to this any longer."

A trader stopped by with his ox cart and examined the artistic little figurines. "Which gods are these meant to be?" he asked. He picked up a couple and ran his fingers over the smooth surface. "Your craft is worthy of promotion in a temple at least. The faces are intricate and imaginative. The grain and the cut make each an original."

Nathaniel nodded as he picked up his favorite. "You have a keen eye to see beauty in these figures. I serve only one deity and he has perfected those in his own image. I simply attempt to copy him."

The trader lifted a larger figurine. "This is surely the goddess Aphrodite. I will pay you double what you ask if you can sell me a dozen every month. The temple in Caesarea would welcome such additions for their worshippers."

Nathaniel frowned and began to pack away his offerings. "These are not gods or goddesses and they will no longer be for sale in this place. You will have to find your goddesses elsewhere." He hoisted his pack and hobbled away.

The young Zealot acting as his liaison with Barabbas and Ox kept pace. "What are you doing? You have become part of the scenery here where we can observe the traffic without suspicion. You must continue your business."

Nathaniel shook his head. "My business here is done," he said.

~ ~ ~

Zilpah and Tikah found Salome sitting at her perch overlooking the lake. The blue skies, smatterings of white fluffy clouds, the scent of orange blossoms and an abundant bird life along the shoreline made it the perfect day. "Why are you up here, Auntie?" Zilpah asked. "Abba told us we can come to see you because he has to go to market again. The old beggar keeps stopping by and he thinks that we might be in danger."

"What old beggar?" Salome asked.

"The one by the market," Zilpah answered. "Abba saw him meeting with a Roman centurion, a rabbi, a tax collector, and a brothel woman. Abba hid behind a wall and heard them talking about working together to find young girls for the Romans. They also talked about finding some lady Zealot named the 'Shadow.'"

"Abba thinks that we need to help you stay safe by watching those people," Tikah added. "We saw the Roman eating a locust-powder biscuit with butter and honey on it. He didn't even get sick. Why don't they eat olives like we do?"

"We are people of the land," Salome said, "so we use olives and olive oil as gifts from Ha'Shem. Through them we are strong, resilient, and healthy."

"Do you think we can go with you to pick blackberries?" Zilpah asked. "Our Abba says you might be able to make us a spread to put on our biscuits. He says you know where we can get pomegranates and maybe even some wild dates and figs."

"Don't forget about the walnuts, almonds, and pistachios," Tikah said.

"Children," Salome said. "Look towards the lake and tell me if that is the beggar you saw with the Roman."

Zilpah squinted into the sun then turned back. "It looks like him," she said. "I told Abba that all beggars appear the same and he told me that I must learn to see their inside like Ha'Shem sees them."

The beggar casually strolled toward them and Salome pointed toward the clouds. "Look at the clouds, girls. Tell me what shapes you see. I see a lion riding in a chariot."

"That's silly," Zilpah said. "Lions don't ride in chariots. I see a ship with two sails. Maybe that's the ship they take the children in."

Little girls should not be imagining horrible thoughts because of cloud shapes. "I see a giant fish and a dragon chasing after it," Salome said, pointing toward another shape. The beggar followed the direction of her hand and crouched where he was.

"Come girls," she said. "I think baby Rachel needs another feeding. We can play this game another day. We can also find blackberries and all the nuts you can eat."

As they neared home, a brothel woman stepped out of the forest, followed by a tax collector. They looked long and hard at the girls. The shadows of Sepphoris had reached the shores of Capernaum.

~ ~ ~

There seemed to be no chance of winning. The Zealots pressured Nathaniel to continue his carving business so he could track the caravans but Sarah threatened to leave him if he continued to prostitute himself with his figurines of Salome. Thinking of the wooden images being used in pagan temples churned his stomach and infuriated his faith. He did love to coax the figurines from the blocks of wood, using the grains to bring life to the sculpture in his hand. But not at the compromise of his faith.

"At least be here when the weather is decent," Ox chided. "Carve other things. Your camels are worthy of purchase. Don't waste your talents because of the ignorance of others."

Nathaniel faithfully fulfilled his role as messenger. The sons of Judas continued to regather followers from the Galil but focused on disrupting Roman legions in the south. They were guerrilla fighters who specialized in ambushes at unexpected places. Barabbas gathered his followers from the lands beyond the Jordan and from the regions around Lebanon and Damascus. While both leaders were Zealots, they failed to find a way to coordinate their efforts and their impact was small. Ox did the best he could to coordinate rescue efforts when needed.

Sarah approached him in his garden one morning. "You are more restless than usual. What is happening with you? My dreams seem too much for you." She rested one hand on his shoulder and stroked his hair with her other. "There is so much more we could do in the vineyard and with the olives. I don't understand your lack of ambition to do anything significant so your family is cared for. Surely, you see what your distraction over Salome is doing to us—to our family."

"It's not Salome," Nathaniel said.

"Then what?" she asked. "You can tell me."

He reached up and held her hand. "The centurion threatened that he would take Hannah if I didn't help him. The Zealots are pressuring me to keep carving so I can be their lookout. The traders want me to make figurines they can use as goddesses in their temple." He released her hand and turned to face her. "Your father wants me to help him smuggle silk through the Roman lines. You want me to tend vines and sell olives. I can't do everything for everyone."

"Surely, you don't believe my father wants you to do anything illegal," Sarah said, stepping back. "Surely, you've misunderstood him."

"Even if I have misunderstood, perhaps you can see that my restlessness has nothing to do with Salome."

Sarah paced the yard, frowning. "You and I need to talk until we decide what we want to do together," she said. "We have children who need our focus. These are dangerous times and we can't do anything to make it harder on them."

Nathaniel rose and followed her toward the house. "I think I need to spend some time finding out what Ha'Shem wants from us."

CHAPTER TEN

Sepphoris / Nazareth – Wasted Disguise

Ten days after Zebedee's last assault on her, a dove feather appeared woven into the fenced chicken pen in Capernaum. Salome looked toward the forest and then released it into the wind. Ten days after, two feathers appeared. *How did these Zealots expect a nursing mother to be risking her life?*

Zebedee was out fishing with the boys and Rachel napped so she hustled up the trail and retrieved the strip of vellum. The call was for Sepphoris again. It was no doubt from Ox. It was time for another trip to Nazareth. Without hesitation this time she hitched the donkey up to the cart, bundled Rachel, left a note for Diana, and set off.

Mariam welcomed her gladly and hugged Rachel as if her own. "I have enough to feed her if you're stuck in town too long," she said. "Abba and Ima will want to see you tonight."

The stew of lentils, onions, leeks, barley, and greens in olive oil supplemented the cucumbers, goat cheese, bread, and dates. It was simple fare but sufficient for the day.

The bang of wooden bowl against platter startled her. Her Abba winked. "If you have so much to do that you have no time to talk with me then you have no time for dreaming." He pushed his bowl across the table toward her. "We will talk tomorrow."

Salome completed her evening chores and prepared for bed. Her father remained silent as she set the washing water by the door. Her mother accepted the pile of folded clothing and set it into four of the six alcoves in the wall. The intense whispers of her parents floated toward her, beckoning her ears to strain and interpret the snatches of sound. There were enough worries. Sleep would be a welcome refuge. Her younger sister, Mariam, was already asleep on the mat edged up next to Salome's.

Mariam's breaths rose and fell in steady rhythm. She slept as if nothing was amiss.

Salome ground her teeth back and forth. How could "little miss perfect" prattle on about how some messenger met with her fifteen years before to tell her she would give birth to the Son of Ha'Shem—God? Ha'Shem has no offspring. A confession of transgression by two irresponsible youths was forgivable, but a belligerent stream of fantasy and continuous deception-no! It had to stop.

~ ~ ~

The two shepherds trudging up the hill toward Nazareth stopped for a moment to talk with Gideon, the gatekeeper, and then walked straight toward Nathaniel who had been watching them from his perch on a rock near the synagogue. They were young with the faintest tufts of hair on their lip and chin. Their step was firm and confident.

"Shalom! Shepherd," they called. "We walk where the sun is hottest near Sepphoris. There are many eagles circling overhead and we fear for the loss of the little goats."

"Shalom. Perhaps you should keep the little ones for when the moon is brightest," he responded. "Are you messengers?"

The two stopped, and the oldest one was smiling. "You don't recognize me, do you?" he said. "I'm Behrouz. I've been with Judas learning to protect this land."

"I thought you were a Parthian," Nathaniel replied. He stepped forward with a huge embrace. Stepping back, he said, "Why didn't you go back to your homeland?"

Behrouz frowned. "As you may know, my uncle was my only living relative and he was crucified by the Romans when I was taken from here. After they beat me and left me for dead, I was taken by a Zealot who nurtured me back to strength. Judas sent a messenger for me to join him and I did." He looked across the valley toward Sepphoris. "I've grown strong enough now to fight and to free other children being caught by these foreigners."

Nathaniel slumped back down on the rock. "You know that you are like a son to me, even if we had such a short time together. Guard your way. Think twice before you follow the schemes of those who are blinded by rage and revenge."

"I would love to see Ima and Hannah," Behrouz said. "Perhaps you might be considering someone to betroth her to. There are not enough women for all of us who are fighting. We are having to be creative to establish families to build up our future."

The thought was startling. "Hannah is so young," Nathaniel said. "Her mother would definitely not be ready to let her go. You are welcome to come for a meal but do me this favor and do not bring this up to Hannah or her mother. I am being watched by village spies so understand that it would not be wise to stay long."

"I wanted to assure you that I am safe," Behrouz said. "You can pass my greetings to my Ima. If this is not a good time to press the matter regarding Hannah, I will make an effort to return another time. Thank you for rescuing me when I was a boy. Perhaps one day I will return the favor." He nodded toward his companion. "Come! We will take the road to Nain and return to Judas. Perhaps Ha'Shem will provide for us another way."

~ ~ ~

As Salome shook off the memories of that significant time in her sister's life the next morning, she took her first steps into the city known as the crown jewel of the Galilee. The city, Herod's tribute to his masters in Rome, buzzed with the energy of prosperous nations flaunting and flogging their wealth.

Her first stop was the bakers for the five buns that hid her message. This time it was the fourth roll that informed her it was time to infiltrate the centurion's fortress. A rabbi's daughter had been taken and was believed to be working in the kitchen. Territory she was familiar with. She withdrew to the market fountain and considered whether she wanted to accept the challenge. If so, how would she risk it all?

Zebedee would have to raise his own children if this went wrong. Her parents and sister would not know how to handle the shame if she was discovered and crucified. And what would Nathaniel think? At least she would have done something good for someone.

She left her message behind the brick at the baker's and waited. All she needed was a hairdresser and someone who could fit her with a special disguise to attract the right kind of attention. She would take on the role of head chef for the centurion during the next week. This role required her to play with fire while guarding her dignity.

Sitting by a fountain in the marketplace, she was approached by an Egyptian woman with a smile as broad as the sky. "Well, by the stars of Aphrodite, if it isn't the face of the mosaic back from the dead."

Rising, Salome grasped the arms of her hostess and smiled in return. "I trust you can take this familiar face and make it so beautiful that not even my mother would recognize me."

The Egyptian took Salome's hand and walked swinging it. "I'm not so naïve. The only one you don't want to recognize you would be that centurion who used to make your heart beat fast. Whatever you do, do not betray him again."

Salome entered the fortress and wandered the long stone halls with their Persian wall hangings. The dining room with dozens of animal heads mounted on the walls sat clean and ready for use. None of the servants acted out of the ordinary. It was time to prepare herself for the next steps—to prove her loyalty to the centurion and to deflect any suspicions.

In an alcove off the main courtyard of the fortress, the Egyptian slave, Hamurti, fussed with Salome's hair and turned her long auburn strands into fountained coils on the crown of her head. Golden ear studs fit on Salome's ear lobes and a golden strand graced her neck. The dress, borrowed from a Phoenician slave girl, was a rich cream linen, embroidered with colorful squares and circles. This all was set off by a woven belt that boasted its own geometric designs. Soft lambskin sandals were wrapped around her feet and ankles.

A bowl of grapes and a plate of fine cheeses sat on the nearby counter. A cup of wine rested within arm's reach on a stool. Time for the fly to be wary of the spider's web. It was all a little too inviting. Hamurti brushed Salome's hair gently then took a moment to massage her shoulders. "Did you know the carpenter?" The massage moved to her scalp and then down her neck.

Salome allowed her head to fall forward. "Which carpenter? Half the men in my village seem to be carpenters."

Hamurti paused, gently massaging shoulders. "The one they crucified."

"They've crucified so many that it seems like a dangerous profession."

"You know who I mean."

"You mean Thaddeus?" Salome focused on relaxation. *Breathe in, breathe out.* "Yes, he helped me with breakfasts for Anthony. He was from Hebron."

"You didn't seem very emotional for losing a good friend." Hamurti dug deeper into Salome's shoulder muscles. "Do you know why they killed him?"

"Ouch." Salome straightened up. "Do they need a reason any more?" She rotated her shoulder muscles.

Hamurti stepped away. "Anthony was jealous."

"Of who?" Salome snagged a grape and popped it into her mouth. *Where was this conversation going?*

"Of someone Thaddeus spent too much time with."

Salome chewed slowly. "I've never seen him with anyone and I spent most of the day at work with him." She spread out her arms, open-palmed. "Maybe it was someone he met after hours."

Hamurti reached for the wine glass. "Did you know he was a Zealot spy?"

"No!" Salome stood and snatched up the plate of cheese. *Relax! Too much reaction.*

The Egyptian held out a comb toward Salome extending the point of her finger. "Be truthful. You had no idea he tried to get near you so he could recruit you?"

"No!" A thick slice of goat cheese provided a mouthful. She held out the plate to the Egyptian who shook her head and took a sip of her wine.

"How can you be so naïve?" Hamurti pointed toward a small stool for Salome to stand on. "Come, I need to shorten this dress. Since this is borrowed, I'll stitch the hem lightly."

More slow chewing. A swallow. "I had no idea." Salome stepped onto the stool and turned slowly as the Egyptian knelt and checked the length.

"Do you know anyone he called the 'Sparrow?'"

Salome spun to face the Egyptian. "I knew everyone in this fortress and no one was called the Sparrow." *Be careful.*

"Wait! Keep still," Hamurti blurted. "The centurion wants to know who else is involved."

"In what?" Salome moved clockwise slowly as the stitching continued. "That was fifteen years ago. Surely, he has better things to think about by now. Why is he so fixated on what happened then with Thaddeus?"

Hamurti rose from her knees and glared. "You must know. Everyone does. He tried to poison the food at the governor's banquet."

Salome lifted the hem of her dress and examined it closely. "How did you know?"

"He tried to recruit me to be part of it." The Egyptian backed away a few steps as if to get a better perspective on the hem length.

"How did the centurion find out?"

"I told him, like I tell him everything that happens here." Hamurti took another step back. "Now, step down."

Salome stepped off the stool and carried it to the corner. "Did you tell him about me?"

The Egyptian's eyes scanned her dress from top to bottom but the intensity on her face seemed to focus beyond the dress. The minute of silence pushed the boundaries of comfort. "You were such a child. Come, sit still over here and let me finish your hair."

Salome turned toward the window. "The centurion is coming!"

"How do you know?"

"Listen!"

The staccato of horse's hoofs echoed off the stone walls and Salome stretched on tiptoe to glance out the window into the courtyard below. "Gentle, little dove," the Egyptian said. "The centurion will be distracted in the baths for some time. Prepare the meal and he will be hungry for more than what you put on the table."

"His stallion walks like a pharaoh," Salome said. "When he races the wind that horse has fire in his eyes. The two of them look like they're in a dance."

The Egyptian knelt at her feet and adjusted the hem of her tunic. Nimble and flexible, she contorted herself on the floor. "Guard your heart, little dove," she warned. "He would never be yours alone. Claiming his heart would be like trying to chain his stallion in place." Hamurti unfolded herself on the floor and rose.

"I'll walk away before he gets close," Salome whispered.

"The one who plays with fire often gets burned. Better to dream alone than to groan together."

Salome examined herself in the surface of the water-filled bronze bowl. Her hair was coiled like an Egyptian princess. The colors around her eyes brought out glory she had never seen in herself. "Hamurti, you are a magician! Whose face is this looking at me?"

"Your people hide their beauty with your faceless god, little dove." Hamurti placed her face side by side with Salome's over the looking glass. "My people draw out the wonder of the goddesses and put them on display to draw awe from all who see. Color on your eyes and cheeks mesmerize a man."

The rose garden was in full bloom as she stood by a window and contemplated her next move. Spending this much time dressing up to distract the centurion so the rabbi's daughter could make her getaway now felt like a betrayal of her marriage vow and her faith. It had all seemed so simple and straightforward. "Adonai, help me!" she prayed. She was in too deep to back out now.

Hamurti stopped in the doorway. "I'm going to the kitchen to let them know that a special lady will be arranging the dinner for this evening. You know your way around. Just act like you are in charge. Give me a few moments."

Salome waited then skipped to the kitchen where six servants chopped vegetables and cooked a variety of fish and fowl. Hamurti strolled past her with a nod. "The centurion wants his cena," Salome called out and smiled when the servants turned, one by one, to gaze at her. The rabbi's daughter had been relegated to washing dishes. Getting the girl away meant no turning back in dealing with Anthony's wrath.

She nodded to the chief chef. "Caleb, this porridge needs to be a special puls. Emmer, salt, fat, olive oil, and vegetables. Set out the eggs, cheese, and honey with fish."

"Are we creating a feast for a special occasion, my lady?" Caleb asked with a bow. "We have shrimp for the appetizer and pheasant for the main course. We could add dormice if you pleasure."

"Add some of the special pork sausages to that," she ordered. "And oysters."

"What have you arranged for the dessert?"

Salome turned toward Marcus, the baker. An observer didn't have to examine his large frame long before realizing he loved to taste his own creations. *"Marcus, the black currants and cheesecake with those sweet wine cakes made with honey and cinnamon should be perfect."*

"Yes, my lady," Marcus responded. "May I suggest some pear with that?"

"Yes, make it your best." Turning to a long-faced woman kneading dough she waved her hand. "Esmie, what else is growing in the gardens right now?"

"My lady, we have apples, grapes, strawberries, gooseberries, plums, melons, and pomegranates. There's a new fruit called a cherry that isn't ready yet." She beckoned to another woman who stood at the door with dirt-stained hands. "What else is out there, Celest?"

Celest rubbed her forehead with the back of her hand and furrowed her eyebrows. "Celery, garlic, cabbage, broccoli, lettuce, onions, turnips, cucumbers, and olives, of course."

Salome nodded. "Dig up what you think might make a good salad. I'll go set the table for the master." She pointed toward the girl scrubbing a pot. "And you, when you're done, help me with the table. Hurry now!"

~ ~ ~

Hunting with a bow proved to be a worthy distraction from his carving so Nathaniel perfected his new skill as a way to feed his family. At first the arrows missed their intended target by wide distances. "Good thing no one is here to watch me," he told the village dog on one occasion deep in the woods. He had seen a family of wild boar running with their tails up during his last effort and he set his sights on coming home with a trophy that would make Hannah smile. Perhaps he'd even stuff it to begin his display.

Seeing Behrouz commit to the cause stirred up strange inner conflicts. How could a Parthian boy ally himself to a cause he had no part in? Could Nathaniel prove himself loyal to the homeland if the time came to test himself? What price was he willing to impose on his wife and daughters for the sake of other families? What did Ha'Shem expect of his people at a time like this? Would he be able to carry on his work of observation and messages without getting further involved with Salome?

Sarah had refocused her energies into the work of olives, grapes, and baby Deborah without further bringing up his previous indiscretions. Moments of intimacy spaced further apart but neither of them talked about the change in relationship. Nathaniel focused on his plans for a new addition to his home. A triclinium with a central fountain and plenty of room for his stuffed trophy animals took shape in his mind.

~ ~ ~

An hour after Salome had finalized the meal, a house slave arrived in the kitchen to announce that centurion Anthony had decided to take his dinner in his quarters. He was tired from a long day. Some wine and some simple food were all he desired. The man snatched up a few things from the prepared dishes and lumped them onto a single plate. "That should do," he announced as he exited.

The echo of Anthony's voice bounced into the kitchen. Familiar giggles followed.

Salome followed the servant down the hall. Hamurti lurked near Anthony's quarters. "The two-faced snake," she hissed under her breath.

Who was she fooling? Dressing up like another girl throwing herself at the centurion for attention? To prove loyalty? To who? To Anthony? To the Zealots? No, she was here for one reason—the girl. She had planned for a few days, but why wait?

In the dining room, she examined the flowers, the cushions, the flickering lamps set into the recesses in the walls. The scent of olive oil floated throughout. Jutting out her chin at the rabbi's daughter, she ordered, "Clear up this place and then meet me in the garden."

She tidied up the dozen varieties of food items on their plates and considered her options. The kitchen servants looked on hopefully. They often enjoyed the leftovers and today there would be plenty.

"Help yourself," Salome said. "I'm done here. Tell the master to find himself another maid."

Once she decided to run, she kept going. After meeting the rabbi's daughter in the garden, she handed her off to another handler outside the fortress gate and never looked back. Twenty minutes from the city gate, near the bottom of the hill on which Sepphoris perched, Salome stopped to watch a Syrian weaver's daughter in a cottage off to the side of the road. The loom was like a musical harp in the hands of the young woman as the warp and woof of the screen became the pattern of a beautiful shawl. The repeated *thump, thump* almost drowned out the sound of horse's hooves pounding on the road outside.

Salome stepped in behind the weaver and watched the centurion flash by on his stallion. A shiver raced up her spine. Even the lowest soldier in the empire's legions wouldn't endure being mocked by a peasant girl who spurned his advances. Even if he might not want her anymore. If Anthony caught her, she might never see home again

"That's a beautiful dress," the young weaver stated. "Do you want me to make you another?"

Salome stretched out the patterns on the dress as if seeing them for the first time. "How long would it take you and how much would it cost?"

The young Syrian shook her head. "My father is the weaver who will work out the pattern, the materials and the costs. I only do what he sets for me to do." She held up a miniature weave for Salome to examine.

"Okay, perhaps I'll be back," Salome said as she headed for the door. Within a few seconds she backed up and shielded herself behind the loom. "Hide me," she pleaded. "There's a centurion outside who is looking for me."

"Get under those carpets," the girl urged.

No sooner had Salome taken a deep breath and pulled the carpets over her, then the centurion's voice boomed into the shop. "Weaver. Where are the carpets I ordered? They were to be delivered today?"

The meek voice of the weaver's daughter squeaked out in reply. "My father loaded your order in the donkey cart outside. He waits for my brother to return from Cana. Even now, he has gone to find one of your slaves to show us the way."

Heavy footsteps sounded across the floor. "Does your father weave for Zealots or do you offer shelter to Zealots or Parthians?"

"Never, sir. We are loyal to the empire."

The voices grew closer. The rich woolen fibers seemed to suck away the air. The burden of the carpets increased as the seconds passed. Irritations like little ants crawled up and down her legs then up her spine and into her arms. *Throw it off and breathe!*

"Do you purchase product from the land of the Parthians?" The voice came from directly above Salome's hiding place. Salome froze like ice.

"I am a simple weaver," the girl responded. "My father purchases all we have from those who keep their flocks close."

"He is a simple man for leaving a beautiful daughter alone." The voice moved away toward the girl. "Perhaps you would like to deliver the merchandise and help me find the best place to put them."

"Sir, I am a promised woman. My father will deal with you."

"I demand an extra carpet for the delay," the centurion said. "Let me see what you have available."

Heavy footsteps sounded again right next to where Salome hid. She bit her lip and prepared to be discovered. "Yes, let me see this Persian carpet. It is a fine weave."

"Kind sir," the girl said. "I beg your pardon, but these ones are spoken for. I can make you two identical ones within the week to cover for the inconvenience."

"Very well," Anthony boomed. "Don't let this delay happen again. I give you good business."

"Yes, sir. You are so kind to understand. I will remind my father to get the order to you before sunset."

The footsteps faded, but not the voice. "By chance, did one of my servants come by earlier? A young Hebrew girl? Perhaps there were two girls, together."

"Were they sent for an order, sir?"

"No, I sent for the one, but she had gone on an errand. If she should stop by send her back to me immediately."

The clip-clop of hooves raced away and the young weaver lifted off the carpets. "I think he knew you were here. It sounds like you need to return soon."

Salome rolled out and onto her feet. "No, I can't return. Please, don't tell him I was here. I've got to run."

The weaver looked out the door. "Are you one of the stolen girls? The ones he brings to satisfy his men?"

"What?" Salome said. "What do you mean?"

"My father says I must stay close to home because the centurion steals girls to satisfy his men."

"No! Those girls are much younger." The street was empty. "Guard yourself and any other girls you know. If you hear anything about a rabbi's daughter, please send a message to my sister Mariam at Nazareth."

"My name is Zenaida," the girl said. "May the gods be with you. Remember me in your prayers."

"I will." Salome quick-stepped around the building to hide in the hedges lining the compound. It was a short sprint to the forest paths from the end of the settlement so she slipped off her lambskin sandals, hoisted up her linen dress, and raced into the cool shelter of the tre

~ ~ ~

The arrow missed the boar by a hand's width and Nathaniel hobbled over to retrieve the feathered missile. He almost gave up his search but he spotted it under a bramble bush. The next hours saw near misses on a buck, an Egyptian goose, and a young bear. He resigned himself to his fate and set up a marked target against a tree trunk. Only when he had hit the tree three times in a row did he resolve to venture after the boar again.

CHAPTER ELEVEN

Nazareth / Capernaum – Deadly Cost

The usual one hour walk to Nazareth took three hours. Salome dawdled in the forest, picked mushrooms and lectured herself on the sheer audacity of attempting to parade in front of a Roman who likely didn't remember the face of half of the women he had been with.

A stream provided a cool place to douse her soles and cleanse the mud from between her toes. She hesitated to put the clean lambskin slippers back on. If she was careful, she could stay on the grass and wash the leather at home.

Where in this forest had Rebekah been accosted? She shuddered. No one could hear a woman scream in this isolated part of the woods. The bird song and sunshine eased her mind and drew her into a slow dance.

She examined the purple star shaped bramble flowers flooding a small section of forest. White bramble flowers were also nearby. She picked a handful to take home for her mother. It's what a good daughter would do. Blackberries wooed her to reach as far as she could for the juicy fruit. The ground was muddy so she chose her steps carefully.

The sudden rooting sounds of a wild boar nearby startled her and, as she backed away, she stepped on a thorn. *Ouch!* The piercing pain caused her to misstep and sent her falling sideways into the brambles. Her coiled hair snatched up some of the white flowers. Without delay, she rolled out of the bushes while the thorny plants scratched at her face and hands and stole tiny patches of skin. The mud clung to her dress and hands.

Salome ripped off the lambskin slipper and extracted the point of a thorn from her foot. "I can never go back now," she said out loud. "Hamurti will kill me. I should have changed. I've destroyed the slippers, the dress and her hairstyle." She reached for the necklace and was relieved to find it still in place. "Now I'm a thief, taking someone's gold. I must look hideous. It's a good thing Anthony can't see me now."

The boar trotted out of the bush, tail held high like a flag pole. It hesitated at the prostrate figure of Salome across its path, grunted, and barged off into the bush on a different track. Birds scattered in all directions.

Salome emerged from a trail, limping at the edge of the forest near Nazareth, where she spotted Nathaniel. Oh great! He held a bow in his right hand and a large knife in his left. The shock on his face told her all she needed to know. "What are you looking at, shepherd boy?"

His mouth hung open like he was frozen in the act of eating a forbidden fruit.

She pushed by him and limped toward the village gate. *Should have stuffed a dust rag into that open mouth.*

Nathaniel rushed up beside her. "Why are you out here in your night tunic?"

"This is not my night tunic," she said, brushing away grass and flower petals. "It's a dress for women of importance."

"Why are you wearing it?" he asked, smiling. "You're not anyone important."

She pulled up the mantle off her shoulders and settled it on her head. "I wore it for my work."

"What happened to your face?" he said, reaching a finger toward her. "Why are your cheeks streaked with colors?"

Salome hesitated at his sincerity. *Does he really care?* She wiped at her eyes. "It's the way we women cover our sadness."

"Did he hurt you?" The tone was angry. "I've got my bow and knife. I'll teach him that he can't treat one of our women like a common whore."

Salome stopped and looked him in the face. "If I need your help, I'll call you. I tried to dress up and make myself beautiful." She walked on. "So, you think I'm a whore. You're lucky we didn't marry."

He kept in step with her, trailing her by a dozen paces as they entered through the town gates. "But I thought all that noise in the bushes was a wild boar. I could have shot you."

She kept her pace, trying to walk away. "Then you really would have some explaining to do with your wife and my husband."

He rushed up beside her and kept even, stride for stride. "Salome, I am sorry I said the other day that you think you're too good for everyone else. Sometimes I think it must be hard to always be so good. It must be like having a pet dragon that always needs to be fed."

The twist in her gut took another turn. She glared, spun, and left. *He's lucky I don't spit.*

Five minutes later, the giggle from Mariam didn't help when Salome walked in the door to her sister's home. The baker's wife, the rabbi, the butcher, and half the village had witnessed her shame and humiliation as she entered Nazareth. She didn't need anyone else reminding her how unwanted she was. She was the good one and she was determined to prove it.

She doffed the muddy tunic and tossed it into a corner. *Last time I borrow anything nice.* The necklace and ear studs got dumped in a bowl. The lambskin sandals were kicked off under a stool near the entrance. Her face was wiped with an old towel. It was then she realized that there was no water to wash with. Mariam had no doubt washed the dishes and discarded the water without refilling the bucket.

Frustrated, she pulled on a drab old tunic used for the garden. She snatched up the bucket and stomped toward the well. The Almighty, no doubt, punished her for flaunting her beauty and daring to tempt an enemy of her people. Her real motives seemed to matter little. She would wash up and learn to be good again.

Who did Nathaniel think he was, comparing her goodness to a pet dragon?

Within the hour she had washed herself clean, scrubbed out the cream linen dress and hung it to dry. A dozen neighbors stood around and watched her, drawing their own conclusions. Not once did she speak up to deny any of the rumors that were no doubt growing. She was the good daughter and people would have to sort out their own conclusions.

Mariam stood with the chickens, oblivious to everyone, singing some psalm. "The LORD rescues the godly; He is their fortress in times of trouble.

The LORD helps them, rescuing them from the wicked. He saves them, and they find shelter in Him."[2]

The hawk circling in the charcoal gray skies reminded Nathaniel of Sarah's comments to Hannah. That one day they would fly free like the bird. He bent and measured the dominant vines to be cut. Twice his arm's length. The one-year-old growth was half the thickness of his finger and provided the long, straight shoots he cut straight at the base and angled at the top. Each section had four buds, three of which would be planted underground with only one showing. The winter would form a callous on those underground and the spring would bring new growth. Focusing on the vines, the olives, the sheep, and his carvings eased his mind and kept Sarah happy.

The local Zealots had become more aggressive in recent months. Members of a patriotic group known as the Sicarii had infiltrated and urged the younger firebrands to use threats against even the Jewish traders who cooperated with the Romans. A wild-eyed freedom fighter taught the young shepherd boys how to use a dagger to fight and even urged them to slice the throats of those who undermined the resistance. A carpenter from Nazareth, who helped Romans build their crosses, was found one day speared against a tree with his throat cut.

One day, Nahum, Nathaniel's assistant, released his shepherd's staff and watched it fall a few finger widths short of his toes. He didn't move. "Shepherd," he said. "How do you know if you are walking on the wrong path?"

Nathaniel patted the ground beside him and waited for the younger man to sit. "By knowing if you are on the right path."

Nahum pulled at a tuft of grass and released it in the breeze. "How do you know you are on the right path?"

Nathaniel sat silently, giving proper space to the weight of the question. "A few ways, my son: Is what you see familiar to your eyes; is it safe to your heart; is it clear to your feet; is it the path the wise ones before you have walked?"

The young man picked up one of Nathaniel's figurines and ran his fingers over the newly carved face. "And what if none of these things are true but the others who are with you won't let you leave to go back?"

"The farther you walk this wrong path the harder it is to go back and the greater the consequences, pressures, and regrets you will have. You are a man and must prepare to act like one."

Nahum rose, brushed off his tunic, picked up his staff and walked toward the flock. He pulled out a dagger and threw it over the edge into the ravine.

~ ~ ~

Over the next year, the world flooded into Capernaum and it grew. Farmers arrived and the overgrown hills covered with oak, pine, terebinth, and olive trees were cut back, the land was terraced, and wheat, lentils, millet, and garbanzo beans were planted instead. More and more slaves were brought in to work the land. Carriages stuffed with young girls from all places east flowed by. Occasionally, even carts of young emaciated boys joined the caravan trail.

Four Zealot families relocated into Capernaum and made themselves known to Salome. "We were told our children would be safer near you," one mother confided. "Ever since someone took one of the centurion's girls from under his nose, he has been merciless with anyone who even seems like a Zealot. He is determined to find someone he calls the Shadow." Salome silently adjusted her plans to stay quiet and safe near home. Perhaps now she could prove to be a good wife.

Reports and rumors of a demoniac in the region faded and Salome refrained from instinctively looking toward the forest before leaving her compound. She was convinced that Bartholomew had saved her from the leopard. Perhaps by sacrificing his own life. As a token, she returned to the trail near his cave once a week and left five small barley loaves and a handful of sardines. They always disappeared. Despite the lack of evidence, the demoniac's shadows slithered into the pathways of her nightmares. Why had he saved her? Would he save her next time or destroy her for trespassing into his domain?

"Yes, he's real," she told the new children who asked her about the rumors of the demons in the forest. "Never go into this forest without an adult who can protect you."

"Can we go into the forest with you?" a young boy asked. "Our Ima says we are safe with you."

"Perhaps one day I can show you another special cave," she said. "Maybe we'll wait until your abba wants to join us for a walk."

Traders set up shops near the crossroads linking East to West and the luxury goods from the Orient and Occident flooded into the quiet community. Salome recreated some of the delicacies from her days in Sepphoris, sold them to traders, and Zebedee grudgingly enjoyed the change of diet for special occasions. *Maybe there's hope*, thought Salome.

It didn't feel right that the only way to be a good wife was to bow like a slave before your husband, washing his feet, cooking his food, and scrubbing his clothes clean at the lakeside. Why couldn't a woman be a good wife and make a difference that mattered?

Salome stood at her perch, watching her children playing with other little ones. Perhaps the best way to be a good wife was to raise her children to be good members of the community. A young couple further down the beach stood side by side gazing at a trio of sail boats drifting by. *Oh, to be young again. To do things over.*

One evening, a singing chant sounded by the lakeshore. A caravan of Bedu on camels snaked their way past the fortress at Capernaum. The beasts grunted and snorted in protest, adding their own noise to the desert song. The riders flowed with the jerking and swaying as if one with their mounts, gently tapping a stick on each neck to keep them moving. The train stopped before Salome and one by one the camels were brought to their knees.

A tall dark sheik in flowing robes and a white head cloth slipped off his camel and stood before her. He retrieved a small bundle from his pack and offered it. Dates. "We seek the one who shall set his people free," the man said.

"As does our whole nation," Salome replied, accepting the gift. "What brings you to this place?"

"We are people of the sand and the stars," the sheik said. "Our elders once honored an infant king in this land. They met him in Egypt but we now must follow the tongues of men who tell us his family has come north."

A fluttering in her stomach arose as Mariam's words shouted in the cavern of her mind: *The Magi worshipped my son but we had to flee to Egypt to escape Herod.*

"There is no one here who has come to set his people free," Salome said. "You must speak to the elders."

The sheik nodded. "We will follow the stars for they speak greater truth than any human tongue. For some reason they brought us here." He turned toward his camel and signaled the others. The groans elevated as beasts struggled to their feet.

"Stay the night," Salome called as the sheik rose on his camel.

The sheik nudged his beast forward and chanted his song. "We follow the highway of the stars. When you discover the truth of who we seek, then great peace will come to you. Release every burden of your heart and exchange it for life."

The chant in no way sounded like Mariam's songs of David but the arrow lodged in her soul had much the same affect. What conspiracy lay in the stars to probe her heart like this?

~ ~ ~

Nahum's anxiety grew daily. He paced the edge of the cliff looking out over the valley. The weaver's brother arrived at the edge of the field and motioned for Nathaniel to join him. All he wanted to know was the price of a lamb for a dinner he was giving but Nahum refused to believe it.

"He was here to find me," the shepherd lad said. "I should never have gone to that meeting. They made me swear a blood oath but I didn't mean it. I would never betray them to the Romans but I can't betray the people of Nazareth either."

Nathaniel gripped his shoulders and shook him. "Nahum. He wanted a lamb for his dinner. Nothing more."

Within hours, Nahum's legs were shaking so much he couldn't stand. He fell to his knees sobbing. "Help me," he called. "Help me."

Nathaniel knelt beside him. "What are you so afraid of?" he asked. "Who is threatening you so bad? What can they do?"

The lad looked up, tears streaming down his face. "If I don't take the second oath tonight, they can go after my brother and my family as well. I know the right path to take but I already have two feet on the wrong path. There's no one who can save me now."

"If anyone comes to hurt you, then come to me," Nathaniel said. "I'll tell them that I'm the one who convinced you to walk away. I'll tell them you're too young. I'll tell them you have a family and a responsibility you need to care for."

Nahum threw himself into Nathaniel's arms, sobbing until he convulsed into silence. Then, without a word, he backed away, hung his head and walked toward home.

A shiver raced down Nathaniel's back. Who were these new Zealots and what did this mean for Galilee?

~ ~ ~

The basalt fieldstones and limestone-block rooms, surrounding a courtyard designed for Zebedee's mother and his brother's family, ceased being sufficient and masons were called to construct another larger courtyard only for Salome's brood. The flat roof provided a great place to dry laundry, fishing nets, and sleeping mats. Salome cherished the moments when she could recline with her children, tell them stories, and feel soothed by the cool breezes off the lake. *It's good for my children not to have to be terrified by Zealots, Romans, and Parthians.*

Every time a young one attempted to crawl onto the waist-high walls along the edge of the roof she shuddered involuntarily before hauling them back. As a child she had walked along the walls in her home in Nazareth without worry. As a young girl she learned to walk along the limbs of the olives near her village without trouble.

That first night, after swatting her son for his attempted hit at her when she pulled him off the wall she slept fitfully. Images of Nathaniel in Nazareth, as a boy, following her into the forest danced across the fringes of her dreams. She had skipped happily toward her tree and started to crawl up the notches and knots spaced in the bark like an unseen ladder.

"Wait for me!" he had called. "I want to climb up there with you."

"This is my tree!" she had declared.

She had sat comfortably on the first large limb and laughed as he tried over and over to find a way up to her. He would always be the gatekeeper's son—nothing special. But he was persistent and found his own way to her branch. He had clung to the trunk tentatively, looking to her.

"If you really know how to climb trees then walk out on this limb to where I am," she dared.

And he had. He had pulled himself to his feet and tried to walk toward her.

Not like that! She had wanted to yell but the words wouldn't come out. And then it was too late. He had wobbled as his foot slipped. A panicked look came into his eyes, a terror crept over his face, and a scream erupted from his mouth. And he was down on the ground, shrieking a blood-curdling scream and holding his foot as he rocked back and forth, curled in on himself.

Her nightmares rarely got beyond this. He was looking at her, wobbling, screaming, crying, rocking.

Someone inevitably shook her, woke her, and it had been her screaming and rocking.

She always shook it off. The last thing she wanted was for her son to end up with a limp. *I have to protect him.* Her boy would do more than guard stupid sheep the rest of his life.

Why was Ha'Shem missing from everything worth loving in this life? Why did Abba never have time to leave work and provide the strength and care that a daughter needed? Even a song from Mariam would be a touch of home worth suffering through. The world was a terrifying place. Storms shook her to the core of her soul and the lake had a steady stream of them.

CHAPTER TWELVE

Capernaum / Nazareth – Stormy Passions

Finding Nahum with his throat slit shook Nathaniel. The young man's body floated half-submerged in the pool at the bottom of the ravine. At first, Nathaniel thought he might have fallen from above and braved the narrow trail to reach him. When he dragged Nahum out of the water and turned him over the truth made him wretch. The dagger had severed the jugular and more.

The carts of children continued to roll through on the road past Nazareth and Sepphoris to satisfy the depravities of the international population. Now, clandestine traders smuggling silk, hidden among other goods, tested the road checks of the legionnaires attempting to thwart the lucrative trade. Crucifixions increased and so did retributions against those who allied their choices with the Roman pressure.

Nathaniel's limp had become part of him and he hardly noticed the awkward gait. His shepherd's staff doubled as a crook for the sheep and as a crutch for him. It was his constant companion. In some ways, it had been a blessing. The Zealots asked only small favors and the Romans overlooked small suspicions. His reputation as a vine grower, a shepherd, a carver, and an advocate for his people grew. Even Sarah and her father expressed their admiration.

All was peaceful until the night he caught the two men trying to take his daughter, Hannah. The danger hadn't been apparent at first. He had rounded the hedge near his home and seen a large-bellied Samaritan holding out an apple to nine-year-old Hannah. A tall Phoenician held a rope and a bag behind his back as he maneuvered to come alongside the child. Nathaniel withdrew his sling, scooped up two stones, and hobbled faster.

When Hannah stood to take the apple, the Phoenician grabbed her wrist and Nathaniel yelled. "Stop!"

Hannah attempted to pull away from her captor but the man quickly bound her wrists. The Samaritan dropped the apple and pivoted toward Nathaniel, brandishing a dagger. Nathaniel released the stone from his sling, catching the Phoenician on the shoulder. The man wrestled Hannah in front of him and held his own dagger at her throat. Nathaniel stopped.

"Drop your sling!" the Samaritan demanded.

"Get away from my daughter!" Nathaniel growled, holding out his shepherd's staff.

The Samaritan stepped toward Nathaniel while the Phoenician, holding Hannah, backed away. "Take her to the cart," he called over his shoulder. "Don't take another step," he yelled to Nathaniel.

"You're out of your mind if you think I'm standing here while you take my daughter."

The Samaritan leered. "You'll be happy to know the centurion asked for her directly and was willing to pay a good price. He thinks she'll bring great comfort to his troops. Once you're dead she'll need someone to take care of her."

Nathaniel reached slowly around his back and gripped the knife he used for his figures. "Watch out for the dog," he said. When the Samaritan glanced toward the Phoenician who had turned away, Nathaniel hurled the razor-edged blade at his daughter's captor. The weapon struck its mark between the shoulders. The man lurched in surprise and reached for the source of pain. The Samaritan took two steps toward his accomplice then turned back toward Nathaniel just in time to be struck by a stone on his jaw.

"Run!" Nathaniel yelled at Hannah. And run she did. With his shepherd's staff he began to beat on both the men, swinging with more power than he had ever imagined he had. In moments, the two scrambled away, uttering threats from beyond the hedges.

~ ~ ~

A month later, for the first time in her district, Salome heard a complete contingent of leather-skirted legionnaires march in their spiked boots, banging on their shields, sounding out their war cries. She was sure it was ready to unleash its fury on the little town. As the Romans arrived in Capernaum in force, she foraged for mushrooms in the forest with her sister-in-law Diana. The wide-eyed terror on the young woman's face froze her own soul.

"What is it?" Salome shouted.

"Romans! Hundreds of them. They're coming to crucify us all." Diana dropped her shawl filled with mushrooms and raced off through the shrubbery away from the noise.

Salome released her own shawl and sprinted after Diana. She caught up with her when the woman stumbled over a tree root and fell on her face. Shaking and sobbing, Diana lay with hands over her head.

Salome knelt and leaned in to shelter her with her own arms. "It's okay, it's okay. We haven't done anything wrong. They're marching to remind the Parthians that this is their land now."

Diana huddled into Salome's chest and held on tight until the march had passed. Finally, the young woman's cries slowed to a whimper.

"What scared you so bad?" Salome asked.

Diana sniffed and wiped her tears, face and nose onto Salome's tunic. "It all came back to me," Diana said.

"What came back?" Salome asked.

"Before you came here, we visited friends in a town by the Great Sea." Diana wiped at her tears with her sleeve. "I used to like watching the Romans marching with their glittering shields and shiny armor."

"That doesn't sound so bad."

"Then one day they marched into our village and took the butcher, the baker, the teacher, and a group of slaves." Diana shook at the memory and Salome held her tight. "They made us all watch as they whipped them until the skin hung off their backs. Then they put huge nails through their hands and feet and left them to scream and die on a cross."

Eyes widening, Salome hugged Diana tighter. "I'm so sorry you had to see that."

"Not only that, but one of the soldiers grabbed Zebedee and I was sure they were going to put him on a cross."

"How, horrible. What happened to him?"

"My Abba ran onto the road and threw himself down at the feet of the soldier. He gave him a bag of money and the man let Zebedee go. I think part of why my brother drinks so much is to forget about what might have happened to him that day."

"Why would the Romans do such a thing?" Salome asked.

"The soldiers said the men were protectors of the Parthians and this was a message to anyone else who wanted to protect Parthians. My brother told me the Parthians come by here many times a year and we can never tell the Romans." She shook her head vigorously. "I don't want to die on a cross."

"Hush, child," Salome soothed. "The Parthians are gone. The Romans are gone. The trouble is gone."

For the first time in her life Salome wished Mariam was here to sing a psalm designed to calm a quivering soul. At least these Romans hadn't come to steal her children.

~ ~ ~

When Sarah heard about the attack on her daughter from the butcher's wife—before she heard about it from her husband—she packed, ordered a cart, and prepared to take Hannah to her parent's home in Cana. Nathaniel's trauma drew no compassion or empathy from her. She claimed that his wanton disregard for their daughter—because of his flaunting of his craft, his refusal to walk away from the questionable life of a shepherd, and his inability to afford proper security for their home—was enough to mark him as an undesirable.

Hannah cowered in her room for days and Sarah raged around the home. "What are you doing to bring danger to this home?" she shouted. When he attempted to defend himself, she continued her tirade. "'This is a peaceful town,' you told my parents when we got married. 'Nothing ever happens in Nazareth. We'll be safe here.'" She snatched up a clay lamp and threw it at him. He dodged and it shattered against a wall. "Do you know what those soldiers do with little girls? Do you understand why I want to be away from here? It's bad enough that those brutes undress me with their eyes—but to put our daughter at their mercy is unforgivable." Within days, Sarah and Hannah were gone again on one of their frequent trips to Cana.

~ ~ ~

The best part of the year was the months after the rains. As the weather warmed, Salome stood on the flat roof of her home talking with her neighbors on either side. Her sister-in-law, Haddassah, could stand within three strides on her adjoining roof as they sorted laundry and scouted for the men out on the lake in their fishing fleet. Haddassah was the primary conduit of family news and kept Salome informed of what was happening in the community. Haddassah always heard from her own sister, Judith, who lived closer to the markets in Capernaum where all news worth sharing originated.

When her neighbor, Abandokt, the Persian wife who lived two roofs over, had trouble in childbirth with her new daughter, Farhad, it was Judith who shared it with Haddassah, who shared it with Salome. When Abandokt didn't appear on her roof for two weeks she knew why and was able to inform the neighbor between them what was happening.

It was on the roof, one summer day, that she heard the latest on the Roman efforts to deal with the Zealots and Parthians. Haddassah almost whispered across the gap despite the stiff breeze blowing in off the lake.

"Did you hear about Sepphoris?"

Any news of Sepphoris sparked Salome's interest. Frequently, she had to block out fantasies of Anthony and his dalliances with the Egyptian slave Hamurti or others in the fortress. On rare occasions, she allowed herself momentary thoughts of when she had served an especially lavish meal and found herself in his arms bathed in words of admiration and affection. Before things progressed farther, she always shook her head and focused on something else, like fish. It was what good girls did.

This time Haddassah was already into her story when Salome shook her head.

"What do you mean, no?" Haddassah asked. "You knew it might come to this."

Salome stared. "Tell me again. I was thinking of making sardine stew for dinner."

Haddassah held up her fingers. "Ten, I said. The Romans crucified ten of the Hebrew slaves for no reason except they refused to lay the mosaic tiles of a lewd encounter between a goat and a goddess. And on the sabbath." She marched down her stairs and up Salome's.

"Do you know who ordered the crucifixions?" Salome asked.

"The Romans!" Haddassah said, pointing toward the fortress. "Who else?"

"Which Roman? Which centurion?"

"What does it matter?" Haddassah stood with hands on hips. "The question you should be asking is which slaves? Three of them were your neighbors in Nazareth."

Images of Nathaniel smiling at her near the sheep pen filled her mind. Images of him staring open-mouthed at her when she emerged from the forest in her cream tunic with brambles in her hair. Images of him lying prone at the base of the tree where he had fallen after trying to follow her onto the limb.

Haddassah grabbed Salome's wrist and waited for her to focus. "Salome. Are you okay?"

The tumbling clouds mirrored the sense in her stomach. "Was Nathaniel one of them?"

"How am I supposed to know?" Haddassah asked. "These were your people. Why do you care about this Nathaniel?"

The tumbling increased. "He was a friend."

Haddassah moved toward the stairs. "I hope he isn't a friend that's going to come between you and Zebedee."

"He's a friend from far away and from long ago." The clouds looked darker. "Zebedee has nothing to worry about. Look at me." She slid her mantle down onto her shoulders. "I'm already thirty. What man would look twice at me now?"

"You sell yourself short," Haddassah said. "If you were dressed like some of the other girls in town, your husband wouldn't dare leave his home to go fishing." She started down the stairs. "Why do you think he sends me shopping instead of you?"

The walls got closer and the vision of the horizon got farther away. Not once had Zebedee tried to take her out on the lake again since the stormy accident. Not once had he allowed her to go into Capernaum's shopping district on her own since then. Only a few times had she been permitted to travel to Sepphoris or Nazareth or Cana or Yerushalayim without a family escort right beside her. The tiniest seed of resentment took root in her soul. She was good and didn't deserve to be treated otherwise.

She was sweeping her roof for the twentieth time when Zebedee sauntered inside the house with the boys trailing behind him.

"Salome," he bellowed, "where's our dinner?"

"Make your own dinner," she muttered before wincing with shame. Good girls didn't disappointment their husbands. "Coming," she announced.

Zebedee stripped off his wet clothing inside the door and left it in a heap. Salome almost tripped over it as she backed into the room, pulling the sleeping mats behind her after having aired them on the roof. *Of all the inconsiderate things.*

James raced by, with a fish head chomping up and down, chasing his sister, Leah. Of course, the girl was screaming as if a dragon had her in its jaws. Salome shielded her ears and stared at the abandoned fishing gear. "I'm going to the market," she called and walked away.

Within a minute Zebedee raced up behind her and grabbed her arm. "What do you think you're doing?"

She stopped in her tracks but stared straight ahead. "I'm going to the market like every good wife goes to market. If you want your dinner then there are things I need."

Zebedee stepped in front of her. "But I didn't give you permission to go to market."

"Exactly." She stepped to one side. "We've been married fifteen years and I've been cooped up in the house like a pigeon in a cage. It's about time I went to the market like every other woman in town."

He held her wrist hard. "But someone might take advantage of you."

"Is that really what you're worried about?" She tried to shake free. "You keep me covered in rags and stinking like fish so no other man will look sideways at me?"

Zebedee stepped away from her. "You've got children. You've got a husband. You've got a home. What else could you want?"

"Leeks." She raised her arms high, waving them frantically. "I want leeks and garlic and onions and peppers and herbs and whatever else I can find at the market."

Zebedee smiled. "And what will you buy them with?"

Salome stood like a statue. She looked back toward home and then toward the market. "I'm going to look for what is available and then I'll know how many shekels I'll need."

"But who will make dinner?" He stood aside.

"Ask Leah." She pushed around her husband and headed for the market. "I'm sure she can make more of that fish stew you live on."

Experiencing the market was very much like what Salome imagined the tilapia felt like being trapped in a fish net. Bodies bumped and jostled and pushed by. There was no room to escape in the covered area. It was more congested than the market in Sepphoris. Merchants pushed products in her face jabbering in numerous languages. Aromas, pleasant, tangy, and repulsive fought to fill her breath. Noises—goats bleating, donkeys braying, shouting, bargaining, bells ringing, crashing, crying—bombarded Salome and she cupped her hands over her ears and broke through into the nearest patch of sunshine. A centurion was leaning up against a stack of crates kissing a woman who was dressed a lot like one of Anthony's dancers.

Salome stepped up behind him. "Anthony?"

The centurion stepped away from the woman and pivoted to face her. It wasn't Anthony.

"Sorry, I thought you were someone else." She backed away.

The centurion stepped forward and grabbed her wrist. "And who did you think I was? A lover cheating on you?"

"No. Ah. No. Anthony is a centurion from Sepphoris."

"Ah. A centurion for whom you were a lover." The man moved closer. "My name is Claudius and I'm happy to take his place."

"No." She backed away. "I only worked for him. Other girls filled that role."

"But you dreamed of stealing his heart." He smiled mischievously. "You wanted to be one of his girls."

"No. I need to go. Release me." She attempted to shake him off.

He gripped her wrist harder. "Perhaps he wanted to impress you with his desire to be the primus pilus, the first spear, the head centurion in all the land."

She looked around for help. Everyone looked away. "I know nothing of his desire for power."

His free hand moved to her shoulder. "Perhaps you only wished for him to use his power on you so you could use your power on him."

"In the name of the Almighty, release me." She raised her voice. "My husband is waiting for his dinner."

The centurion released her. "Hurry then, but if you change your mind, you know where to find me. You might want to change what you're wearing when you come."

Salome clawed and elbowed her way through the shoulder-to-shoulder wall of bodies until she broke free a few hundred yards from the lakeshore. She fought for breath as the tears streamed down her cheeks and sobs ripped at her chest.

Arms wrapped around her and stifled the scream in her throat. Throwing an elbow did nothing so she collapsed to the ground.

"Salome. Hush. Salome. It's me. Haddassah. Zebedee sent me."

She stumbled home. "Haddassah, you're the bravest woman I know," she whispered. "How you survive that market every day is beyond me. I think I'll stay on the roof and pray from now on."

"No, girl. From now on we will fight this market together."

That night, when Zebedee expressed a desire for intimacy, she rolled over and ignored him. She might be a good wife but the leering face of the centurion would not let her forget how vulnerable she was.

CHAPTER THIRTEEN

Nazareth / Capernaum – Unveiled Hostilities

The tragedy of Nahum and the near tragedy of Hannah burrowed like ticks into Nathaniel's brain. Alone in his home, he lay for days in the dark, refusing to eat. Only when the rabbi stopped by did he begin to emerge from the valley of shadows.

The rabbi had called "shalom" and then walked in without waiting for an invitation. "It's darker in here than a viper's den," he said. "And what is that smell? It's like a bear has been hibernating for a year." He pulled aside the blankets hung over the window and tossed them outside. "No wonder you can't keep a woman around." He nudged Nathaniel with his foot. "Am I defiling myself by touching the dead or has a taxidermist stuffed you like one of your animals?"

Nathaniel shielded his eyes with his arm and turned his back. "I am an unworthy shepherd unable to protect even my own little lambs."

The rabbi sat on a stool. "So, should I fall on my face, knowing that you have set yourself up in the place of Ha'Shem?"

Nathaniel twisted around and sat up. "What do you mean?"

The learned scholar nodded and rubbed the beard on his chin. "It seems to me that only Ha'Shem has the power of life and death. Was it not our ancestor David who proclaimed that the Lord was our shepherd? Are you now so arrogant that you, a sheep, would claim the flock for your own?"

"That's not what I mean."

The rabbi rose. "Then you should return to the lambs out there and allow your shepherd to have his way. If you remain here, you will never see your wife and daughter again." With that he left.

Every muscle ached as he rolled out of bed. His head pounded. The arrogance of the rabbi was annoying. He washed his face, neck and body before slipping on his tunic. The foot-washing basin was barely wet so he grabbed a bucket and headed for the well.

The day was gray and cloudy, matching his mood. Someone had dropped a liberal helping of seed out for the hens. He rested his forearms on the top bar of the pen and propped his chin up on his wrists. What could he do? His legs would buckle before he made it to the well.

The gate slammed and Aaron, the lone remaining shepherd boy, walked into the yard. "Nathaniel, I can't look after the flock by myself anymore," he said. "That centurion came by looking for you. I don't want to die like Nahum."

Nathaniel hugged the lad and set him down on a stump. "What makes you think you might die like Nahum? Have you also pledged yourself to the Sicarii?"

Aaron shook his head, no. "The centurion told me that the Sicarii had killed 700 women and children in a village near here. He warned me that they were determined to slit the throat of every Galilean to make the Romans look bad. They even killed a priest on his way to the temple."

"We need peace," Nathaniel said. "Do you know of anyone else who can tend the flocks with you?"

"There's a new boy named Caleb who has moved here with his Abba. They're carpenters but he might be able to help a little. Yeshua, or his brothers, might also be able to help."

"See!" Nathaniel said, patting him on the back. "You're already managing the flock and finding ways to prove yourself a worthy shepherd. Let's go look at those sheep right after I get some water from the well."

~ ~ ~

The arrival of the Roman cohort meant an increase in the building of their new fortress along the beach. The front edges of the project reached right to the level area of the beach where the fishermen repaired their nets and boats. The fishermen protested silently by refusing to fish.

With the soldiers came dozens of girls and women designed to service them. Salome thought little of it until she saw Zebedee talking intimately with one of them. When he next sought out her attention, she deliberately ignored him and paid the price in a night of brutality. She endured, knowing that the bruises would show up in the light of morning.

When Zebedee reached for her at first light, she clung tightly to her blanket and refused to turn to him. He pulled forcefully at her cover and a surge of rage burned through her. She swung her elbow, cracking his nose. At his howl of pain, she forgot everything, threw off the covers and checked his face. Blood trickled into his beard. She grabbed her tunic, covered herself, and rushed for a basin and towel.

He was pinching his nose and holding his head back when she returned. She dropped the bowl of water and cloth at his feet, snatched up her special tunic and left the house. Not a word was said. She humbled herself, went next door, and borrowed more clothing from Diana.

An hour mingling among the vendors at the city market passed without a purchase. These men and women were acquaintances, if not friends, by now. They greeted her and offered their best merchandise but the dark pit inside could have swallowed the world and not been full. She sat on a rock and stared vacantly at the gulls drifting over the lake.

What am I doing here? Why are we playing this game? I need to be where I am needed and wanted. I need to do something that will still change the world. What's the point? My chances are gone. The whole family thinks I'm trash. They wouldn't care if I was here or not.

She wandered the forest for hours and then meandered toward the fortress project. She could see it perfectly from her place on the hill. The sun soothed her spirit as her hands gently massaged the painful targets Zebedee had created in his forcefulness. Who was she kidding? There was no place to go except to sit and watch the men going back and forth—hauling heavy sand, rock, and timber.

Guilt crept up like a slithering snake through the grass. It came when she perched watching a group of six larger slaves hauling massive building stones for the expansion of Capernaum's new fortress and commercial district. The straining muscles, sweating torsos, and masculine grunts, captured her desires to find someone strong enough to protect her. As men strained together against creation to move dirt, break rock, and build structures that would withstand the forces of nature, she fantasized an embrace that dissolved all cares. Only one problem: good girls didn't put their hopes in slaves as their protector.

A Nubian was the first to notice her stares and reciprocate them. His body, clad only in a loin cloth, was bronzed darker from the sun. He was a head taller than most and was confident in his walk, despite his designation as a slave. He made a point of lifting rocks heavier than most could carry and walked off the direct path back toward the construction site.

At first, Salome lowered her eyes, allowing the hot flash to wash over her neck and face. The slave paused his gait and waited for her to look up again. He raised his eyebrows and again she lowered her eyes and tugged her head scarf tighter. She glanced around her but no one else seemed to have noticed the exchange. The next time the Nubian passed, she refused to turn away. His eyes seemed to pierce into her soul and she gasped at the sense of vulnerability. She scrambled to her feet and walked back into the forest where it took hours of self-chastisement to thwart her imaginations and restore her sense of goodness.

The next night, in atonement for her wandering desires, she gave herself freely to Zebedee and worked hard to prove she was the good wife he believed her to be.

The temptation, however, burned in her as she wandered to and from the marketplace, snatching a glimpse of the Nubian, wishing for an hour to sit on her perch and drink in the perfectly sculpted flesh of a powerful man. Of course, her Zebedee was strong from his work with the fish nets. But he was covered in loose, drab, fishy tunics that appealed to no one's imagination. And when he forced her, the pain dug deep into places that would never heal.

And who knew what he was thinking? He had already proven himself. Why did husbands have a right to crave the flesh of other women but wives had to keep their eyes down, their heads covered, their bodies stifled?

Of course, Mariam would never do such a thing. Being good meant that one had to keep one's thoughts and actions under control. A good wife had to be a stone, a cold, unfeeling, untouchable stone.

~ ~ ~

Nathaniel's vines withered with his spirit as he walked unseeing through the patch of ground he had staked his future on. Others had taken over the care of his flock and his carving knife lay idle on a stool where he had abandoned it. A small streak of blood still stained the handle. The rabbi dropped by his home daily to encourage him to get out for a walk but without Sarah and Hannah nearby, the shroud of loneliness entombed his heart and mind.

One morning his wanderings took him as far as Sepphoris. He noted the rabbi's donkey cart standing behind the synagogue. He sat by a fountain in the main plaza watching the vendors hawk their wares. The gentle breeze rippled the colorful cotton canopies over each booth giving the impression of a gently rolling sea. It was there that a girl about Hannah's age approached him.

The girl stood before him and awaited his acknowledgement. Her eyes and lips had been colored to make her appear older. Her hair was coiled on top of her head in the style of the Egyptians. Her crimson himation covered a silk sleeveless chiton that reached her knees, meeting the strips of black-leather sandals that wound up her calves.

"Kind sir," she said. "You look lonely. Perhaps you could use some comfort."

Nathaniel startled at the proposal, knowing the intent. He looked around the plaza for the girl's handler and saw at once an older Persian hovering nearby. He patted the space beside him at the edge of the fountain and waited for her to sit.

"You should be at home helping your mother or else playing with your siblings," he said.

"I have no mother," she responded. "I have no family. I have to work so I can eat."

"Do you have anyone else you know who is like family?"

"I have an uncle near Jericho," she said. "He once tried to rescue me."

"How long have you comforted men?" Nathaniel asked. The Persian examined a piece of pottery at a nearby vendor but he was trying to listen in on the conversation.

"Ever since the raid on my village," she answered. "It seems now I know nothing else. If you desire, I can take you to a room to meet your needs."

"When have you eaten last?"

"Yesterday morning."

"Come!" he directed the girl. The Persian set down the pottery.

She followed Nathaniel to the bakery, where he purchased some sweet raisin bread. "Eat it slowly," he said. "When I bump into your master, run down that alley and hide under the covering of the donkey cart until I come for you later. If anyone asks you why you are there tell them Nathaniel sent you. I will take you back to your home when I can."

Nathaniel moved directly toward the Persian who was now examining leather goods at another booth. With his staff, he struck the Persian on his ankle and shouldered him over onto the table. "You son of a dog," he yelled. "How dare you steal our treasures."

The Persian clutched his ankle and supported himself on his elbow as Nathaniel towered over him. The leather-goods vendor and others surrounded the two and raised voices soon filled the air. "I took nothing," the Persian pleaded.

Two legionnaires arrived and grabbed the Persian. "What have you taken?" they demanded. In the melee Nathaniel slipped away and noticed that the girl was nowhere in sight. The rabbi's donkey cart was also gone.

~ ~ ~

The work of the Romans in building their fortress in Capernaum gave Zebedee and Jonas an idea. They took several of the men who had worked for the Romans, hired ox carts to haul limestone blocks from the quarries, and started to build a large compound to accommodate their home and business. Salome's father Heli advised them on the best materials. Salome mixed the clay, shells, and pot shards into a mortar that bound the irregularly shaped blocks. Once the walls were completed, she coated it with a flat paste to smooth things over.

Yuseph took time to cut the timbers and fit them into place on the roof. The trusses fit perfectly atop the walls before wattling and straw mats were set in place and then covered with a hard clay. The stairs leading up to the roof were framed and covered in clay. Zebedee dug a mikvah, a ritual bathing pool, within one of the rooms.

Salome had often expressed how much she missed the one at her home in Nazareth.

"You've got the lake like everyone else," Zebedee had replied. "Does every woman think she's a queen? If I make such a pool, you'll have to haul the water to fill it. I can't imagine what everyone might say."

Within a month, under the sizzling sun, the new expansion was ready for habitation and guests.

The first person to inspect the place was a tall, dark-skinned tax collector named Levi. His long-fingered hands seemed fit for handling coins and for pawing through everyone's belongings. Still, he was an amiable fellow, joking with the men and willing to barter over the tax due for the materials used. He had transferred into the Galil area from Damascus.

Zebedee wasn't so amiable as Levi sorted through things and calculated the total tax in his head. "Write it down," the fisherman growled. "I want to see this for myself. I can't believe any self-respecting Jew would work for the Romans in emptying our coin holders."

Levi smiled. "Oh, you have coin holders. That's two extra shekels for the coin holders."

Salome laughed out loud and gained a scowl from her husband.

Jonas followed the tax collector, answering questions about the type of wood, where it came from, how it was hauled, who did the labor.

When he was done, Levi nodded sagely and pulled out a parchment. He called the men over and Salome stood nearby. "It seems to me that you men have figured out a way to build a quality home for half the cost of the Romans in Capernaum. I would love to hire you to build my home on the edge of town. In exchange, I will pay you twice the price of the tax you owe."

Zebedee stood stunned. Jonas smiled and nodded. Salome hurried away to prepare a celebration feast.

It wasn't only babies who brought surprises.

~ ~ ~

The rabbi had kept the girl until Nathaniel arrived. Together, they found her home town near Damascus and arranged to have her smuggled there with a caravan. It gave Nathaniel a new lease on life and he doubled his efforts to bring the vineyard back to health and strength.

News of his efforts reached Cana, and Sarah, Hannah, and baby Deborah returned home. While the relationship continued to be tense with Sarah, Hannah was quick to express her joy at reconnecting with her father. "You are the best abba ever," she declared as she snuggled in his arms.

His efforts with a bow had improved enough to secure a few trophies, including the wild boar. He stuffed what he could and had another experienced Egyptian teach him the art of preserving smaller game.

Ox and another Zealot attempted to recruit Nathaniel into their efforts but Nahum's death at the hands of the Sicarii stifled any temptation to prove himself heroic. "My family needs me," he said. He pledged himself to guard Hannah and kept her close whenever possible.

~ ~ ~

On a day when the gray clouds threatened to dump a lake-full of moisture onto the heads of the ant-like humanity scrabbling across the dusty terrain below, Nathaniel and his family pulled into Capernaum in a donkey cart. Hannah waved and ran off to find the other children. Instinctively, Salome ran to Nathaniel and hugged him.

Sarah stood holding a little one, mouth agape.

"We've been friends since we were the size of lambs," Nathaniel offered in explanation. "We used to explore the trails around Nazareth together. Sarah, this is Salome, and Salome, this is Sarah. Hannah has run off to join your boys, and this is baby Deborah."

"What are you doing here?" Salome asked, reaching for the donkey and pulling it toward the stables. "Oh, praise Ha'Shem for the life of this little one and for your union of joy."

Nathaniel took the little one from Sarah and followed after the cart. "I probably should unpack all this stuff. We're here for the betrothal feast of our distant relative Shimon, who I believe is going to be in partnership with your husband."

"That's wonderful! Who is Shimon going to marry?"

"I see you still have your humor." Nathaniel said.

"What do you mean?"

"Shimon is marrying your sister-in-law," Sarah announced.

The news was like taking an unexpected punch in the midriff and her soul absorbed the darkness of the weather overhead.

Nathaniel put his hand on her shoulder. "Sorry, you really didn't know, did you? I think the family wanted to surprise everyone."

"They certainly did that," Salome responded, choking out the words. "I guess I better get over to help the women. That's what every good girl would do, right?" she said, looking at Sarah.

The women, including Haddassah and Judith, looked up in surprise when she marched in and surveyed the vast spread of cooking pots and trays scattered around the kitchen area. "Well, it looks like you all managed to cook up a little surprise for me. And when I was starting to feel like I might belong in this family." The tension was intense.

Haddassah faced her and stood her ground. "We knew you were busy trying to get your own house in order with the new mikvah and larger kitchen and new rooms for guests. We didn't think you needed one more thing to do."

"And I suppose I was too busy to be told about my sister-in-law's betrothal."

"Actually, both Dinah and Donna are getting betrothed," Haddassah said.

"Oh, then that explains everything. Why my own husband hasn't told me a thing about his sisters."

Judith stepped up beside her sister, Haddassah. "If you want to work, then there is plenty for you to do." She gestured toward a stack of dirty pots. "If you wish to mock us and pity yourself then your own house still has plenty of work to absorb your anger."

Salome glared at Judith and Haddassah then turned toward the woven basket filled with sardines. "I assume you're having fish stew. At least I know how to do that by now."

When Salome emptied the basket into a large pot, she looked up to see Sarah, Nathaniel, and the little one staring at her.

"Right, I need to help you find a place to rest." She abandoned the sardines in their pot and moved to the door. "Leave the fish. I'll be back to make the stew once I take care of my guests."

Once she had settled her guests, she stood staring out at the lake as Nathaniel stepped up beside her. "I think I've decided something important," she said. "I've been feeling trapped in my marriage with this family. I need to decide to choose to be where I am, to do what I need to do because I want to do it."

"That's a noble goal," Nathaniel said. "It may not be as easy as it seems. I've been trying to do the same thing. When it gets hard, remember that I'm cheering for you to find the love you have always wanted."

"Yes, and you'll be muttering under your breath that I shouldn't be trying to be good to earn that love. You think I need to starve my dragon."

"I couldn't have said it better," he said, smiling. "I hear the baby. I better go and help her settle."

When Zebedee and the boys walked in the door for supper, Salome refrained from mentioning her surprise. "I guess you should know that we have guests from Nazareth here to celebrate your sisters' weddings," she said off-hand. Zebedee nodded and kept filling his mouth with the fish stew.

"It's Nathaniel," she said. Zebedee stopped chewing, swallowed, half-lifted his spoon, let it drop a bit, and then dipped it quickly to take another mouthful.

"He brought his family," Salome added.

"Hmmm," Zebedee nodded as he stuffed a chunk of bread into his mouth with the stew. After dinner he went to his sleeping mat without further discussion.

CHAPTER FOURTEEN

Capernaum / Nazareth – Unleashed Tears

The double betrothal ceremony was a time for great dancing and feasting for the Capernaum and Bethsaida fishing communities. Dinah, Zebedee's second youngest sister, was betrothed to the fisherman named Shimon, and Donna, the youngest sister, was betrothed to Shimon's brother, Andrew. There were limited options for the fishing community to find suitable partners. With all the preparations, celebrations, and arrival of more guests, Nathaniel and Sarah were gone before there was time for any significant conversation. Watching Nathaniel disappear up the hill toward his home in Nazareth, with his little family, left Salome empty—again.

"He'll be back before the harvest," Haddassah said over her shoulder as Salome scrubbed at another pot. "It's good he has a family so both of you can keep your friendship without trouble."

"You wouldn't understand how many regrets I have around that friendship," Salome retorted.

"Then tell me," Haddassah said. She sat on a stool and waited.

Salome leaned back against the counter. "When I was a girl, we would dance in the meadow without any inhibition. He would bring his lambs and we lived as if there was not a worry in the world." She set down her towel. "I was always afraid of water and one day I went by myself to a pond to make myself get over this fear. I stepped in over my head and started to gulp water. I didn't even know he was around but he jumped in and saved me."

"You sound like your heart has been captured by him. Why was there no betrothal?"

Salome turned and scrubbed at the pot again. "My Abba tried to convince me to consider him but by then I was focused on a few Zealots who I thought were older, more mature, more passionate. Thaddeus encouraged me to carry a few messages." She wiped her forehead with her wrist. "He got crucified. Then there was David. I wanted to restore the honor of my family after my sisters were taken advantage of and he taught me how to use the bow, a dagger, and a spear." She sighed. "Nathaniel came to warn me about the trouble my older sister had experienced but I dared him to walk out on a tree limb. He fell and broke his foot. I could never have spent life with a man who only reminded me of my guilt."

"So, you make your choices based on guilt?"

"I make my choices based on bringing honor to my family and my people."

Haddassah sprang to her feet. "Don't tell me anymore. I always knew you were one of those freedom fighters using my brother to cover your own exploits. Why did you have to come here and bring this plague on our family?"

Salome hung her head over the basin. "Somehow, we are related. My Abba thought this was the best thing I could do to restore the family honor and be safe away from all the trouble."

Haddassah marched to the door. "You should have stayed where you were. My brother knew from the start that you had no desire for him. If you have a heart for our honor then leave the children and go back to where you're wanted."

The months flashed by and Salome passed on what little instruction she knew about preparing for marriage but the girls managed the arrangements in stride as if it all was the next step in growing up.

Dinah seemed delighted when Shimon and Andrew arranged with their father Jonas to build homes close by and to enter into a business partnership with the Zebedee clan. Six vessels now worked to haul in the catch for the expanded enterprise and the accumulating wealth made life comfortable for all of them.

Salome retired to her perch on the hill most afternoons and watched the boats set out for the evening catch. When her sons begged to go and Zebedee took them against her protests, she walked the path to where she had laid her memorial for the lost child and resigned herself that soon another rock would mark a grave in her growing family.

Being good had been a useless pursuit. Her family and community still suffered under the pressure of the Romans, the Zealots continued to radicalize and demand greater demonstrations of loyalty, the Messiah was nowhere in sight, and her marriage was in shambles.

The tears still streamed down her face when she heard the twig snap behind her. She wiped her face with the sleeve of her tunic and turned quickly. "Nathaniel!" she choked out, "you're back!"

"You seem sad," he said, crouching down. "I'm here for a few days on business. Also, for the weddings."

She looked away toward the lake. "You probably shouldn't be here, alone, with me."

He laid a hand gently on her shoulder. "We haven't had a chance to talk since I was here last."

She moved to brush him away but froze when her fingers touched his. "Something Sarah and Zebedee are no doubt happy about."

He released his touch. "There's something I need to tell you."

She turned to see his expression. "If it's about the betrothal, you're a little late," she said.

He smiled. "No, it's still not about the betrothal. They tried to take Hannah."

Salome inhaled and covered her mouth. "How? When? Is she okay?"

"I stopped them but the centurion has his eye on her," he said. "I also met a young girl who propositioned me in the marketplace."

"What?"

"She belonged to a Persian," Nathaniel said. "I distracted him and the new rabbi in Nazareth helped me rescue her. This business with the children is getting worse. I don't think I can sit back and do nothing."

Salome nodded. "That's a good thing. Ox can help you."

Nathaniel put his hand on her shoulder again. "I need you to work with me."

She shook her head. "Zebedee would never let that happen. There has to be someone else."

Nathaniel stepped back and surveyed the lake. "I saw Hamurti in the market a few weeks ago."

Salome wrinkled her brow. "How is she doing?"

"Hamurti married a nobleman from Ethiopia and still lives in Sepphoris." He stood and rubbed at his knee. "She wanted me to tell you that she no longer assists in preparing the stolen girls for the men."

"I suppose that is a good thing," Salome said. "Is Anthony still there?"

"Anthony will soon be transferred to Yerushalayim," he said. "There's another reason you might want to get involved again. Most of your kitchen crew were crucified."

Images of faces flooded her memory. There was Caleb, her chief chef, a Hebrew always willing to turn a meal into a feast fit for a king. There was Marcus, her rotund baker, always laughing as he created another sweet treat. There was Esmie, her multi-talented helper willing to solve any hospitality issue. And there was Celest, the gardener who could make any fruit or vegetable grow bigger, faster, and larger than anyone else. They were not just servants but friends. The tears flowed again.

Nathaniel knelt and took her in his arms. "It's hard to lose the ones you love."

And with that she sobbed away the years of regrets and fears.

"Ima?"

Salome broke away from Nathaniel and wiped her eyes again. It was Leah, unsure of what she was seeing.

Nathaniel stood to his feet and stepped back.

"Come child," Salome called to her daughter. "Your Ima felt hurt and Uncle Nathaniel was helping her with her sadness."

Leah stayed where she was. "Does Abba know you're sad?"

Salome rose to her feet and walked to Leah. "Abba is very busy with his work. We have all been so busy with the weddings. Uncle Nathaniel has been my friend since I was your age and he understands my tears."

"Ima, Rachel needs attention. She stinks again."

"Leah, you're old enough to help her."

"She wants you. And besides, a Roman soldier is looking for you."

Salome's arms shook as she looked toward home. Spinning toward Nathaniel she spoke tersely, "Did he follow you? Did you bring him here after all these years?"

Leah spoke up. "Ima, I think he's the new centurion in Capernaum. He says his servant is sick and that someone said you might know how to help him."

Salome released her breath and the relief washed over her. "Good, good. Yes. We need to help the Romans so things will stay peaceful around here. Hurry. We need to go."

Without looking back at Nathaniel, Salome hurried home, gathered a few ointments, and accompanied the centurion toward Capernaum's fortress where the servant lay with fever. It was time to do good and to earn good favor.

~ ~ ~

"Can we go for a sail, Abba?" It was Hannah, fascinated at the white sails skittering across the surface of the lake. "I want to catch a fish," she added.

Nathaniel had been waiting for Salome's return for much of the early afternoon. The cooler evening breezes would soon arrive. "I haven't sailed boats here," he answered. "But some of Aunt Salome's family know how to sail. Someone will have to look after baby Deborah."

Sarah scowled at him from behind her daughter. "It's Aunt Salome now, is it? Maybe you'd like her to look after baby Deborah for longer than a boat ride?"

Nathaniel shrugged. "I'll go find someone who can take us out on the water. You can find someone to look after the baby." He meandered toward a group of men lounging near a dozen boats being readied for the evening fishing. It didn't take long before he gestured to Hannah and waited for her to skip towards him. "One of the grooms, Andrew, will take us out for a short ride before they have to work again."

The water, smooth as glass, provided the perfect surface for the skiff to race with a stiff breeze. In no time, the shore was a distant strip of brown and the figures on it as small as ants. "Wheeeee!" Hannah cheered. She put her hand over the edge to feel the spray as Sarah anchored her tightly by the other arm. "Ima, don't squeeze me so tight," she protested. "This is fun."

Sarah inched closer to her daughter. "It's okay to put your hand out but I need to keep you safe. The water is too deep for you to swim in and we don't have time for trouble."

Andrew cocked his head back and chortled. "There's no fear in that child. She'll make an excellent fisher's wife one day."

Sarah sneered. "So that's what it takes to be a fisher's wife—to be fearless. I'm surprised that Salome has done so well. Nathaniel told me that when she was young she fell into some water and nearly drowned." She tucked a blanket around her legs and draped the rest of it over her daughter. "Some people aren't always what they seem."

Andrew shook his head. "Actually, Salome is still afraid of water. Zebedee took her out in the water and the boat tipped and she nearly drowned again. I've never been able to figure out why she agreed to this kind of life so close to what she fears."

Sarah squinted her eyes and peered at her husband. "Unless there is something she fears more in her home town. Or, perhaps something she loves too much to be near."

Nathaniel caught Andrew's attention. "I think it's time for us to get back to shore. You have a bride to take care of and we may need to leave sooner than we thought."

~ ~ ~

As Salome left the fortress, Jairus, the ruler of the local synagogue, stopped her with a look. "What brings you to the house of a gentile?"

"I try to help anyone I can." She lifted up her jars of ointment. "Philemon was sick with a fever. If we keep the Romans happy then peace will be something we might not have to fight for."

Jairus nodded. "Well said. Philemon has been good to my daughter, helping her with our ducks and chickens. I trust you were able to help him without defiling yourself."

Salome smiled. "Since the centurion built the synagogue for you, I think he has shown himself worthy of our honor and respect. If the centurion's servant is blessed then ultimately, we will be blessed."

"Zebedee has chosen a wise woman for his wife," the synagogue ruler said.

"Something you should remind him of, if Ha'Shem should prompt you." Salome nodded and turned, only to almost trip over a woman crouched low in pain behind her. Two of her clay pots dropped on the cobblestones and shattered.

"Unclean. Unclean." The woman uttered as she raised an arm to cover her face.

Salome knelt and picked up the pieces. "Rest easy, Bernice. I see the doctor in Sepphoris wasn't able to help you."

Bernice picked up one last piece of the shattered pottery and laid it closer to Salome. "Nor the doctors in Caesarea, or Damascus. I have spent all I have. This bleeding disease leaves me weak and unable to even go near my own family. Please, Salome, if you ever hear of anything that might help, let me know."

Salome watched Jairus walk into his synagogue and then observed Bernice huddle in a stable filled with scattered hay. It didn't seem right or fair that life should create pain so indiscriminately. What sin had this woman committed that Ha'Shem should punish her so severely?

With one last nod, she gathered her tunic and traipsed home. Perhaps she could invite Nathaniel to stay for one more day. She looked first toward the stable but didn't see Nathaniel's donkey. A quick walk around the neighborhood made it clear. Nathaniel and his family were gone.

~ ~ ~

Sarah and Hannah were in good spirits after the wedding ceremonies and Nathaniel reclined in the cart allowing his two donkeys to trudge up the road. The forest road was shaded and cool, surrounded on every side with birdsong and animal calls.

Baby Deborah nursed and then slept with the gentle swaying of the cart. Sarah and Hannah sang psalms and played a game trying to guess what each other had seen in the sky or trees.

Travelers were numerous and friendly, sharing news of what was still ahead. "They're selling honey around the corner; the farmer is giving away corn near the stream; there's a Roman checkpoint this side of Sepphoris."

Nathaniel passed his own news back. "Zebedee's youngest two daughters are wed to the sons of Jonas. It's going to be crowded ahead if you're not careful. They're selling fresh fish and honey on the turn off to Capernaum."

Hannah stood, waving at every passerby while Sarah kept her eyes focused on the road ahead. "Do you think that the trade in children will stop now that the centurion is moving on?" Sarah asked. "I still get nervous every time we're on our own like this. The Romans could swoop in and we'd be helpless to stop them."

"We've got people looking after us," Nathaniel assured her.

"If you mean Barabbas and his gang of cutthroats," Sarah said, "I'd rather head straight to Cana and stay with my parents. At least they have security guards around their vineyard who know how to fight. They've all been mercenaries somewhere." She urged Hannah under a blanket when she saw horsemen galloping down the road. None of the three were legionnaires but Hannah had to stay hidden until the trio were well out of sight.

"I hate to live in fear," Nathaniel said as Hannah resurfaced to join him on the driver's seat. "When I see how free Salome's children are I wonder if we should move down there."

Death-stares rarely get as intense as the one Sarah shared. "If you are looking for ways to get more hugs from your childhood friend then you can take us to Cana right now and not come back."

Hannah turned in her seat. "Ima, I don't want to go there. I want to go home."

"We're taking a different way home, Hannah," Nathaniel said. "You and baby Deborah will get to see some of the places your Abba liked when he was younger. I need to visit a friend."

~ ~ ~

Nathaniel's plea for help niggled at Salome's mind all through the weddings and beyond. How could she do anything more? She was keeping her own children safe and Ox was sending others to move into town in hopes that she could coordinate their care. Zebedee would not hesitate to stop her involvement in something that might bring danger to their family.

Twice, dove feathers had appeared near the chicken pen and twice she had released them into the wind at the shoreline. Oh, that she could be a bird and ride the winds to freedom!

"You look deep in thought," Jairus, the synagogue ruler, noted as Salome gazed out at the birds drifting over the fishermen at work. "There is so much to occupy a bright mind like yours. The ingredients for healing medications with so many different diseases, the crowded conditions in the market, the health of your children or perhaps the latest recipe for fish stew."

Salome smiled. "If you can keep my trust, I am actually thinking of how the Almighty raises up some to rescue those who are vulnerable and how others who would like to be his instrument of peace and healing are kept confined to helplessness."

"Deep thoughts for sure," Jairus said. "Perhaps you might think of the prophet Moses having to herd sheep for forty years while his people suffered under slavery. Or perhaps Gideon threshing wheat in a pit while his people were being oppressed? Or perhaps Joseph in a prison or Daniel in a lion's den."

"I get your point," she said. "You think the Almighty may have his timing for all things and that the timing may not always be what I would plan."

"My daughter said something interesting the other day," he said. "She said that your daughter, Leah, was confused about who you loved more."

Salome laughed. "I try to love all my children the same," she said. "Of course, the boys might not believe that."

"She wasn't talking about your children," Jairus said.

The truth struck home. "Oh, if she's wondering about my relationship with Nathaniel, we've been friends since we were children. My Abba tried to set up a betrothal for us but I was young and foolish and refused him. We sometimes laugh about what could have been but we are both married with our own families. Leah has nothing to worry about."

"Perhaps you should make that more obvious at home," Jairus said.

CHAPTER FIFTEEN

Capernaum – Risky Courage

The family from Nazareth planned to take three days to get home after choosing a longer route and enjoying the birdlife, the new scenery, and a company of dancers in one of the caravansaries. They sampled pickled fish in Magdala and ogled the red earthen towers forming an entranceway to the interior of Galilee. Hannah loved the adventure and the gently rocking cart kept baby Deborah calmed or sleeping.

At a roadside market stand, Sarah discovered a brilliant sapphire mantle of spun silk. Her joyful smile and impromptu dance, spinning around with the mantle fluttering in the breeze above her head, inspired Nathaniel to ask the Indian merchant if he had others. The man beckoned him to follow, and he dug into the back of a covered cart. Shimmering sheets of glistening gold, brilliant blue, and grassy green unveiled themselves.

"How much?" Nathaniel asked.

The vendor glanced around and then whispered. "A special deal for you, my friend." He pulled out a silk cloth and wiped the sweat from his dark face.

Nathaniel inched closer. The smell of curry and other spices filled the space. "What is my part of the deal?"

The hawker winced. "For one small act of kindness I will give you the length of your daughter off of any bolt of your choice."

Sarah had put down her scarlet mantle and was looking his way as she draped Hannah in a similar mantle. "What is the act of kindness?" Nathaniel asked.

"A simple thing, really," the Indian vendor said.

Sarah raised her eyebrows and took a step toward her husband. "Hurry, tell me now or we do not have a deal," Nathaniel urged.

The Indian said. "A Parthian dealer has secured these from the Orient and needs them delivered to a friend outside Sepphoris." He lightly rested his bony fingers on Nathaniel's wrist and leaned closer. "Surely, it would be little trouble to conceal these beautiful materials under your belongings until my friend finds you. The Roman elite long for these touches of heaven but the common soldier understands little of such longings. No one would suspect such a beautiful family."

Nathaniel pulled back. "Do you know what the price is for smuggling goods like this?"

The Indian bowed quickly with his hands clasped together in front of him. "Yes, for me the price is great. For you, perhaps it would be simply a misunderstanding."

"How will your friend find me?"

The smallest of smiles and another bow. "He will find you." The vendor watched Sarah take a step toward them. "Make it two lengths of your wife and we will settle this deal," he said.

Nathaniel nodded. "I will take my wife for a brief walk and you can load my cart so the material will not be seen. I bear no responsibility if your friend does not arrive one day after I reach home."

The Indian turned toward Sarah and threw his arms wide. "How fortunate you are my friend to have found such a lovely mantle. You will be like a queen among the women of your village. Come, we must wrap it and see if there may be a sari to match it."

By the time the little vendor had wrapped his charm around Sarah and Hannah, Nathaniel was sure he had more than compensated the man for any special deal given for his little act of mercy. Baby Deborah cried out and Nathaniel convinced Sarah that they must walk and talk about the purchase before finalizing a price. When he returned and dropped a pouch of coins into the merchant's waiting hand, he received the faintest of nods and a simple bow. "Please save these special garments until after you are home and free from the dust on the road."

Less than an hour up the road, the family covered their faces as a contingent of Roman cavalry riders, spewing a dust cloud, stormed by them in the direction of the roadside dealers. The three of them choked and coughed before pressing on.

Sarah waved at the receding dust. "What has got into them? You'd think they'd found some Parthian smugglers." She pulled her simple brown mantle tighter around her head. "I'm sure glad I took that vendor's advice and kept my material wrapped and out of this dust."

~ ~ ~

Blistering sunlight sucked the moisture from her lips and cheeks as Salome stood knee deep in lake water, hands resting on the stern of her son's fishing boat. James had coached her patiently day after day for a week while Zebedee was away—assuring her that she had nothing to fear. Twice, she had successfully perched in the craft for several minutes before hurtling into the water and heading for shore.

"Come on, Ima," James coaxed. "You've done this before. There's not a cloud in the sky. You'll shrivel up like a raisin before you drown."

Salome pushed herself up and over the stern, laying still as the boat rocked. A curious gull floated overhead and she prepared to move quickly if necessary. What was there to be afraid of?

The boat rocked harder. "James, stop it!" she warned.

"Ima, I think something's wrong" he said. "Diana is running toward us."

Salome struggled to right herself and got up on her knees. "What's wrong?" she called.

"Salome, you've got to get away." She bent over, gasping. "A Zealot ran to our house and said the Roman centurion who is after you will be here any minute. He said your life is in danger."

She scanned the hills and paths around her home. "Where can I go?"

"Out! Onto the water," James urged. "Ima, you have to do this."

She grasped the sides of the boat in a death grip. "I can't, I'm scared."

James scrambled aboard, rocking the boat even more. "I'll take you."

His pleading eyes betrayed his eagerness. The lake suddenly seemed endless. "James, you're too young."

"I've watched Abba. I can do it."

"Hurry!" Diana said. "He'll find you if you don't go now."

"Stay low and trust me," James urged. "Here, put this blanket over you. I'm going to paddle with my hands."

The rocking boat, the suffocating heat, the blinding fear slowly coiled like boa constrictors around her soul. "James, what's happening?" she called.

"Ima, he's on our roof, looking this way. Stay still."

A shudder convulsed her as she stretched out her legs for comfort. "Who is with him?"

"Another soldier." The boat continued to rock. "Okay. They're coming down the stairs."

"Good, maybe they'll leave before I bake to death." She tried to appear calm. After all, this was her son.

"Ima, the soldier is pointing toward Abba's boat." James pulled at the sail she lay on. "They're running. I think they're going to come after us."

Salome threw off the blanket. Anthony and a soldier raced across the sand. "Hurry, we have to put up the sail!"

James' eyes opened wide. "But, Ima. I thought you were too afraid."

"I've watched your Abba put up this sail over and over." She hauled on the material, setting it in place on the mast. "If we don't get far enough ahead, they'll catch us and that isn't something either of us wants. Pray hard for a wind."

The sail was up in a minute but hung limply in the doldrums. The two Romans fit oars in place and pulled hard. Salome blessed her husband for storing the larger sail for his boat while he was away. The Romans would not have the advantage of a larger sail should the wind arise.

"Adonai, hear us!" she called. "Adonai, ruler of the land, of the sea, of the wind. Take us to safety in our time of need."

James turned. "Ima, I didn't know you could pray. Abba said that your family didn't teach you such things."

"There's a lot of things your Abba has never bothered to find out about me." Salome tugged hard on the sail. "Adonai, we are your people, the sheep of your pasture. Send your wind as you did in days of old."

The Romans closed the gap quickly with their strong strokes.

"Adonai, hear us!"

And then the smallest ripple appeared on the glassy surface. A quiet breeze danced across her cheeks and played with her hair. The sail caught and the ship lurched.

Salome got to her knees and held tight to the mast as James handled the rudder. The Romans seemed to move in reverse toward the shore.

"You won't get away with this, you Zealot!" Anthony howled.

In response, the wind blew harder and the ship skimmed across the surface. Breathless terror and tearful joy swept over her, as powerful as the wind. This is what Zebedee had desired for her.

"Won't they just wait for us until we get home?" James yelled the obvious.

"Then we won't go home." What had she done? Her family and community were now at risk. What good had her little adventures accomplished?

~ ~ ~

The friend Nathaniel wanted to meet waited calmly in a tree at the side of the road halfway between Magdala and Nazareth. Nathaniel knew he was around by the call of a hoot owl that sounded as he passed. "I need to go into the forest for a few minutes," he said.

"Don't bring trouble on us," Sarah said. "This silk will only atone for so much."

Nathaniel nodded as he pulled to the side of the road. "It's for the children." The forest path was littered with a carpet of leaves and the coolness was refreshing. Without any dust from the road, it was easy to breathe. The clearing he expected was just out of sight from Sarah and the children. He didn't have to wait long.

Ox and two others stepped into the open. "You were fortunate to avoid the Romans searching for silk," Ox said. "Your baby daughter travels well. Does your wife know we are here?"

"I assured my wife you were with us," Nathaniel answered.

"The less she knows the better," Ox continued. "The new centurion at Sepphoris seems to be more intent on satisfying the Romans than the old. Anthony hasn't left yet but he appears determined to impress his replacement with what he is capable of in suppressing Zealots, increasing trade, and stealing children. No family is safe at the moment."

"What do you want me to do?" Nathaniel asked.

Ox leaned closer, as if the very forest had ears. "In three days, we will raid two of the bathhouses and three of the temples at night to take back as many children as possible. The four of us will drive carriages through the night to Damascus. We will have others who will take the children back to their homes."

Nathaniel looked back toward the road. "What if we're caught? With my foot I can't run."

"Prepare your wife," Ox said. "She should go to her home in Cana with the children. Be at the market bakery by daybreak and ask the baker for three fresh rye buns. Check inside for a message. If something is wrong you will know it and you can go home."

~ ~ ~

James sailed the skiff expertly toward Bethsaida. The same winds that pushed their sail favorably toward the northern village had churned up the waters into a squall that threatened to capsize Zebedee's fishing boat with its Roman crew. The soldiers were a speck among the whitecaps when Salome felt free to breathe again.

"Who are those men?" James shouted above the wind. "Isn't that the centurion you told me not to talk to?"

Salome weighed her options and decided on truth. "I used to work for that centurion at Sepphoris when I was young," she said. "He's determined to steal our children and to destroy our freedom fighters."

"Are you a freedom fighter?" James asked.

"I'm your Ima, but I try to help whoever needs help."

"It looks like he'll have to wait another day to catch you," James said.

"James, you are amazing, son!" she exclaimed. "I didn't know you were so good at this."

"Abba taught me years ago," James said. "I've been all over this lake while we fish."

"Maybe your Abba knows more about parenting than I realized," she said.

When the pair pulled into shore, the first person to greet them was the servant for the centurion in Capernaum. Salome tried to shield herself with the wet blanket but the man shouted "Shalom" and waded in to pull the skiff onto the beach. "What brings you so far from home on a stormy day like this?" he asked.

James spoke up without hesitation. "Shalom, Philemon. A couple of soldiers were after my Ima and we needed to find a place to hide away for a couple of days."

"This is a good place," Philemon said. "It is peaceful. Since you helped me with my illness, I have been resting here. My thanks to you again for your kindness. I hope I may repay it someday."

"Perhaps you can help us find a place where soldiers wouldn't look for us," Salome suggested.

Philemon looked across the lake toward Capernaum. "Sometimes these Romans do strange things." He helped Salome out of the boat. "I don't always understand the ways of my master but at least he is good to your people. My brother lives in this town and I'm sure he would be willing to hide you for a few days. I'm going back to Capernaum tomorrow and will let you know if there is any trouble waiting for you over there."

"Bless you," Salome said. "We would be grateful to your brother and his family. Please assure my husband and the others that we are well."

~ ~ ~

The second morning, as Nathaniel limped toward the village well, a shepherd boy fell into step with him. "The bakery is closed," he said.

"Shalom," Nathaniel said. "That is of no concern to me. I'm here to find water."

The boy's eyes furrowed and he jutted his chin toward Sepphoris. "The messenger you met on your journey told me to tell you that you don't need to send your family away because the bakery is closed."

Nathaniel stopped, eyeing the lad. "I was going to go to the bakery tomorrow. Why does it matter if it is closed today?"

The young man clenched his jaw. "The bakery is closed now every day. The baker ran into trouble with the occupiers."

"Oh! You're trying to give me a coded message," Nathaniel said. "Sorry, my mind was preoccupied with how to persuade my wife to leave town. Thank you. Perhaps someone will find another baker."

"We first have to rescue this one," the shepherd boy said. "You will hear more when it is time to go again. I think we have a traitor in our midst."

~ ~ ~

A week after landing in Bethsaida, James slipped back into the bush behind his home and whistled. Salome popped up from cover. "They're gone," he said.

"Where's Philemon?" Salome asked.

"He's back with the centurion," James replied, "playing his part as a servant. Since you healed him, he's been strong and healthy. He says he's glad he could help us."

"Come!" Salome whispered. The pair skirted the butcher's shop, the tailor, the tiler, and then skipped across to Shimon's before arriving home. "Anthony almost had us."

"Philemon doesn't think Anthony or Claudius knows exactly who you are," James said as he closed the door behind them. "He thinks you're a Zealot messenger but no one special. He's really looking for someone his men call the Shadow. He says she's a beautiful young woman who tempts men with her eyes." James chuckled. "Imagine him thinking you might be her. He'll be back if he thinks you're causing more trouble."

"Imagine that." Salome moved a stool and straightened out a sheepskin rug. "Not assuming that his high-class chef might be hiding out as a stinking fisher's wife. I'm sure he must suspect something."

James picked up a bread roll, tried to bite it, and then used it like a rock against the wall. "For now, let's lay low at home and hope he doesn't come back anytime soon. Somehow, we need real food."

~ ~ ~

Sarah was the envy of her neighbors in Nazareth and the attention frayed Nathaniel's nerves as much as the smuggling had done. One wrong word to the wrong ear about the luxurious silk clothing and the Romans would know exactly what happened. The bright colors amidst the dull brown, olive, and tan garments of the villagers were impossible to ignore.

The Indian vendor's friend had shown up within hours of Nathaniel's arrival at home and informed him that the Roman cavalry riders raided the merchant but found nothing thanks to Nathaniel's gracious act of courage. Nathaniel had the courage of a kitten as he ventured out of his home.

After two days, his nerves were so much on edge that he forbade Sarah and Hannah from wearing their new clothes in public. "You can save them for special occasions like weddings," he instructed. "That material is expensive. Besides, we don't want the neighbors all jealous and talking because we have something better than they do."

The heavy mood around the home strained relationships but allowed him to walk with more confidence around Nazareth—until the baker's wife stopped him as he leaned over the sheep pens watching a pair of lambs romping together.

The woman appeared like a specter out of nowhere and stood next to him. "I'm surprised you haven't got a tunic to match the gorgeous one you got your wife. Yes, you're the talk of the village and the envy of every woman. Tell me your secret—did you have to sell your entire flock for such a treasure?"

Nathaniel turned and leaned back against the rails. "Shoshanna! Shoshanna! Doesn't the Torah teach us about coveting and envying and gossiping?" He smiled slyly. "Surely, you wouldn't want me to include you in any guilt I may have in trying to bring joy to my wife and daughter. I wish I was worthy of all the honor given by our women but in truth much of what you see was a gift. Let us agree to have that little secret between us."

He was glad Sarah knew nothing about his role in transporting the three bolts of silk when two legionnaires dropped by the house. Nathaniel was in the vineyard and missed the interrogation. His wife came to him later weeping that the soldiers had confiscated one of her new dresses. Fortunately, they only knew of one and warned her of smugglers in the area.

Nathaniel vowed to never compromise himself again for the sake of his wife or anyone else. He was certain he now knew who fed the Romans with the information they wanted.

CHAPTER SIXTEEN

Capernaum / Cana – Painful Harvest

The new rabbi at Capernaum's synagogue was a restless soul. Salome watched his stocky frame frequently pace the shoreline in his thick dark tunic, sandals in hand, as he waded in and out of the water. He appeared to be a man of deep thought as he rubbed his jaw through the salt-and-pepper beard sprouting down to his chest. Although he never seemed to initiate contact with the local residents, he was responsive to their requests.

A week after the rabbi blessed the new added rooms to the home of Zebedee and Salome, Ima died in Nazareth from a fever. A month later, Abba fell head first off a wall in Sepphoris. Two rocks were set in place where they were laid to rest. Anna. Heli. In a few weeks, Salome, Mariam, and Rebekah were all the family left. Sharing grief by sharing space seemed a good way to start the healing between the sisters. They huddled in Rebekah's home in Cana.

A songbird caught their attention. Morning after morning it competed with the rooster to announce the dawn. Only it never stopped throughout the day. Annoyed, Salome walked to the fringe of the vineyard in Cana and spotted the nesting orange-tufted sunbird. The long, black curved bill refused to quit the harsh alarm call. She grabbed a long stick and lifted it toward the hanging grassy nest. "Got some eggs in there, do you?" she said. "Let's see how you feel if someone yanks them out from under you?"

Rebekah marched across the edge of the field. "Salome! What are you doing?"

Salome dropped the stick. "Dumb bird won't be quiet."

Rebekah scanned the swaying nest. "She's proud of what she's done."

"They're going to die."

"*So?*"

"So, I can solve her heartache now." Salome stepped on the stick. "We take chicken babies. Why not hers?"

Rebekah cocked her head and frowned. "What is happening with you?"

Salome clutched the back of her neck. "It's a good thing I don't have my sling."

"Salome!"

"I don't know what to do anymore." Heaven never seemed so far away. "Ever since Abba and Ima died, I want to scream at the world. Nothing is right anymore." The tumbling clouds held no meaningful shape, no hope. "I used to be the one who was there for them. With what happened to you and then Mariam, I was the good daughter. Life wasn't supposed to turn out this way."

Rebekah stepped closer. "When you lose someone you love, it changes things. You first."

"I thought the world was chaotic when Anthony was after me," Salome said. "It got worse with Zebedee. Now, it feels like I'm in a house with no walls, no floor, no ceiling." Salome kicked the stick she had dropped. "I don't know which way to turn. I'm out of control. Maybe I should have let Zebedee drown me."

Rebekah reached out and pulled Salome close. "When those Romans had their way with me, I was sure my world was done. I didn't know how to face Abba and Ima." She squeezed harder. "When they sent me away, I thought all hope was gone but Adonai met me here and gave me a family to love and care for."

"I don't like feeling this way." She squirmed out of Rebekah's embrace. "It's like I can't do anything right."

"It's okay to feel like you do."

"Even when I feel like using my sling on Mariam?" Salome grinned mischievously. "I can't handle it when she marches in with that perfect son of hers while my little terrors destroy every hope I have to look like a good mother."

"Better liven up, your little sister has just spotted us and is on her way here to join in the misery." Rebekah waved. "Turn around and I'll knead your shoulders. Just breathe."

"What options do we have?" Salome turned and attempted a wave of her own. "Yuseph is trapped in his work at Sepphoris, Zebedee keeps expanding the family fishing business and your husband is traveling to sell your wine as far away as Rome."

Mariam approached, arms wide open, and the three embraced. Three sisters facing the world together as one. "So, what are we talking about now?" Mariam said. "Have you got another recipe in mind?"

Salome laughed. "Fifteen years into my marriage and I can't remember not eating fish as a part of my daily diet. Please inspire me with something new."

"I have a new walnut and pheasant recipe," Mariam said. "Yeshua loves it."

~ ~ ~

The shepherd boy made another attempt to pass a message to Nathaniel. The thump of his shepherd's crook betrayed his presence in advance. "I hear you," Nathaniel said.

"Another message from the traveler," the lad said as he took his place beside Nathaniel. "When the bread won't rise the clay will." He stood silently, waiting for a response. After a minute he tried again. "When the bread won't rise the clay will," he said.

"Why can't you tell me that the potter is the new messenger?" Nathaniel asked.

The youth shook his head. "We have to speak so the Romans won't understand us. We are trained for this."

Nathaniel looked around, limped over to a bush and glanced behind it. He hobbled to a rock and pushed it over. "Funny thing," he said. "I've been here day after day and never seen a Roman who might overhear what someone is telling me."

"The potter will see you tomorrow morning," the lad said and left.

The potter wasted no time in handing him a piece of broken pottery. The simple inscription was clear. "³ Damascus. Sunrise."

The shudder up his spine almost made him drop the fragment. He handed it back to the potter who crushed it.

At sunrise, the covered carriage, drawn by two horses, awaited him at the bottom of the main road from Nazareth. A Bedu trader motioned him inside where they changed outerwear. A small parchment with a crude map to Damascus was shoved into his hand. He took over the driver's seat and the former driver limped back up the hill to the village.

As he passed the base of the cliff, where the Zealots had hidden from the Romans after damaging the waterwheel, three youngsters dressed as Arab children stepped out of the brush and climbed into the back. The two horses traveled faster than Nathaniel had ever gone before and he worked hard to guide them when needed and to rest them when possible.

The carriage came equipped with food, lukewarm tea, and extra blankets for warmth at night. The three girls, dressed like boys, seemed content to talk among themselves and approached him shyly during their overnight stay on the side of the main road. They slept in the carriage and Nathaniel attempted to rest as he sat against one of the wheels. Now he found himself drowsy and drifting during the trip as hour after hour of dusty roads flashed by.

Five Roman security checkpoints came and went without hindrance. His paperwork received a brief glance each time and his load was never inspected. If this is what working for the Zealots was like then he might be able to handle the risks.

Sarah welcomed him six days later after he exchanged the covered carriage for a donkey cart two hours from home. His cart was filled with blocks of cedar, olive, and oak sized for carvings. The legionnaires, who stopped him along the way, had the same questions. "Where have you been? How long have you been away? What do you have in the cart? Have you seen anyone with three children moving away from the area in a hurry?"

The rehearsed responses tested his moral compass. "I left Magdala yester-day . . . Long enough to pick up some wood for my carvings . . . I've seen no one in a hurry with children."

~ ~ ~

Three weeks into her stay in Cana, Salome strolled through the olive groves outside the village. Some of the finest orchards in the land were rooted in this soil. The gnarly trees, twisted and knotted, betrayed their years of endurance in the poor soil. Several of the trees had grown hollow. There were a dozen with a girth that would take three men holding hands to circle. Dense foliage provided welcome shade for workers and observers alike. One giant had toppled and small shoots grew from the roots. Perhaps she should pluck an olive branch like Noah's dove and take it back to her sister as a token of peace.

Sarah, Nathaniel's wife, stood among a dozen women beating the branches of the trees to release the berries. She was clearly in charge, directing the others on which tree to beat and which baskets to fill. She was also very pregnant.

"How happy your husband must be to see such life," she called.

Sarah turned, hesitated a moment, and then smiled in recognition. "Ah, the fisher's wife. The lamb who grew up with my Nathaniel." She turned and waved a "come" signal to two young boys holding donkeys loaded with wicker baskets. "Your husband releases you from making fish stew, does he?"

Salome nodded in agreement. "Yes, I am here for a breath of fresh air."

Sarah stepped over branches and berries and strolled over, rubbing her belly. "This little one will also need a breath of fresh air in the next month. Come, join us for some freshly made cakes. I am overseeing the harvest for my elderly parents."

"It seems like you will have plenty of oil to share with your neighbors," Salome noted.

Sarah lifted the cover off of a large clay pot. "These are the finest berries. The oil will go to the temple to anoint the priests for their duties. Some will fill the lamps of the Menorah during the Feast of Tabernacles. We have been blessed."

Salome accepted the offered cake and held it up for the blessing. "My Abba used to say that the olive symbolized beauty, strength, prosperity, and divine blessing. He told us the Torah instructed us never to beat a good tree twice so that the stranger and the orphan could gather whatever was left."

"Ha'Shem is truly generous to all," Sarah acknowledged. "Nathaniel created a large stone roller to crush the berries. It takes two men to operate it. If you are able, you can help us load the baskets on the donkeys so we can take them to the press."

The baskets were filled and the donkeys led away. "I could use some good olive oil for my healing work," Salome said. "It is good for wounds on the outside and for digestion issues on the inside."

"It's also a good laxative," Sarah said. "Help yourself to anything you can carry. You have earned it with your work and if Ha'Shem provides for the stranger, who am I to withhold his blessing from a friend of my husband."

Salome unwound her mantle and carefully filled it with berries. Sarah wandered off with the women and waved farewell as Salome wrapped up the gift she had been given. The walk to Rebekah's included many stops to rest and it was evening by the time she arrived. She divided the berries into thirds for her sisters and, after an evening of celebration and dancing, fell into a deep sleep free of terrors and regrets.

The next morning the three sisters stood watching the children playing a game called "trap the deer." It involved tapping the shoulder of someone running to declare them the hunter. All the other players were deer and had to avoid the hunter. "Wouldn't it be wonderful to bring our families together in the same community?" Rebekah said. "You could move here to Cana. We have plenty of room."

"I need to get back to Zebedee," Salome said. "He would never leave Capernaum and he doesn't like it when I'm gone too long."

Mariam grabbed Salome's wrist. "I'll come with you and you can stop in Nazareth on your way."

~ ~ ~

The small caravan dropped off Salome and Mariam with their children at the bottom of the hill. "Something's about to happen," Nathaniel said aloud to a nearby ewe. He was whittling from his observation point overlooking the pool in the ravine as they climbed and entered through the village gate. His impulse was to welcome them home but since Sarah wasn't with them, he remained where he was. Sarah would be back from her parent's home in Cana any day. With their third child on the way, he needed to focus on looking after his own family.

On the surface, life in Nazareth was serene. The sheep had grown fat and woolly on the rich grass and shearing time would be soon. He had secured his markets for the wool and had begun negotiating with a vendor for his wines. The Zealots kept a low profile since Nahum's tragic death and the Romans had reduced their patrols. He had been called on for only one trip to Damascus.

Caravans, loaded with spices, cloth, and other riches continued to plod by on the road below. Vendors from Nazareth and Sepphoris lined the roadway with their own wares to sell to the pilgrims and travelers.

While the world outside seemed orderly and under control, the young shepherd's—Aaron's—inner world imploded. He grew impatient with any sheep that wandered from the flock and appeared to take perverse pleasure in slinging stones that startled the animals. He spent hours hurling javelins and daggers into tree trunks and lost his temper when the arrows from his bow missed their targets.

After a significant outburst accompanied by threats and curses, Nathaniel hobbled over to him and put a hand on the lad's shoulder. "I know you miss your companion," he said. "Cursing every tree as if it's a Zealot or a Roman isn't going to bring him back. What do you remember about Nahum?"

Aaron dipped his shoulder and shook off Nathaniel's hand. "I don't know. He said he was going to drive out the Romans. He said he was going to change our world and bring peace again."

"Desiring peace is a worthy cause that takes great character, "Nathaniel said. "Your bar mitzvah is soon and the depth of character within you will be what others remember about you. It may be a much bigger struggle to conquer the enemy within than the enemy without." Aaron took out his sling as he spied an ewe following a trail of grass that would lead it away from the flock. Nathaniel laid a hand on his wrist. "Try compassion and mercy before judgment and punishment," Nathaniel said. "On the sheep and on yourself."

"I should have been there for him," Aaron muttered. "I wanted to tell him not to get involved but we both thought that maybe Judas or Barabbas could chase the Romans away. My grandparents told us stories of the great heroes of our nation and we wanted to be like Gideon or Samson or David. Where is Ha'Shem when we need him?"

Nathaniel extended his arm and gave Aaron a side hug. "He may be closer than we think if we can only wait."

Aaron pocketed his sling and walked toward the straying lamb. "All I can say is that if Judas or Barabbas are not the ones we hope for, then the true Messiah better come soon."

~ ~ ~

Sardine season dawned bright and Zebedee's fury escalated. Herod Antipas had raised the taxes on each fish caught or processed, on each net owned, and on each man hired to catch the fish. The tetrarch continued to build his new city and palace along the lake, naming it Tiberius, in honor of the emperor who had granted him rule of the troublesome territory.

The trouble flared clear the first time Zebedee hurled his clay mug, shattering it against the limestone walls. "Woman!" he barked. "Why do I carry all the weight of this family?" The pieces lay broken like the man who threw them. "The more I try to get ahead, the more I seem to get behind. Why do the rich have all the power to walk over us?"

The broken pieces were scooped up without saying a word. Salome dumped them in the trash behind the house and returned cautiously. The last thing I want to do is to get hurt.

"What are you doing to earn your keep?" Zebedee said. "Other wives sell their wares in the market to support their husbands. Didn't they teach you to do anything in Nazareth?"

How did her mother have it so easy?

~ ~ ~

Nathaniel met Yeshua, Mariam's oldest son, when he took time away from the vineyards to check on his flocks. The young man sat erect in the opening to the sheep pen. He whittled a piece of olive. "Shalom," he said. "I am the door and I am the good shepherd."

"I see," Nathaniel said. "Shalom to you. Thank you for guarding the sheep from all the wolves and thieves. I thought you were the carpenter's son."

Yeshua stood and turned to examine the flocks. "My Abba is in Sepphoris. He also has sheep that must be guarded." He held up the small shape he was whittling. "My attempt at a sheep."

Nathaniel emptied a bucket of water he had brought for the trough. "Not bad. I, too, used to carve. Did I see your aunt Salome in town recently?"

Yeshua nodded. "She visited her sister in Cana with my mother and then passed through on her way back to Capernaum. What made you stop carving?"

Nathaniel paused, bucket still in hand. "I used to carve and sell figurines but the purchasers wanted to use them for worship in ways I couldn't agree to." He smiled. "Did I hear you went to Yerushalayim for Passover last year?"

Yeshua laid his carving on a fence post. "Yes! I had to be about my father's business in the temple. As you know, Adonai must be above all. There can be no other gods before him." Nathaniel arrived home in wonder at Salome's nephew. *Who was this young man and where had he gained his learning?*

CHAPTER SEVENTEEN

Capernaum / Nazareth – Healing Hope

After the centurion's servant recovered from his fever, more and more residents stopped by to ask Salome for help in healing. Salome anointed some with oil, called on Haddassah to offer prayers, recruited Abendokt to apply some of her herbal remedies, or gave some visitor a hearty meal and a chance to vent. More and more people claimed to have improved health from their visits with her. Only Bernice seemed to be beyond help.

When a leper stopped by, complete with the putrid smells of rotting flesh and pustules, Salome was horrified. Haddassah erupted in a verbal tirade and the beggar left, needs unmet. When Zebedee found out that his wife had welcomed a leper into his very sanctuary he railed on Salome. She was forced to scrub the entire home from top to bottom and the whole family slept in the stable for a week.

Once Zebedee had moved on to use his tongue for other scourging, Salome humbled herself and closed up her clinic. Instead, she visited her Egyptian friend daily to absorb everything Abendokt could teach her about remedies that could be obtained from trees, plants, roots, and other sources. She ignored the use of amulets, chants, and incense common with some of Abendokt's work while focusing on the core ingredients in the remedies.

With no local priests or prophets, the people were left to concoct their own solutions to the injuries, diseases, and plagues permitted or designed by Ha'Shem. Abendokt was generous in sharing her wisdom.

"Salome, many of the foods and spices we eat are also helpful for medicines. Pomegranates, dates, olives, garlic, beet, hyssop, cumin. There are plants for liver ailments, others to counteract snake venom, some for eye diseases, others for stomach worms, and even some for skin diseases."

"Our holy men prefer to pray and to quote the Torah," Salome said. "It is through repentance and sacrifice that our healing is assured."

Abendokt nodded thoughtfully as she continued to pull small jars off her shelf and place them on the table in front of Salome. "The spinach beet is good for the heart, the eyes, the stomach. The wild rose to stop bleeding. We will take time to walk and gather myrtle and watercress. I know our people use opium from the poppy plant to dull their pain but many of your sages say this is not good for the clarity of your mind in prayer. Other medications can help with having children and some can keep one from having children."

"This is all very good, my friend," Salome assented. "Our people see that Ha'Shem alone is our healer and he alone is the one who asks us to be humble and to come closer to him. Our healing and our redemption as a community of people are tied together."

"So, your people ignore the healing properties of the creation around you to wait for what you cannot see?"

"The Torah speaks for the Almighty when it says, 'There is no god besides me. I put to death and I bring to life, I have wounded and I will heal, and no one can deliver out of my hand.'"3

"Perhaps there is room for both. You can see that these creams, oils, and ointments are designed for healing. Your people may believe that there is sorcery and evil in what I offer so perhaps you can convince them otherwise."

Salome worked with Abendokt, watching how she collected, created, and applied her healing products. While the local Hebrew residents often refused the touch of the Egyptian, they sometimes agreed to allow Salome to apply the same treatments.

All this changed when the rabbi's wife came requesting help to heal a skin disease. When the skin disease healed with special creams, she requested help to get pregnant as she had been barren.

Within six months she was with child.

The rabbi burst into Salome's home enraged. Spittle flew from the corners of his mouth as he yelled. "Ha'Shem had cursed my wife to be barren for sins that she alone needed to confess. And now, without sacrifice and confession, you have bewitched her womb. This child will never be mine and I command you to cease your sorcery before the town tears down your home and destroys your family."

Zebedee raged as he scooped up bottles, ampules, jars, and clay pots filled with herbs, spices, creams, and oils. "Woman, they want to burn us all together." He dumped the lot into the flames set aside for the meal preparation. The sizzling and explosions sent him crawling out the door where he yelled back inside. "I warned you but it is clear you have never been one who will listen. There is not a good bone in your body. I'm not sure how you bewitched me into marrying you."

Being good was hard when no one was willing to change.

~ ~ ~

Twice more, the friend of the Indian merchant stopped by Nathaniel's vineyard to coax him into another smuggling effort. "Your father-in-law assured us that you could be reliable for us," the man urged. The first time Nathaniel was civil but firm in his refusal. The second time his anger flowed out like lava and he threatened to fetch the centurion to stop the whole operation. "You have bought my silence but not my help," he conceded.

Sarah's fear increased again after several of the villagers accused her and Nathaniel of being enemies of Rome and of being enemies of the freedom fighters. Nightmares increased and she kept Hannah from leaving the home on her own. She refused to release little Deborah into any else's care. One sabbath afternoon she hitched up the donkey cart, loaded it with her prized possessions, and left without telling anyone but the baker's wife.

Shoshanna was only too happy to inform Nathaniel when he returned home from the synagogue.

For a week, Nathaniel sat on the edge of the ravine. Images of Salome grew in his mind as he imagined what marriage to his childhood friend might have been like. Memories flowed. There was the time Salome goaded him to climb an oak tree only to have him fall and break his ankle. He still limped because of it. There was the time he caught her slinging stones wildly in an attempt to hit a sandal she hung from a limb. She had taken the sling her Abba had made for a brother who had died and was railing against Ha'Shem for his failure to hear their prayers. She was a passionate, playful, and precious friend.

154

~ ~ ~

Levi, the tax collector, came by to collect on his debt. The men grudgingly gave up their fishing to take up the masonry and carpentry tasks of building the next home—his. Salome guided the donkey as it pulled the cart of materials back and forth between the quarry and the construction site. Levi often walked alongside to calculate the size of the load.

Zebedee was especially fascinated with the building materials used by Levi and raved about the invention to Salome. The tax collector had imported cartloads of volcanic ash that had been pulverized and mixed with lime and gravel. When mixed with water, a hard material was created to form a solid floor and a base for the home.

Salome was intrigued by Levi's clear records, using his fingers, hands, arms, and foot to find precision with a small scale and a larger scale to assist. The man's integrity, even though this was his own project, impressed her. Here, at last, she met a man who tried as hard as she did to be good.

Noticing how the Galilean men shunned Levi and did all they could to avoid him, Salome pushed to find out more. "How did you get into this business of tax collecting?"

Levi rubbed his thick beard thoughtfully. "The story could be long or short," he said. "I will start with the short version. If you need to hear more, I will consider it."

"Okay, tell me enough to understand," Salome said.

Levi continued to walk along the road toward the building site with one hand on the donkey's neck. "The year before I was counted as a man," he said, "my father was imprisoned for debts. A ship he owned carried all the grain from our farm on its way to Alexandria. It was taken by pirates and sunk by the Romans who tried to capture it back."

"That's terrible," Salome said.

The tax collector nodded. "The Romans insisted we pay our taxes but we couldn't so they took my father. When I came of age, the governor who knew our family suggested that I apprentice as a tax collector in exchange for my father's release. My uncle agreed and I learned the trade."

"Is there no way out?"

"Yes. This stop is my final commitment but I needed enough money to still purchase a house. I apprenticed under a wise teacher and have never taken one shekel more than I was owed. Ha'Shem has blessed me with good health."

"You came from Damascus. Why did you come here?"

"I grew up in a world where none of my family knew much about Ha'Shem." He traced his hand along the black cross on the donkey's neck. "Have you ever wondered why Ha'Shem created donkeys here to be made with big black crosses on their backs? Why is it only here? Such answers I seek but cannot find."

"I've wondered that myself," Salome mused. "Why would Ha'Shem give us animals that carry the sign of our own torture on their necks? It was almost as if he anticipated what we would face. We work like donkeys and carry death on our backs." She shuddered. "You were going to tell me why you came here."

"Yes. My family were involved in international trade and accepted many ideas and teachings. It was all very confusing so I wanted to move here and learn more about the Torah."

Salome stepped up alongside Levi on the other side of the donkey's neck. "I wonder if others ever wonder why all donkeys have a black cross on their necks? Perhaps you will find a teacher who can tell you such mysteries."

"Perhaps," he said. "You need to get your donkey home. Your family will be waiting for their meal soon. Thank you for lending this fine beast for my work."

Salome halted by a table outside the work site. "I have time and another question. How much land do you have for your home and garden?"

"I have two yokes' worth—that's the amount of land a pair of yoked oxen can plow between sunrise and sunset."

As Levi dumped out a bag of coins on the table, he asked her to verify that he was paying the correct amount for the gravel. "It is good to establish everything with a witness," he said.

"You have so many different coins here," Salome noted. "How do you know what each is worth?"

Levi laid out the coins like a teacher preparing to tutor a child. "With Babylonian coins like these, one shekel equals twenty-four giru. One *mina* equals sixty shekels. One *talent* equals sixty mina. Our system is simple, one shekel equals twenty *gerah*. One *litra* equals sixty shekels. One *kikkar* equals sixty litra."

"What about these other coins?"

"There are gold, silver, and copper coins from different nations but that is far too complicated for the time we have. We need to get this load of rock back to the site. Time is money and I promised these men to be fair."

The house took two days longer than the agreement set out so Levi generously paid out what he owed the men and they went home happy. The roof hadn't been done but at least the walls were up.

The Galil was a strange place for a tax collector to come learn about Torah. Still, Salome was glad that if they had to have a tax collector that they at least had a good one.

~ ~ ~

Meeting Mariam at the well in Nazareth was no longer a surprise for Nathaniel. His regular rendezvous continued with the Zealot messenger—now Lydia, the potter's sister—as messages flowed back and forth, and sitting at the village watering hole also helped him catch up with much of the news and gossip in the community. Yuseph worked in Sepphoris and was rarely home during the day.

He was sitting on a bench near the town center when Mariam approached with her gourd. "What keeps you away from your sheep this day?" she asked. "You look weary."

Nathaniel slumped his shoulders and let out a sigh. "Aaron is distressed from Nahum's death and I don't always have the words I need to calm his soul. Sarah is afraid for Hannah more than ever. We lost a lamb over the cliff when a bear chased it." He clasped the back of his head with both hands. "Any words of wisdom?"

Mariam leaned against the edge of the well and set her gourd aside. "I find my wisdom in the psalms of our ancestor David. His words ease my soul and clear my mind. There are many times I am overwhelmed and Ha'Shem meets me in the Law and the Prophets but especially the songs of our people."

"When did you ever find yourself overwhelmed?" Nathaniel asked. "You always appear so calm."

Mariam fidgeted with her head covering and smiled. "Try mothering six children," she said. "The outward appearance is not always what Ha'Shem sees. You have heard the news of how Herod destroyed the little ones in Bethlehem and how we escaped. That was a time of fear for me as we rode into Egypt and faced new customs, new language, new expectations, and the loss of our dreams." She stood up and paced in front of the well. "We saw the great pyramids built by our ancestors so long ago and realized that the Almighty had saved his people before and could do it again. We did find others of our faith who had also run from Herod and we kept our traditions and hopes alive. Some days the words of the psalms seemed empty and distant but I sang them anyway." She shrugged and looked at Nathaniel. "Yuseph and I are simple people with a simple faith. Adonai has provided and protected and so we await his time for what is ahead."

"And what is it you await?"

"We await the moment when his great light will shine in the darkness. When peace shall overcome our fears. When truth will triumph over the lies that fill our minds."

Nathaniel stood up as Mariam retrieved her gourd and lowered it into the well. "Do you believe the Messiah is already here?" he asked.

"I do," she said.

"Do you believe that the sons of Judas or Barabbas can free us from the Romans?" Mariam hesitated as she drew up the gourd of water. "I believe one greater than them has come to free us in ways we cannot yet imagine."

Nathaniel spotted Lydia. "Good talking with you, Mariam," he said. "We all hope the true Messiah will come soon." In moments, the exchange was made and he headed home pondering what it must have been like to see the pyramids. His people had accomplished great things. If they could only stay together, they could do more great things.

~ ~ ~

Yeshua's affinity for Capernaum was noticeable along with the special rapport developing with James and John. Yeshua wandered the hills and the shoreline praying and talking with Ha'Shem. Mariam and Yuseph were committed to the feasts in Yerushalayim and inevitably more tales grew from a trip when Yeshua was twelve. Salome had overheard the first version of this story when her sister was talking with Zebedee after a dinner while she alone cleaned up. Zebedee had lounged on a stool with his back against the wall while Mariam stood, swaying. Her sister had been pregnant with her fifth at the time.

"Yuseph and I had the scare of our lives this last time in Yerushalayim," Mariam confided. "You know we have no small clan now that we reconciled with my oldest sister Rebekah. Everyone in Nazareth and Cana chose to travel together in one large group."

Salome had set down the dish she was scrubbing and stood near the doorway. One couldn't trust this girl to ever settle for being who she was. Everyone knew Salome was the good daughter. Mariam had to prove that she was the perfect daughter.

"So, what happened?" Zebedee had asked politely, picking at his nails and digging out the dirt while attempting to listen. At least he was good to her family members.

"We visited our friends in Bethlehem and then we went through the feast days and Yeshua loved the wonder of the temple and all the rituals." Mariam had continued to sway and rub her belly in the center of the room. "All the children knew to stay near our group so when we left the city, we assumed our oldest son was somewhere in the group. There were a hundred or more of us in the caravan when we started."

"No doubt to keep you safe from the bandits." Zebedee had picked up a fish knife and trimmed his nails. He was patient when he had to be.

"Yes," agreed Mariam, "but when we settled for the night, I looked for Yeshua and no one had seen him. We were already at Jericho and the night made it impossible to return. I'm afraid I did not speak well to Yuseph for his neglect of our son."

"That does sound scary," Zebedee had said with a smirk. "What did you do?"

"At first light, we secured passage with a trading caravan going back to Yerushalayim and made it to the city by late afternoon. We looked everywhere without success."

"I can see why you were worried," Zebedee said, looking up at Salome with a crooked smile. "How did you find him?"

"The third day we walked by the temple and asked a priest we knew. He told us he'd seen Yeshua with some of the rabbis in the temple courtyard. I sent Yuseph in to get him and he came out right away."

Zebedee stopped working on his nails and listened. "What did he say for himself?"

"He said, 'Why were you worried? Didn't you know I had to be in my Father's house doing my Father's business?'"

Zebedee rose and stretched. "I'd love my sons to be saying that," he said. "What do you suppose he meant by that? Did they need a carpenter in the temple?"

Mariam moved to take over the abandoned stool from Zebedee. "The Almighty is his Heavenly Father and he had to be there. Yuseph says that the rabbis were very impressed with Yeshua's knowledge of the Torah and said he asked many intelligent questions."

"Of course, he did." Zebedee had nodded and walked toward his room. "Every mother is proud of her son's achievements—even when he creates heartache."

Salome had picked up her dish and moved back to her washing bin. Unbelievable! The next thing Mariam would be saying is that her son was the Messiah. She abandoned her husband and sister and went to check on the chickens. That cave in the forest seemed like a real temptation at times like this.

She took up a broom and cleaned around the chicken pen. The poor girl must be trying to distract herself from losing our parents in such a short time. I wish I could. It's a pity she always has to draw attention to herself.

Salome found excuses over the next year to avoid visiting Nazareth. If Mariam and her brood chose to trek this way, what could she do? She was the good sister and hospitality was a mark of goodness.

CHAPTER EIGHTEEN

Capernaum / Sepphoris – Mistaken Identity

Nathaniel had grown used to watching for Salome's visits to Nazareth. She had never responded to his request for help and he didn't pressure her. She would come if the time was right. The visits showed him that things in Capernaum had not gotten better for her. He stopped looking for her once the vineyard demanded his full-time attention.

His trips to Sepphoris lessened as the Romans increased their crucifixions and as the radical branch of Zealots increased their attacks on Hebrew carpenters and others who worked to rebuild Herod's palace. Work was shifting toward Tiberius where Herod focused on another fortress to honor the emperor and to halt the potential expansion of the Parthians.

The Zealot leader, Ox, walked around the corner of his home as Nathaniel was skinning a deer he had hunted. The elusive man wore a raggedy peasant cape and hobbled with a cane. His beard was cut shorter and appeared darker. Without stopping, he passed by whispering, "Meet me by the pool at the bottom of the ravine. Anthony has delayed his departure. We need to move to the next step."

Nathaniel noticed the rabbi watching him from the road and continued to skin his deer. "Hungry for some fresh meat?" he called. The rabbi watched the beggar disappear into the bush and raised his eyebrows. Nathaniel waved, kindled a fire, and roasted the meat. The rabbi left.

He wrapped a few bites of the deer meat in a piece of flatbread and tucked the meal into his tunic. A butcher knife got wrapped and put into the same pocket. It was mid-afternoon before he ventured toward the ravine and the pool where Ox would be waiting. Slipping out of the hidden trail at the far end of Nazareth, where he had seen the Zealots smuggling the carpenter's two daughters after their rescue, helped avoid unwanted observation. Although the slope was steep and overgrown, he braced himself with his walking stick and navigated his way to the bottom.

His ankle throbbed as he rested by the pool. No one was in sight and he regretted his adventure, wondering if he misunderstood the Zealot leader. He refreshed himself in the pool, scooping up water like one of Gideon's men, dousing his head. As he shook off the water a hand grasped his shoulder. The edge of a red cape fell over his arm. He froze in place.

"So, you're the rebel leader we've been looking for." The voice was that of Anthony, the centurion. "You may have saved your daughter but it appears your craftiness hasn't been enough to save yourself."

Nathaniel squeezed the water from his beard and shook his head like a dog. "Hello, centurion," he said, smiling. "What brings you here? I already submitted my report and don't have much to add."

"Mocking me for not catching you earlier will not make this easier on you," Anthony growled. "While you were spying for us you should have been watching your back. We know who you are, Ox."

Two legionnaires twisted his arms behind his back and force-marched him toward the road. "You are making a huge mistake," Nathaniel argued. "Your spies have misinformed you. I am not who you think I am."

A legionnaire extracted the knife he'd hidden in his robe after butchering the deer. "Looks like something big enough to cut a man's throat," the soldier chirped. "I'd say we have our man."

"I'm not the one you want and that knife is not what you think it is," Nathaniel protested.

One of the legionnaires raised his fist and smashed it into the shepherd's jaw.

~ ~ ~

The worst part of the year was the rainy season. Fresh water was collected off the roof through spouts into rain barrels but the family was trapped indoors huddling by the fire. Salome was left trying to stop her children from terrorizing each other. James and John showed a thundering temper and it shocked and shamed her to have Zebedee witness his sons at their worst.

"This doesn't come from my side of the family," Zebedee said after the second time ordering the boys into quiet. "What is there about your family that is causing this?"

"What do you mean?" Salome responded. She was busy digging a trench with a pointed stick to keep the stream of water from flooding in under the door.

Zebedee moved a stool away from the door. "Your whole family was unbalanced before we ever met."

"How dare you!" She dropped the stick and wiped the damp dirt from her fingers onto her tunic.

"Face it! Your oldest sister was raped by a gang of Roman soldiers." Zebedee foraged in a cupboard for a roll and took a bite. "Who knows what Rebekah was up to in order for that to happen? What self-respecting woman would be out in the forest on her own?"

Salome squared off with her husband, reaching around him to shut the cupboard door. "That was no fault of her own and she has proven to be a perfectly good wife and mother in Cana." The rain spilled over from her small trench and poked a liquid finger toward the living room. She raced to stop the flow.

Zebedee continued from where he stood. "Maybe so, but your younger sister got herself pregnant before her wedding and she still won't admit how that happened." Zebedee kicked off his sandals and stepped into a basin of water used to clean feet. "Your whole family still tries to cover up for her. I heard how your whole village mocked you as 'the Virgin's sister.' You didn't have a name."

Salome stepped back from the rapidly growing puddle. "Mariam has proved to be a perfect angel with that tribe of hers. She can't help it if that oldest son of hers doesn't do anything wrong. Yuseph dotes on him even if he might not be the real father."

Zebedee stood in the foot washing basin as Salome knelt to build a small dam against the flow. "And don't deny that you never really wanted to be here. I overheard my father telling our neighbor that no one would marry you in Nazareth and so they brought you here and asked for a small dowry in exchange."

The sting of the verbal slap across the face of her soul paralyzed her tongue. The shame of her family sat like a millstone around her neck and she slumped to the ground in the muddy patch by the door.

Her children were not going to bring shame on this family. She knew how to be good and they would be good as well. It would only get harder in the years to come—especially when the rainy seasons went on and on.

~ ~ ~

Being tied up and dragged through the streets of Sepphoris was the most humiliating experience of Nathaniel's life. The betrayal by Ox in abandoning him to the Romans by the pool tapped into a fury he'd controlled when Sarah had left him. The centurion had taken his walking stick and made him limp for the hour-long walk into the fortress. The beatings with that stick had raised welts across his back and legs.

For the first minutes, he had hoped that Zealots would rush out in an ambush and overwhelm the centurion and his two legionnaires. Nothing happened. The baker's wife and her two sons stood open-mouthed on the road as he was herded past them. The rabbi folded his hands and closed his eyes as he stepped aside. The traders and pilgrims continued their tasks and journeys as if all was routine in their world.

The centurion had attempted to beat a confession out of him. "Where is your daughter?" "Where are the other Zealots hiding?" "Who is the Sparrow?" "Who is the Shadow?" "Are you the one called Ox?" "Who were you planning to kill with that knife?"

The weaver's daughter and her father stood on the porch of their shop as he walked up the hill. A few jeers from people he didn't know punctuated the silence as he passed. Most lowered their eyes or turned away.

Spending his first night stripped and beaten in a cold stone dungeon, suffocating in darkness without food or water, completed his humiliation. Where was Ha'Shem when a man needed him? He began to pray and beg for mercy.

~ ~ ~

It was two weeks before the news of Nathaniel's capture reached Capernaum. Jairus shared it with Salome as she skipped stones on the beach. "Your friend was taken by the Romans," he said.

"Which friend?" She dug out another smooth stone and waited.

"I think you call him Nathaniel," Jairus said.

There was no hiding the impact of the news. "What have they done with him?"

Jairus cleared his throat. "The centurion has accused him of being the Zealot leader for this area and that can only mean one thing."

Salome turned to him. "A Zealot leader? There is no way Nathaniel is a Zealot leader. They will never be able to prove that."

"Sometimes these Romans don't need proof," Jairus said. "Sometimes they just need lessons."

As usual, Zebedee had left to fish well before dawn. When he returned with his haul of fish, sorting them for market, repairing his net, inspecting his boat, he went on with his day as if nothing had changed.

Salome left the children with Haddassah and visited her Persian neighbor, Abendokt. The woman was sitting cross-legged in a corner breastfeeding her newborn. "Teach me how to speak in your language," Salome said. "Teach me how to ask 'How are you' and 'How is your daughter, Farhad.'"

Abendokt settled the child who had pulled away from nursing at the sound of a newcomer. "Ours is an ancient tongue. It may require more than a minute to learn all you need to know."

"Teach me something."

"Why is this important to you, my friend?" She stroked the head of her son. "I am honored that you wish to speak to my heart but it seems that perhaps it is someone else's heart you are focused on."

Salome slumped down against the wall next to Abendokt. "Yes, of course you're right. It's Zebedee. He has me trapped like a rabbit in a snare."

"Surely, you have your family and your community all around you." She gave the child her other breast. "What else could he give you?"

"Freedom!" Salome paced in circles. "After fifteen years of marriage I don't know anything more than baby talk and fish stew. When I was young, I used to climb trees, chase sheep, explore the hills, experiment with foods and spices." She stepped into the doorway. "If something doesn't change soon, I am going to go crazy."

The woman swaddled her child and laid it to rest. "It is hard to be good all the time, isn't it?"

"Yes!" Salome leaned against the doorpost. "Teach me something that my husband doesn't have to control."

Abendokt stirred up the fire in her hearth and set water to boil for tea. "First, tell me why being good is so important to you."

Salome slumped down on a stool and pondered. Finally, she shook her head, rose, and paced. "'Good' is just what is expected. It's what Ha'Shem expects. It's what parents expect. It's what everyone expects. It's what you have to do to be loved."

Abendokt pulled out another stool and sat. "So, you don't think you'll be loved if you don't prove that you're good enough?"

"Of course not." Her mantle felt dirty and oily. "You don't deserve to be loved if you haven't earned it." She slipped her mantle off and folded it in her lap. "I don't know what I have to do to be a good wife anymore. I've given myself to Zebedee whenever I can but he stinks like fish all the time. I've given him children but it never seems to be enough. I've learned new things to earn my way but he's never happy with the outcome." She rose and paced the small space before her friend. "I've kept the house clean and fed him what he wants. I've resisted temptations with other men and forgiven him when he didn't resist his. I've tried to make a difference in my country by working for great causes but he wants me to stay quiet and busy at home." She stood in the doorway looking outside. "I don't know how to be a good wife when my husband is never satisfied and never happy. Sometimes I want to run away. I guess I want to be loved but I can't figure out how to be good enough to get that love."

Her neighbor nodded and looked toward her sleeping daughter. "How good does Rachel have to be before you love her?"

"She's a baby," Salome answered. "She gets loved. She doesn't have to earn or deserve it."

Abendokt smiled. "How did you learn that you had to be good to be loved?"

"My Abba and Ima kept telling me that I was such a good girl. I wanted to be good for them."

"Did you want to be good because you saw how disappointed they were in your sisters?"

"Perhaps." A small tremor niggled in her back. "I didn't want them disappointed in me. I saw how sad and heartbroken they were. I heard it in their whispers around the house."

Abendokt reached over and laid a hand on Salome's knee. "So, even when your parents aren't around you still feel that you need to be good to please them?"

"Of course."

"Who is substituting now for your Abba and Ima so that you have to be good and please them?" Abendokt rose and poured the tea.

"Enough!" The warm cup provided a welcome distraction. "Please, tell me something I can remember to take me through my day."

Abendokt raised her tea as if in a toast. "The child you have today is as precious as the man who will one day lead our village."

Salome wrapped both hands around the mug. "That's it?"

"That's it. If you convince the child that he is precious today you won't have to convince him of that when he is old. If you convince your own heart that it is precious today, you won't have to convince yourself tomorrow, no matter what others might say."

"I better talk to James and John."

~ ~ ~

Nathaniel shivered in the dense darkness, coughing and desperately trying to remember life on the outside. His primary focus centered on the early years of his friendship with Salome, the sparkling smile of Hannah and the joy of the three Damascene girls reunited with their family. If this was the end to life it had been good but it had not yet been enough. He wanted more.

"Ha'Shem," he prayed, "please, give me one more chance to make a difference."

Apart from the intermittent torch of a legionnaire bringing a watery stew, no light penetrated the dungeon under the fortress in Sepphoris.

CHAPTER NINETEEN

Capernaum / Sepphoris – Disordered Discovery

Salome had cleaned up after celebrating James's coming-of-age ceremony when an unexpected visitor dropped by Capernaum. The marketplace was now familiar territory with Haddassah at her side and the encounter with Claudius was a distant memory. She focused her goodness on serving her neighbors and tried to add adventure to some of her meals for Zebedee. Once again, he complained at missing his simple fish stew. When he offered a satisfied belch on occasion, she took that as a sign that his complaints were out of habit rather than displeasure.

Salome pounded out her frustration on the doughy mixture writhing in the wooden bowl sitting in the middle of her makeshift kitchen. The songs she used as her soothing technique evaporated with the mist on the lake at midday. While the words she used to express herself weren't recognizable Aramaic, the tone of her voice did not disguise her displeasure.

"Shalom!" a familiar woman's voice called. "Salome, I brought company."

Salome tried to blow the hair hanging over her eyes. What was Mariam doing here? Don't tell me there's another child on the way. She shook her head and used her forearm to part the bangs to one side. "Shalom, I'm in the slave quarters."

Mariam released her children to find their cousins and then rapped on the doorframe. "Coming in, ready or not," she teased. "Salome, you'll never guess who traveled all this way from near Yerushalayim?"

"I don't suppose you're going to tell me that it was Yeshua who floated here all on his own."

Mariam stopped in the doorway. "Oh, you poor thing. Let me help you with that bowl. You should do that out in the sunshine so the yeast can work better."

"So, now that you have a handful of mouths to feed, you're the expert on baking?"

Mariam stepped fully into the small space. "I'm here to help. We'll go clean out the guest rooms but first I want to introduce you to cousin Elizabeth."

Salome held out her hand. "Wait, first, what is the news of Nathaniel? There's no one I can ask without Zebedee getting angry. Please, this keeps me up at nights." She begged her sister with her eyes. "Tell me the truth."

Mariam marched over and gave Salome a hug. "No word, yet. I think he's still in the dungeon at Sepphoris. That's not good but it's better than the cross."

Salome slumped down on a short rickety stool. "He never deserved any of this. He asked for my help and I couldn't help him. All those children and no one to save them."

Mariam took her sister's face between her hands. "What are you talking about? The Romans are after the Zealots and this is all a mistake. You're not still involved with them, are you?"

Salome forced herself to her feet and stepped toward the wash bowl. She hesitated as an elderly woman with a cane shuffled her way into the room. The woman stopped to let her eyes adjust to the darkness and then appeared to look around for a place to sit. A wisp of gray hair peaked out from her white head scarf and her gnarly hands shook.

The old woman, Elizabeth, spread her hands wide. "May Ha'Shem bless this home with life and hope as He has blessed this land with the coming of His Messiah."

Salome hesitated a moment to digest the blessing then continued her hospitality like a good host. "I'll need to get some water to wash your feet. Let me find you a better stool. I know it's around here somewhere."

Salome rushed to the rain barrel while Elizabeth stood patiently in place. Fine time to come with guests. We're almost out of rain water and not a drop in the sky to refill this emptiness. She watched Mariam stopping to talk with her sons. Avoiding work again. *I'll probably have to make up those guest beds after I finish dinner and clean up.*

The stool wasn't where it was supposed to be. She found it lying sideways in the chicken pen acting as a perch to a possessive hen. She shooed the fowl away and used some of her water to cleanse away the droppings.

Elizabeth was stooped a little lower and leaned heavily on her cane so Salome quickly placed the stool behind her and eased her down onto it. She ladled enough water into a washing basin, eased the sandals from off of her guest, and poured the cool water over the dusty feet. A quick foot massage was greeted with small purrs of pleasure from the senior.

"What brings you so far?" Salome asked.

Elizabeth sat unspeaking for several minutes until Salome wondered if she had heard the query. "What brings you so far?" Salome asked again.

"I heard you," Elizabeth said gently. "I was remembering how far this journey has really been."

Salome took up a towel and finished drying her guest's feet but remained quiet.

"It started nineteen years ago, a few months before your sister came to see me." Salome retrieved some house slippers from behind the door and slid them on the waiting feet. "My husband Zechariah was a priest whose time had come to offer the incense. It was a once-in-a-lifetime opportunity—an unforgettable experience."

She set about preparing the tea. "What happened?"

The old woman set her cane across her lap. "Your sister never told you?"

Salome poured the tea. "Not that I remember."

Mariam raised her hand. "I think I'll go set up the guest room while you two talk this through." She smiled at Salome and left.

"I was barren and clearly past my childbearing years," Elizabeth said. "Although Zechariah and I tried to live blamelessly before Ha'Shem, there seemed to be no blessing for us. The contempt and questioning from others was humiliating."

"That must have been hard." She handed the tea to her guest.

"Zechariah saw an angel as he lit the incense," Elizabeth said, blowing on the hot drink. "The angel promised that he would have a son within the year but my husband doubted this in his heart. He was struck dumb until the child was born."

"Perhaps my mother mentioned something about a child but I didn't remember it being such a miracle."

Elizabeth pointed toward the door where Mariam had exited. "It was a miracle but not half as much as the miracle living inside your sister."

Salome furrowed her brows. "What do you mean?"

"Surely, Mariam has told you of how the angel appeared to her and promised that the seed of her womb would be the Son of God."

"She tried to tell us but who could believe such a thing," Salome said with a shrug. "She said she was a virgin. That no man had touched her in this way. If you knew her, you'd know she's never been good enough to be given that honor."

The old woman stopped for a sip of tea. "And so, she was a virgin—in line with the promise of God to the prophet Isaiah. Surely you are aware of the prophesy? And why do you think a person has to be good enough to be favored by the Almighty?"

More tea was poured. "I am so busy with life that I leave the higher things of God up to my husband and the other men."

"A woman ought to use her mind to enlighten her spirit and satisfy the thirst of her soul," Elizabeth said. "Your sister does this well."

"Of course, she does."

"The prophet said that the virgin will be with child and will bear a son."

Salome wasn't going to be swayed so easily. "Even I know there are other ways to understand that prophesy."

"But have you considered the way that God has chosen to fulfill it through your sister?"

Salome paced the room and played with the idea like a cat with a mouse. Mariam. Mother to the Messiah. *No.* Having a child while a virgin was impossible. "It's impossible!" she concluded. "Ha'Shem doesn't break the natural order to please the whim of some peasant girl in the middle of nowhere."

"Do you think Mariam wanted this?" Elizabeth asked, holding her cane in one hand and her tea mug in the other. "That Ha'Shem bent to her will?" The tea was threatening to slosh over the edge from her movements.

"Of course," Salome said, steadying the old woman's hand. "I don't believe Ha'Shem bent to her will, but I think my sister wanted this so badly that she would say anything and believe anything to make it happen."

Elizabeth raised her cane and pointed it toward Salome. "How well do you know your sister?"

"Too well," Salome said, backing up a step. "I lived with her for her first fourteen years. I've heard her songs and prayers enough to make me glad I'm away from all that."

"I think you need to get to know your sister all over again."

Footsteps sounded at the doorway and Mariam burst in. "Well, it looks like you two are getting to know each other well. The beds are all made and I've put some bread into the purni oven to bake. The chickens look hungry and the little ones would love to help me feed them. Where do you keep the feed?"

Salome looked at her sister as if seeing her for the first time. Without saying a word, she walked to one of the six clay jars sitting in an alcove halfway up the wall. She lifted the lid and waited as Mariam dug both hands into the mouth of the jug and pulled out the feed.

Turning back to Elizabeth, after her sister left the room, she conceded, "She does seem to have changed."

Elizabeth adjusted her cane and hoisted herself to stand in the entryway. "Where is your synagogue?" she asked.

"There are several," Salome responded. "We go to the one near the marketplace. The boys have studied hard there."

The old woman nodded. "You Galileans are some of the most righteous Jews. You work hard to make sure your children know the Torah. Your rabbis are renowned for their great memories in reciting the Torah, the writings, and the psalms."

Salome laughed. "It's no wonder. We argue about every possible interpretation."

Elizabeth winced as she took a step toward a stool and lowered herself back down. "I think I need to rest," she said. "How do you train your sons so well?"

"Not just our sons," Salome corrected. "Our daughters can argue the hind leg off of a bullock when it comes to Torah." She handed over a glass of water to Elizabeth who sipped it gratefully.

"Our boys memorize Torah from five years of age. At ten, they study the traditions and interpretations. At thirteen there is the fulfilling of the commandments and at fifteen they learn the rabbinic interpretations. My boys will soon be facing the bride-chamber and a vocation with their father. Perhaps one day they will find a rabbi to follow."

"My John has followed the same path and will one day want to gather followers for his role as the Messiah's path layer." Elizabeth handed her cup to Salome and worked hard again to stand. "Ha'Shem has been merciful to us. I do miss my Zechariah though. He used to help me understand what my son was trying to argue."

"I'm not sure we mothers will ever understand the passions of our men," Salome said. "Why don't you rest while I get dinner together?"

Once dinner was prepared, Mariam called in the children. James led the procession, joking with cousin John while blocking out his brother John and the little ones from accessing the house. Salome didn't wait for Zebedee to say anything. "James, come right here and sit. You're old enough to know better."

James held his ground. "I'm a man now and don't need anyone to instruct me on the way to act. These little ones need to learn to respect their elders."

The heat flushed up Salome's neck and cheeks. She ignored the rebuke and turned to Mariam. "Where's Yeshua? I haven't heard a word from him all day."

Mariam sat cross-legged, patted the cushions beside her for the little ones, and then opened up the food pots for inspection. "Yeshua has gone to Yerushalayim for the Feast of First Fruits. He is very eager to learn all he can from the Torah. The teachers there are getting to know him very well."

"You let your son go to Yerushalayim on his own?"

"He went with a caravan. He's old enough to look after his own needs. There's not much more I can teach him."

~ ~ ~

It seemed like months before Nathaniel was dragged by two legionnaires outside. He could no longer distinguish between fantasy and reality. They dropped him by a fountain and dumped buckets of water on him until the filth washed away. The sunlight on his body felt like a warm towel but it blinded him enough to keep his eyes shut. The humiliation of being doused while naked in front of jeering onlookers hardly penetrated the invisible armor of illusions he embraced to comfort himself.

A Nubian servant arrived to drape a tunic over his body before he was force-stepped back into the fortress. This time he stumbled along tile floors bordered by carpeted walls and flickering torches. The surface under his bare feet was cool and smooth. At the end of a hall the soldiers moved him into a room where a throne-like dais sat. Nathaniel was deposited in the center of the room, forced to kneel with his face to the ground, and left alone.

Sometime later, loud footsteps and the clanking of armor alerted him to the approach of someone. He looked up briefly. The glistening bronze armor and ostrich feathered helmet let him know it was Anthony. Three others accompanied the centurion.

The centurion grabbed Nathaniel by the hair and lifted his face up. "So, this is the proud rebel leader taking up my hospitality. It appears that until now we've pampered you. Once we've found your daughter, you'll know the terror of Rome."

Nathaniel remained with his palms flat on the floor with his pointer fingers and thumbs forming a triangle that his forehead rested on. He stayed silent.

"Have you nothing to say for yourself?" Anthony yelled. "Do you know what we'll do to your daughter? Tell us who else is allied with you in this city. Give us the names of the workers who dare to undermine the might of Rome and the glory of the emperor." He paced the floor and finally brought his rod down on Nathaniel's back. "Why is it that none of those we torture seem to know you? What hold do you have over these followers?"

"May I speak?" Nathaniel mumbled. His throat felt raw and his voice was raspy.

"Louder!" the centurion commanded. "Speak up!"

Nathaniel lifted his head a few inches off the floor. "They cannot tell you who I am because I am not who you think I am."

Anthony's sandals stopped inches from Nathaniel's nose. Another hard stroke landed. "Who are you and why were you at the pool when we found you?"

Nathaniel cleared his throat. "I am a shepherd, the son of the gatekeeper at Nazareth. I am a vinedresser. The pool is part of my community, where many of us rest."

The centurion laid down three more strikes across Nathaniel's back. "You lie. You are the one called Ox who leads the rebels against us. You slit the throats of your neighbors to keep them afraid of us. You will hang on a cross in the plaza as a warning to others."

Nathaniel shook his head, focusing through the searing pain across his spine and shoulders. "I am Nathaniel. I have no connections to leading the Zealots or to the Sicarii you speak about. You can ask the villagers."

Anthony retreated to his dais and sat, chin on fist. "Whoever leads this rabble thwarts my authority and threatens my status before the governor. Dozens of caravans have been attacked and children stolen from us. You can tell your people that we have found another way to get our goods to market."

"Those are not my people," Nathaniel said.

Anthony rose again and stood over him, rod in hand. "Will you turn over these traitors when you know them or would you rather die in their place on our cross?"

Nathaniel hesitated long enough that another round of strokes sliced his back.

He nodded. "Yes, you will have your traitors."

Sandals marched and the room emptied. The two legionnaires entered, pulled him to his feet and dragged him outdoors. At the city gate they threw him down in the dirt and left.

CHAPTER TWENTY

Nazareth / Capernaum – Broken Maze

After James's defiance in front of Mariam and Elizabeth, the week-long visit went very smoothly. Rachel connected well with her cousins and loved playing a mother role, even though she could hardly toddle after them. Salome spent her time learning Persian with her neighbor Abendokt, chatted with the vendors in the marketplace and walked for hours along the lakeshore. Not once did Zebedee attempt to interfere with her choices and not once did Mariam attempt to join in her escapes.

Sitting on a small cliff overlooking the town one afternoon, she saw Elizabeth's son, John, hiking up the hill toward her. He dug his walking stick into the ground as if it was a hoe digging a bed for a seed. His tunic appeared dirty and ragged from his time outdoors. She waited until he arrived.

"Good day, Auntie," he said as he took a seat beside her. "I see why you come here. The view of Ha'Shem's creation is especially majestic."

Salome scanned the lake, the basalt hills, the bobbing fishing vessels, the growing city, and the gulls floating above it all. "I didn't always think of this in a good way. It felt like I was abandoned here, away from my family and friends. It felt like a punishment from the Almighty for trying to be someone he didn't want me to be."

"Your mind carries such deep thoughts for such a perfect day," John noted.

"Forgive me," Salome said. "I rarely speak my mind here. I have been wondering why you are called John when no one in your family line is called John."

John clutched his chin between thumb and forefinger and rubbed thoughtfully. "Many ask me this question. All I can say is that the angel who met with my father instructed him to call me this name. He says I am a gift from God who will show the way for the promised one."

"So, your mother and father continue to fill your head with the teachings of the Torah and with thoughts of a coming Messiah."

"Yes, it is true," John agreed. "My father passed away last year and my mother will not last much longer. I will soon seek wisdom among the desert people who have established their communities to prepare for the coming."

"Why are you here?"

"My mother believes that Yeshua is the Messiah and wanted us to meet with other members of the family so we can act together when the time comes." He waved his hand toward Nazareth. "He was supposed to be back from his pilgrimage but it seems that we are destined to go our own ways for a while."

Salome stood and brushed off her tunic. "I need to go for a walk. Perhaps when your mother passes then all of this talk about Messiah will drift away on the wind. It must be hard to live so long with a dream that doesn't seem to come."

On the final day of the visit, the old woman, Elizabeth, called to Salome as she prepared to leave the house at dawn. "Salome, may I have a word."

Salome reluctantly pulled up a stool and sat near Elizabeth. A pigeon pecked at fallen seed in the doorway.

"You've never asked me how I know your nephew is the Messiah," Elizabeth said.

"That's not a conversation most people have with strangers," Salome responded.

"I am not senile, you know." Elizabeth raised a handful of gray hair. "My son has been designated as the one who will prepare the way for the Messiah. I may never see it come to pass but I know these things as surely as I know the sun will rise tomorrow."

Salome stood and paced. "I don't know how you people relate with Ha'Shem in the south, but here in the Galilee we have stopped hoping for the Messiah in our time. We have had three men arise and try to fight the Romans. Two of them are dead now."

"The Spirit of God is on my son and on your nephew." Elizabeth smiled. "They aren't men who will remove the curse of Rome. They are here to remove the curse of sin that has kept us apart from the Almighty. They are here to restore us as the people of God and to take that message to the nations and beyond."

No wonder her sister was conned into this movement. Salome knelt beside the woman and gently tapped her wrist. "I can understand now why my sister is entranced with the teaching about Messiah. You clearly had great importance and influence in her life from the beginning when she struggled to find meaning for her pregnancy." She moved to the door and examined the rippling sails on the lake. "Should you ever decide to return to Capernaum again, know that this is a good home, with a good family, who live with a good faith. We trust Ha'Shem to do his will in his time."

The rest of the morning was focused on feeding chickens, baking bread, making fish stew, and saying farewell to her sister's tribe. She welcomed the relative quiet that settled over her home, ignoring the screams and protests coming from the younger ones as they were teased. *Perhaps it is God's blessing to live so far away from the center where religious devotees and Zealots twist the hearts and minds of those who have time on their hands. May the Almighty preserve us.*

As she sat on the roof, observing the glorious reds and yellows of sunset across the sky, Zebedee joined her. "Another glorious night ahead," he said. He laid his hand gently on her shoulder as she tensed up. "I never realized how good it is that I married you instead of that younger sister of yours. You've learned your place here and you keep us out of all this fanciful talk about Messiahs and fighting for our freedom." He sighed and sat on the ledge. "I guess I was so harassed by my sisters growing up that I've been reacting against any thought that another woman might want to control my life. I know I've been hard on you at times but we have a good family. You haven't been like my sisters."

Salome sat, drinking in the sunset and the affirmation. "I know you work hard and I know it isn't easy to go out every day with hope and to sometimes come back with nothing. Your boys need a father who can be strong. Someone who can show them how to care for their own families one day." She laid a hand on his wrist and leaned forward towards Zebedee. "Your sister told me about the Roman that took you to be crucified before we met. That must have been terrifying for a young man like you. I guess I can relate with that fear when I think of what it was like to almost drown."

Zebedee jerked to his feet. "What are my sisters filling your head with now? How can you even think that my near-crucifixion is like your drowning? The moment I think you've come to respect and support me I find out you're slandering me behind my back." He pivoted toward the stairs. "Forget we even had this talk. I've got work to do."

~ ~ ~

Nathaniel lay alone in his own room, thankful for the rabbi who had found him lying in the garbage outside the gate at Sepphoris. The religious leader had summoned volunteers and a cart to get him back to Nazareth. After washing and clothing him, the man had welcomed his own wife and daughter to provide food and an extra blanket.

The shock left him shivering as the welts on his back shrieked their presence. The bloodied wounds stuck to his tunic until the second day when a neighbor gently peeled the robe off of him. A medicated cream and smooth strips of cloth covered the welts and allowed him to rest easier.

On the third day, the baker's wife brought him a savory stew. As she set it before him, she whispered. "Ox thanks you for your silent sacrifice. He was told of the trap moments before meeting you. He wishes a quick healing." In moments, she was gone.

The word from the Zealot leader rallied his spirits enough to get him off of his bed. The sense of betrayal had sucked his soul dry. With a short explanation, a touch of understanding brought a spark of light into his dark mind. The Romans had turned a respectful citizen into a raging lion. There was no way he would betray the freedom fighters now.

~ ~ ~

Rachel, the youngest daughter, was sunshine in a bottle. From the time she woke in the morning she lived to please Salome. Her one irritating practice was that she had latched onto Mariam's habit of singing. Still, her childish songs took the edge off of Zebedee's distractions, the constant bickering of

James and John, and the stubborn belligerence of Salome's oldest daughter Leah.

At the market, Rachel cheerily waved to the different vendors and welcomed the constant gifts that they put into her chubby little hands. She toddled after the stray dogs and avoided being nipped as they chased after scraps. Mothers and grandmothers alike squeezed her cheeks and remarked what a beautiful child she was. Salome quietly thanked Ha'Shem for giving her one good child. Mariam and Yuseph had some kind of spell over their brood.

The first year where the rains never came created a harder time for Capernaum than expected. The lake level lowered, the fish vanished, and the farmers hoed fields of dust without success. The market produce was shrunken and withered and half the vendors never arrived to sell anything. The people of Yerushalayim willingly paid higher prices and much that was available was diverted there.

One evening, three of Zebedee's hired boat hands stayed out late trying to find an elusive school of fish. Salome saw the storm clouds roiling at the far end of the lake and noticed two fishing boats still far out from the shore. "Zebedee!" she called. "There's a storm coming and your men are out on the lake."

No response came so she hurried downstairs and found Zebedee asleep on his mat. She laid her hand gently on his shoulder and shook him. "Zebedee, hurry, your men are out on the lake."

"Leave me alone," he snorted.

"But, your men," she said. "There's a major storm."

"They're men," he retorted. "Unlike you, they can take care of themselves. One little storm won't hurt anyone."

Salome rushed back up the stairs and shielded herself under a sleeping mat as the rains split the sky and poured like a waterfall over the community. The lightning strikes illuminated the boats rising up and cresting on large waves before crashing into the valley. Then there was only one boat. Then there was none.

The bodies of Zebedee's three boat hands were discovered early the next morning by fishermen walking the shore. Two other men from the other vessel had also perished.

THE GOOD WIFE

Zebedee was inconsolable—walking the beach, cursing the heavens, collecting the remnants of his fishing boat washing up along the shore. Salome did her best to remove herself from the premises, seeking wisdom from other women who understood the ups and downs of fishing life.

CHAPTER TWENTY-ONE

Nazareth – Shared Stories

Once his healing was complete, Nathaniel moved to Cana and worked on reconciling with Sarah. He committed himself to laboring in his father-in-law's vineyards, learning everything he could to prove himself. He welcomed the long walks with Hannah and worked quietly to establish his ties with the local freedom fighters.

After a year, he returned to Nazareth and put his knowledge to work in his own vineyard. His trust levels were low and he kept his conversations with neighbors short and superficial. The seasons passed and one day Sarah, Hannah, and Deborah returned back to Nazareth.

Along with them, came his Uncle Zeke and Salome's Uncle Avraham. Uncle Zeke was no less exotic in his attire and Uncle Avraham was no less expansive in his girth. The hunter and the shipping tycoon had joined forces to expand both their business operations.

"The world seems smaller every day," Uncle Zeke said to Nathaniel after Sarah had alighted from his carriage and headed toward the washing facility. "What a fortunate nephew you are. I met your lovely wife and daughter in Cana when I delivered a pair of lions to the governor. I confirmed our previous plans and expressed my deep regrets that you had been ill and unable to join me."

Nathaniel watched Hannah lift a large basket from the back of the carriage. She had grown. "Let me help you with that," he called.

"No! It's just an Egyptian goose from your Uncle Zeke. He had it stuffed for your collection."

Uncle Avraham finally emerged from his coach and arrived panting and sweating. "We hear good things about your vineyards, young man. Your uncle and I have joined forces to ship wild game to the Roman arenas, but we are also looking to expand the variety of wines we ship. We hear you have been taught by the best vintners."

Nathaniel nodded. "It appears you are in need of hospitality as we discuss our futures."

~ ~ ~

Zebedee joined the ranks of men trekking to Sepphoris where jobs were still available. Four months passed and Salome wondered how his needs for intimacy were being met. The women and their children at the lakeshore community struggled the best they could to dig up roots from the forest, trap small game, and pool their resources. Leah left to help Rebekah in Cana with another pregnancy. It was one less mouth to feed.

Ha'Shem, where are you?

Rachel's howl set Salome racing from the rooftop where she aired the bedding. The little one lay near the chicken pen where the last hen clucked and pecked uselessly at the dust. The bite mark on her arm was easy to see. Blood was pooling around her. A distinctive paw mark of a dog or wolf was impressed into a dark muddy patch.

"James," she screamed. "Call Abendokt, quickly. James, where are you?"

"Rachel, Ima is here. Rachel, look at me." There was no response. Salome snatched up her daughter and raced inside. A small chunk of flesh was missing from her arm. She soaked her head covering and bound the wound tightly. A cool rag on the girl's forehead kept her hoping for a noise, a whine, a cry, a scream, anything. Nothing.

Diana poked her head in the doorway. "Salome, what's wrong?"

"A wolf got my baby," she said. "Call Abendokt! Tell her to bring her salves and medicines."

"Salome, there's word she practices the secret arts," Diana said. "The women think she may be behind the drought. There's a council to send her away."

Salome picked up Rachel and rushed out the door past Diana. "I don't care what the women think. She understands the ways of plants and medicines from her people. I need her."

Abendokt was only two doors away, but in the time it took to stumble her way to the door of the Egyptian, Salome could see that something had changed. The usually bustling household was strangely silent. She hammered on the door with one hand while holding Rachel with the other.

A neighbor stepped out of the home next door. "You might as well stop pounding. The sorceress is gone."

Salome's tears didn't open Rachel's eyes that day or the next. She lay helplessly beside her little one while the site of the bite grew red and puss-filled. She inwardly cursed Zebedee for destroying her own supply of medications. Diana brought her some turmeric that they mixed with honey and plastered over the wound. The third day Rachel's eyelids fluttered and she groaned, "Bad doggy."

James and John took turns begging small bits of food from the neighbors and market vendors. Leah had returned home the week before and helped scour the forests for roots and edible plants but her complaints made it clear she didn't appreciate the task. "Why do we stay in this place. Ha'Shem has obviously cursed us all. We're turning into animals."

An unexpected encounter changed everything.

She was on her roof, fanning Rachel and drying out the bedrolls. A man stood on a nearby hill staring at her. She stared back as he began to move toward her. His confident walk flashed memories of her encounter with the Parthian archer and his daughter. The man kept coming. It was a brazen act, stepping into the open where anyone loyal to the Roman overlords could report you. The man walked with purpose. She stayed in place, one hand on the chest of her restless girl.

The Parthian warrior moved into her territory and took the steps up to where she stood alone and vulnerable. He looked down at Rachel and then knelt beside her with his hand on her forehead. Salome waited.

The man opened his traveling bag and pulled out an elixir in a small gourd. He held it up to his lips and made drinking motions.

Salome accepted the offering when he held it out. "Show me," she said.

The man cradled Rachel's curly head in his arms and moved the gourd to her lips. "Sips," he said. "Sips."

When Rachel shook her head, resisting the liquid put into her mouth, Salome took over and stroked the girl's hair, singing a lullaby, calming her to try. The Parthian brought out a clay jar filled with a paste. He motioned for Salome to rub it on the child's wounds. Salome did as he instructed through his pantomime.

"Good mother," the Parthian said. "Good mother."

"Thank you," Salome answered.

"You return arrow, help my daughter." He pointed up the hill toward the place where Salome had found the arrow in her dog's neck. "Now, I help your daughter." The Parthian stepped carefully down the stairs and walked back into the forest. Within a few hours he was back with a large basket of food items. He moved up the stairs to the roof and laid it at her feet. "Children, good. Leave now."

James appeared at the top of the stairs as the man disappeared among the trees. "What are you looking at, Ima?"

"An angel," she answered.

"I thought you didn't believe in all that kind of thing," her son persisted.

"I do now." She lifted her daughter and looked skyward. "We're going to visit Aunt Mariam in Nazareth."

"Will Yeshua be there?" Rachel cuddled in close.

"One never knows. He may be off working with Uncle Yuseph in Sepphoris or he may be off on a pilgrimage. Whatever, we will visit. This place has nothing more to offer us for now."

~ ~ ~

For some reason, Nazareth fared better than the lakeside communities and the village was closer to where Zebedee worked, so Salome moved in with Mariam for a few weeks. The temperature was slightly cooler under all the trees and the variety and abundance of nutritious food improved the mood and health of all of them—even Leah.

Nathaniel and his wife, Sarah, were now key leaders responsible for the prosperity that could be seen. Sometimes it didn't pay to be stubborn. Maybe I should have accepted his betrothal. At least I'd be closer to home.

As if reading her thoughts, Zebedee arrived from work in Sepphoris and fussed over the children—apart from Rachel who clung to Salome. The cheery child who loved dogs had disappeared and, in her place, toddled a terrified, whimpering girl who made strange with everyone and everything. Her world had turned upside down but at least her wound had healed and she was quick to eat whatever she was offered.

All that changed when the eighteen-year-old Yeshua walked through the door and smiled at her. She cocked her head and frowned back. He lowered himself to sit cross-legged across from her. With quick hand movements he hid his eyes and contorted his face making gurgling noises. Within five minutes she was sitting in his lap and playing with his fingers.

Salome was stunned. Even Mariam hadn't been able to draw out the little one. The quiet didn't last as Mariam's children James, Joseph, Shimon, Judas, Assia, and Lydia arrived for supper with several friends and Salome's children, James, John, and Leah interspersed. They were like one big happy family. Rachel sat drinking it all in from the safety of Yeshua's lap. Could there be something special about this Galilean or was he able to charm his way into people's lives?

The morning Yeshua left he brought a small Egyptian duckling with a significant limp to Rachel. "This creature needs someone special to take care of it so that it can live," Yeshua said. "Can you do this for Ha'Shem? Can you feed it and protect it?"

Rachel cupped the small creature in her hands and pulled it toward her cheek to rub her face against it. "Will you come to visit ducky when you're here?"

"Of course, little one. I'll come and see you wherever you are."

When Yeshua walked out the door with a smile and a bow, Salome slid into place next to her daughter. "That looks like a special little duckling you have there."

Rachel held out the feathered creature in her cupped hands. "Yeshua says I need to care for him because he can't walk like other duckies."

Salome petted the downy back. "Do you know the story of the duckling who got hatched with the chickens?"

The little girl shook her head vigorously.

"Well," Salome said, "it so happens that somehow a duck egg got mixed up with some chicken eggs and a duckling popped out. He wasn't like the other chickens. He didn't have the right feet for scratching and he didn't have the right beak for poking up worms and bugs. When he opened his voice, it didn't sound the same. He never understood why he was different from the others in the henhouse. Then one day a beautiful bird flew out of the sky and landed nearby. "Quack!" said the bird. "Quack!" said the duckling who was now grown up. Finally, the duckling understood why he was different. His creator had made him to be a different kind of bird than all those around him."

Rachel lay her head against Salome's chest. "Ima, are you telling me this story because you think I'm different or because you're different?"

~ ~ ~

One afternoon, as Salome traipsed through the village—exchanging chit-chat with Othniel the tiler, Agatha the butcher's wife, Daniel the weaver, and Phoebe the seamstress—she chanced by Yuseph's old carpenter shop. She glanced inside the door and noticed movement. It was Yuseph.

"Peace to the carpenter," she called.

"And peace to the fisher's wife," he replied.

"May I come in?"

"Please, find rest for your wandering feet."

Yuseph, plane in hand, shaped a yoke for oxen. Shavings skittered across the floor as the door opened wider. The scent of freshly worked wood filled the air. "Perhaps you are too busy," Salome noted. "I assumed you spent all your days in Sepphoris."

Yuseph set the plane aside and pointed toward a stool. "There is always time for family. When a project is finished at Sepphoris, I like to come home and do things for the community."

Salome ignored the stool and wandered to a carpenter's bench where an assortment of tools lay in orderly fashion. "I am sure your neighbors appreciate your kindness. What have you made for Mariam lately?"

Yuseph brightened. He moved toward a corner of the room and lifted up a blanket. "This is a storage cupboard for her spices and I'm starting a new platform that allows our bed to be off the floor. I saw the idea from an Egyptian at Sepphoris."

Salome ran her fingers along the shelving of the cupboard. "She is no doubt being treated as a queen. Perhaps, if all goes well, I should order one for our home in Capernaum."

"I'm sure Zebedee would be happy to improve your place."

Salome sauntered back to the stool and slumped down on it. "I'm not so sure. He's a simple man with simple tastes. He thinks all our money should be saved to buy land or seed for crops, so that we're not totally dependent on the fishing."

"He sounds like a wise man" Yuseph said. "Is there anything you wanted from me, here, today?"

Salome stretched out her legs and crossed her ankles, trying to appear relaxed. "Mariam and I have had many talks about your early days."

Yuseph set the plane down. "You mean our betrothal?"

Salome shook her head. "Not your betrothal. Before, and after."

"Okay. You wonder about all the rumors." Yuseph leaned back against the bench facing her.

"Yes, I want to know the truth." The last little shaving hanging off his beard was such a temptation to pluck. And such a distraction. She shook her head to focus. "Why you and Mariam couldn't wait for the little one is none of my business. You have restored your reputation in the community enough to do business here."

"The Romans at Sepphoris don't care about anyone's reputation." Yuseph reached for a glass of water and handed it to Salome. "As long as you can be a master craftsman, they will hire you to help them out. Your sister has had a harder time in the area of reputation."

"I heard rumors about Bethlehem, about Magi, about Herod and babies who were killed."

"I'm not sure what you heard but I can tell you what happened."

"Okay." She took a long swig of her water and set the glass down.

Yuseph pulled up a stool and sat on it, facing her. He set his thumbs under his chin and stroked the beard on the front of his chin. He looked up and away as if pondering a distant memory hard to gather. "Yeshua was born in a stable because there was no room for him in the inns. Shepherds came to the place where we laid him in a manger and they told us that angels had appeared to them saying that Yeshua would be a savior who would save his people from their sins."

"That must have been a hard night for Mariam—giving birth in a stable."

Yuseph crossed his arms and furrowed his eyebrows. "It was, but Ha'Shem was gracious. One of the guests at a nearby inn was a midwife who helped us."

"It is good to have good people to help."

"Yes, we met two more good people when we took Yeshua to be circumcised on the eighth day. After the days of purification, on the fortieth day, we went back to the temple. An old man named Simeon and an old woman named Ana prophesied over Yeshua, saying Ha'Shem had told them about his coming. They said some things that disturbed your sister but everything was peaceful for a while."

"What about the Magi?"

"They came later after we had settled into the community." He reached for another piece of wood and set about to measure it. "I had submitted my claim to my lands in the community from my ancestor David and we intended to raise Yeshua there. They had some great vineyards that had been growing since the time of Solomon."

"Do you still have those lands?"

Yuseph stood up and leaned his back up against the carpenter's bench, crossing his ankles. "No, Herod claimed them for himself, saying those lands belonged to the king of Israel and not any commoner who claimed heritage with an ancient monarch. He was no better than Ahab stealing the vineyards of Naboth."

"Why did he even notice you in the first place?"

"The enrollment for taxes was the first thing." He finally brushed the shaving from his beard. "Next, was the coming of the Parthian Magi who stopped by his palace looking for a newborn king of the Jews."

"So, the rumors are true?"

"Yes, the elders pointed the Magi to Bethlehem and the Magi found us in our house. Yeshua was almost two so we had almost forgotten about the wonder of that first night when the skies lit up."

"What happened with the Magi?"

"There was a caravan of hundreds of camels, horses, donkeys, and footmen so it was impossible to ignore them. A dozen or more of the men arrived at our door bearing gifts of gold, frankincense, and myrrh. It was a humbling thing to hear their story of signs in the heavens and their journey to honor God's anointed one."

"What did you do with all the gifts?"

"Well, that night, Ha'Shem warned the Magi about Herod's intention to harm the child and He warned me that we needed to flee to Egypt. So, I woke Mariam and we went to Egypt."

"And all the babies were butchered."

Yuseph hung his head. "Yes. By God's grace, we survived. Assia was born in Egypt. When Herod died and his bloodthirsty son took over we knew that Bethlehem was lost to us."

"So, you came back to Nazareth."

"And here we still are."

"It is good to have you here. Thank you for telling me your story."

Salome left for home. It was strange how stories from years ago could take on a life of their own. Everyone liked to create stories where they were somehow the good ones. It was comforting to know that Yuseph and Mariam were no different.

CHAPTER TWENTY-TWO

Nazareth – Refreshing Encounter

Within hours of her arrival, Nathaniel knew that Salome was back in the village. Sarah met the fisher's wife at the market in Sepphoris and relayed the information to her husband, seeming to monitor his facial responses as she told of the encounter. Nathaniel looked her in the eye, understanding her desire for commitment, and finally shrugged and walked outside to chop wood for the fire.

The grape harvest was so lucrative that he purchased horses for Sarah, Hannah, and himself and took them riding over the hills. The sunsets were glorious at the end of a hard day and the smothering cloak of Roman occupation seemed a distant reality.

Once a week, without fail, a cloaked messenger would arrive at his door with a message from Anthony. "Do you have any names?"

The answer was always "no," but the silent pressure was a grim reminder that the dungeon on the next hill was closer than he might think.

~ ~ ~

With life settling in, Salome lapped up her freedom on quiet afternoons and set out into the forest. One afternoon she snatched up her sling. Some of the same paths from her childhood lay well-worn and established, some were new and some were overgrown. She barged through tall grass and bush to find the pathway where she had encountered the wild boar. The blackberries and brambles towered over her. The birdsong filled the cathedral and something tugged at her soul. She shook it off and plunged deeper into the forest.

She sat by a stream, removed her sandals, and soaked her feet in the cool waters. Her neighbors in Capernaum still suffered from the heat and draught. What right did she have to such peace and beauty when her good friends nearby still suffered?

The clearing she stumbled into had a vague familiarity. Her skin almost crawled. There were no obvious threats from wild animals on the perimeters. There were no strangers. And then she saw it. A tree. The tree. The tree where Nathaniel had fallen.

With fury, she took out her sling, snatched up some pebbles and shot wildly at the leafy villain. The tears coursed down her cheeks.

"Ha'Shem. Why can't I ever be good enough?"

With Zebedee at work all week, and the children busy with so many play-mates, Salome relished the liberty instead of freedom she once enjoyed in her childhood. She explored the forest paths, usually with one or two children in tow, and she harvested mushrooms, berries, and tubers to help with the increased demands of meal time. When the children decided not to come, she would pull out her sling and improve her aim at the tree.

One afternoon, standing by the sheep pen, she felt a familiar presence. Without looking she spoke. "So, we meet again where we finished it all."

Nathaniel chuckled. "I always knew we had a special connection. Do you remember when that pup stole your meat and I caught him with a noose around his neck?"

Salome turned slightly and shuffled to make room for Nathaniel along the rail of the sheep pen. "How could I forget. You saved my neck and my Abba's favorite dinner."

Nathaniel grasped the rail with both hands and leaned in toward Salome. "Do you remember what you said to me?"

Salome looked away at the sheep. "I believe it was 'thank you.'"

He put his hand out for a lamb to nuzzle. "After that."

She ruffled the top of another woolly head. "Something like, 'perhaps I misjudged you.'"

"Oh, so you do remember?"

"I think I also said perhaps we should talk sometime."

"And I said perhaps it's too late."

"So, you did." She laid her head on her arm on the rail and looked at him. "Didn't I once tell you on the day I turned you down that someday Ha'Shem would provide a good woman for you?"

"For that you were wrong." He poked her side and she giggled.

"What do you mean?" She bent down and snapped off a small wildflower that she raised to her nose.

Nathaniel stepped away toward a path and Salome followed. "Sarah is way more than I ever deserved. I feel that with my physical limitations she is being held back from all she could be. If it wasn't for my parents and hers agreeing to this, we would never have gotten betrothed."

Salome stepped up and elbowed Nathaniel in the ribs. "Now I know it." She tossed the flower at him. "You fell on your head out of that tree, didn't you? And here, I thought it was your leg that got damaged."

"It was my leg."

"And is it your leg that helped you produce children?"

"No. I have three wonderful gifts. Two daughters and a great wife." He picked up a different wildflower and handed it to her.

She took it and set it in her hair. "Is it your leg that helped you and Sarah become the leaders of Nazareth in olive-oil production, in sheep products, in carpentry?"

He stopped in place. "Well, no."

She turned, backing away. "See, it is your head that makes you talk like a fool."

"No one else I know has dared call me a fool," he said, feigning pain. "You talk as if we were still youths lost in our own world."

Her chuckle rose easily. "I haven't talked with a man like this since the day I left this place."

He fell into step beside her as she baby-stepped back toward the sheep pen. "I've missed our talks."

"Consider yourself fortunate," she said. "My Zebedee tried to have a talk with me once or twice and decided that fishing in storms was much easier."

He bumped her with his shoulder, knocking her off stride into the fence rail. "It can't be that bad."

"Oh, it is," she said, regaining her balance. "Why do you think he's up here working in Sepphoris and leaving the rest of his family out of his reach?"

"He hasn't had the chance to get to know you." Nathaniel perched up on the fencepost. "Perhaps if he saw you tumble in the brambles with a wild boar that would increase his appreciation for you."

"Yeah, only he probably would have used his bow and arrow to shoot me and then explained that he thought I was a wild boar." She stopped a stride away as he turned to face her. "By the way, thanks for not shooting me."

"You're welcome," he said. "I still laugh sometimes for no reason and Sarah asks me why. I tell her that I've found some strange things in the forest and they make me laugh."

"Does she know about us?"

Nathaniel tilted his head and smirked. "There was never any us for anyone to know about."

"You're right," she said. "Perhaps you lived in my dreams and fantasies more than in real life."

He slipped off the rail and stood facing her. "This is dangerous territory for old friends."

"You're right," she said, turning away. "Let me ask you about Mariam."

"Your sister?" He followed her stride. "What about her?"

"You've seen her around the village. Tell me what she's like as a mother. How did Yeshua turn out so good? Don't people talk about what happened?"

Nathaniel set his foot up on a stump and picked off a blade of grass to chew on. His furrowed brows framed his face along with his generous beard. "Salome, you can't always live in the past. Sometimes people know each other's faults and then they get around to being neighbors and looking out for each other's children."

"But she fabricates everything about herself and her children. She always has to be the center of attention. She acts like she is little Miss Perfect."

Nathaniel set both feet on the path and straightened up to his full height. "That is the bitter piece of you I thought I had seen. Salome, we've grown up now. Unless you learn to see your sister for who she is you'll be trapped in your own bitterness and you'll pull all your family members in there with you. You've been so worried about being the good one in your family that you've missed out on what real life is like." He reached up, snapped off a twig from a tree, and tossed it into the bush. "Do you remember me saying that goodness was like a dragon for you? That you had to keep feeding it with acts of niceness to draw attention to yourself? Before you accuse your sister of anything you need to look deep within yourself."

She turned her back to him. "I wish you would stop talking about the dragon."

He put a hand on her shoulder and then removed it quickly. "Would you rather I talk about the wolf of jealousy you seem to also be adopting?"

Salome sat down on the stump Nathaniel had been resting his foot on. "Fine, I'm listening. Tell me about the angel who lives in Nazareth. But first, I had a friend who told me that I could be loved without having to be good enough. Do you think that's true?"

Nathaniel chuckled. "You've never had to be good enough with me," he said. "Just be who Ha'Shem made you to be. Love is not something people owe you for what you do. Love is the connection two people have by sharing who they really are."

"Aren't you the wise one," she said. "Okay, talk to me about my sister."

"Walk with me," he said. "I want to show you something else Sarah and I are working at."

She followed his lead. "What is it?"

"Come and see."

Within minutes, the pair stepped into an opening overlooking a long hill filled with grape vines. "Vineyards!" Salome exclaimed. "As magnificent as King Solomon's."

Nathaniel smiled, pleased at the affirmation. "Perhaps! The grapes are almost ready to harvest. Perhaps you would like to tread the winepress one day and take some of the juice for your family."

Several men and women cut off purple fruit clusters and placed them in baskets that other women carried up the hill.

"Where's the winepress?" Salome asked.

Nathaniel pointed to the far side of the hill where a temporary shelter had been constructed to shield those treading the grapes from the sun. Ropes hung from the matted ceiling so those in the press could hold on and keep their balance. A larger cistern was cut into the rock and a small channel allowed the juice to run into a lower cut cistern where it could be collected and cooled while it fermented.

Salome stepped forward and examined a large cluster of grapes. "Ha'Shem has blessed you. This tells me that you have no intentions of moving anywhere else."

"These vines are new plantings from ten years ago. You may remember that as children we were never permitted on these lands owned by Aretas. The grapes are large and plump because we have much rain and a small underground creek on this side of the hill."

"Your wine must be highly sought after."

"This wine is for common drink. The rich wine comes from the vines on the other side of the hill where it is rocky and the roots have had to dig down deep for nourishment. We have had one strong vine that yields smaller and sweeter grapes."

"So, if you were to describe my sister, which kind of grape would she be?"

Nathaniel backed away and held his finger to his lips. "First, did you ever ride a horse?"

Salome stopped in the middle of the path. "No, when would I ever have had the chance?"

He spread his arms like an eagle. "How about today?"

"What do you mean?"

"See my new barn over there?" Nathaniel pointed toward a cedar-planked building with a flat roof and broad doors at the edge of his vineyard. "There are three horses in there. How would you like to ride while we talk?"

"I'm afraid I might fall off."

"Let me teach you," he said. "You might be surprised how easy it is to make a dream come true."

Nathaniel's arms were so strong and steady that her fear was brief as he boosted her onto the horse. She imagined Queen Salome riding before her troops.

"Are you going to be okay now?" Nathaniel asked as he swung up onto his own mount.

"Do you know why my parents called me Salome?" she asked.

"Perhaps a relative's name?"

"No. They named me after the last of the great monarchs from the Maccabees—Queen Salome Alexandra. They hoped I would bring them great happiness."

"So, that is why you are a woman of such confidence and determination," Nathaniel said. "Perhaps I should have been bowing instead of trying to woo you in my younger years."

Salome stared hard at the man riding so comfortably slightly ahead of her. "You were trying to woo me?" she asked.

Nathaniel turned and smiled. "Perhaps it was only in my dreams. Come. Let's ride to the hill across from Sepphoris and I'll tell you all I know about your sister."

It was a cool swish of evening breeze that drew their attention to the sun sliding quickly toward the horizon of the Great Sea. Hours passed and Salome wondered if someone had bewitched her sister and turned her into a different being. The Mariam who Nathaniel professed to witness with her family and the villagers was a stranger she almost wished she had known as a good friend.

As Nathaniel and Salome emerged from the forest to connect with the village path a group of workers coming from Sepphoris crossed in front of them. Zebedee was at the forefront. He stopped in his tracks with a glare at Nathaniel. Without asking for an explanation, he grabbed hold of Salome's hand and dragged her off the horse and toward home—to Mariam's place.

It was there that she gained a real appreciation for her sister. Zebedee dragged her into the home and threw her down onto the floor in front of the family gathered for dinner. Rachel raced to hug Salome but Mariam marched up to Zebedee and ordered him out of the house. Before he uttered a word, she pushed him outside and shut the door behind them.

Yuseph encouraged all the children to keep eating and then slipped outside where escalating voices could still be heard. In a few minutes, stillness prevailed. Mariam stepped inside and lifted Salome to her feet. "We should talk," she said.

Jealousy isn't always easy to talk about but the two sisters unleashed a lifetime of pent-up conversations. "I need to be me," Salome muttered through her clenched jaw. "Zebedee is off running after half the women in the country, like he's some Roman centurion, but the moment I talk with a friend he turns into a gladiator. You don't know what it's like living with these crazy fishermen who talk about nothing else but fish."

"He saw you with Nathaniel," Mariam said.

"Yes, he saw me riding on a horse along a trail coming home with Nathaniel. I see him drunk out of his mind in the lap of an Egyptian harlot. Somewhere in the Torah there has to be some law about that."

"There are many laws in the Torah," Mariam said. "If we forced everyone to follow every law that's been written we would all be blind and toothless. We would have no children or spouses."

Salome couldn't believe her ears. "Aren't you little Miss Perfect raising the Messiah in your own home? If the rabbis heard you, I'm sure you'd be stoned as a rebel and a sorceress."

Mariam rubbed her temples with her thumbs as she listened. "You may not understand, but raising the Messiah is not an easy task."

Salome turned away. "And I suppose you think that being related to the one raising the Messiah is easier?"

"In our home we speak of the spirit behind the Torah," Mariam said. "We speak of God's grace and compassion displayed with his people. We listen to how the Torah is to be applied with everyone we meet."

Salome furrowed her brow. "You read the Torah and discuss it?"

"Yes," Mariam affirmed. "Yeshua and James are especially keen on debating the teachings but Yeshua says we must live it and not only listen to it."

"But, you're a woman."

"Yes, Yuseph has taught me many things during our time away. The Torah was our life."

"I don't think Zebedee even knows how to read." Salome pressed a hand hard over her racing heartbeat. "He never opens a Torah. We hardly ever talk about it and when it's time for fishing we hardly ever get to synagogue."

"How do you think such a man might feel when he has nowhere to go to help him understand the world outside his little home? He only knows the traditions and practices he remembers from his own home and what he might hear from his friends."

"So, what do you think I should do? I can't let him humiliate me in front of the children. Imagine what they are learning from their home about how women are to be treated."

"Perhaps this is your time to teach your children how to respond to injustice, oppression, abuse, anger, and jealousy."

Salome paced back and forth chewing on the edge of her thumbnail. "You might have to teach me."

Mariam nodded. "We'll learn together with our children. We'll share stories and ask them how each person in the story should respond so that they show the heart of Ha'Shem."

"Every story I know turns into a nightmare. That's not what I want my children learning."

"Follow my examples. I'll share a few and once you get the idea then you can share a few. Children learn quickly if you give them a chance."

Zebedee never mentioned the encounter on the trail but he hired stone-masons to build a separate home in Nazareth for them to reside in. "Within the year, when the weather turns, when the fish come back, when I have enough money—then we return to Capernaum. We have a business to run."

CHAPTER TWENTY-THREE

Nazareth – Clearer Understanding

After Zebedee's abuse against Salome, James openly defied his mother, refusing to acknowledge a single request for his help around the home. Leah disappeared for hours at a time into the surrounding communities. John lost himself in the play with his cousins and Rachel returned to her clinginess—rotating between Salome and her pet duck for a sense of security.

It would have been easy to slink into the new quarters and hide away in a darkened corner but Salome's pride drove her to prove her goodness. The dragon found many ways to expand its grip on her. She dug out a garden, purchased some chickens, and set to sewing new bedding for everyone in the family. In the early afternoons, she left Rachel asleep with Mariam to wander the village streets, greeting all who would speak to her.

The baker's wife tried to snare her again into the happenings at Sepphoris. "The Zealots smashed two marble statues of a goddess and the new centurion is threatening to crucify more carpenters if he can't find out the culprits . . . . The Parthians have established a secret trade in silk that comes all the way from the far east . . . A new theater is being built where all the immoralities of Rome will be on full display . . . The markets are opening up to fruits, spices, and foods from Ethiopia, Egypt, Libya, Spain, Britannia, Gaul, and Persia. We are now on the major trading routes from east to west. The peace is holding."

One morning Salome wandered into the carpenter shop where Yeshua was finishing up a baby crib. He acknowledged her with a nod and kept on with his work. The scent of shavings filled the air with a sense of accomplishment and adventure. One never knew what a piece of wood might become.

"I remember when your Abba made a crib for you," Salome said. She picked up a broom and herded the shavings into a heap.

"I don't remember seeing it," Yeshua responded. The plane took another shaving off the wood and it drifted onto the floor alone.

Salome kicked the shaving across toward the others. "Your Abba and Ima had to leave for Bethlehem because of the edict from Caesar and it was left behind. I'm not sure who ended up with it but it was a beautiful bed."

"How is your stay?" Yeshua asked. He set down his plane and ran his calloused hand over the smooth surface. "May the Almighty Father grant you the best blessings while you are here." He retrieved a crib bar and set it in place.

"Thank you," Salome replied. "Why do you call Ha'Shem, Father? Do you not have your own father?"

Yeshua ceased fitting the bar in place for the crib and stood to his full height. "The One we call Ha'Shem has created all things. As our ancestor David said, he even fashioned us together in our mother's womb. When you see this baby crib you might say that since I am the creator of what you see that I am its father. Such is Ha'Shem with me."

"But I have heard you call him Abba. That is not simply acknowledging him as Creator. You acknowledge him as if he himself is the source of your being and the one you have intimate relationship with."

"This is true." Yeshua moved aside a plane and leaned up against the carpenter's bench. He removed a shaving lodged in the folds of his carpenter tunic.

Salome stepped closer and ran her fingers over the smooth surface of the crib's railing. "And what does this Abba of yours require for this intimate relationship?"

"He requires that I love him with all my heart, soul, mind, and strength. And that I love my neighbor as myself." Picking up a wooden mallet, Yeshua carefully tapped several more of the crib bars into place.

Salome wiped off the carpenter's bench and hoisted herself up to sit. "But what about the 613 laws Moses commands for us all to follow?"

Yeshua kept tapping away at the bars. "All these laws are summed up in these two commands to love."

Salome set the broom aside. "Where did you learn all this?"

Yeshua sets his palms flat out on the carpenter's bench and smiled. "I read Torah and Ha'Shem guides me into what is true."

"You are exceptional," Salome said. "I wish my James and John had a desire for something besides fishing."

Yeshua nodded. "Perhaps one day they will."

"I pray that it would be so."

She left him to his work and walked the streets of Nazareth, wrestling with the idea that Ha'Shem might desire an intimate relationship of love with his own creation.

The hook in her heart proved impossible to resist. The time for spring planting arrived, the rains diminished and her feet grew restless for the paths around Nazareth. Her aim with the sling continued to improve again. Zebedee's ongoing work in Sepphoris gave Salome space and allowed her to set her own tone in the new house he had built.

The question of intimacy with her Creator played in her thoughts. Could Ha'Shem really be like a father? What kind of father was he like? Certainly not like Zebedee.

On a beautiful spring morning, while the children were preoccupied with their own play at Mariam's home, Salome wandered to Nathaniel's vineyard. The humiliation after her last encounter remained fresh in her memory so she avoided going near her friend's home. With no one in view she wandered up and down the rows of freshly planted vines. She noted that each shoot had been carefully rooted two paces apart.

One plant withered in place and she knelt to examine it closer. As she did, she heard voices nearby. It didn't take long to identify that the voices belonged to Nathaniel and his daughter Hannah.

Nathaniel spoke gently and patiently. "Dig deep enough so that your elbow is even with the ground. That's right. Good work." They were planting new vines.

Salome peered through the rows of vines until she spotted Nathaniel. His head and shoulders were visible. She crouched low and moved away. The snap of a twig underfoot froze her in place.

"Who's there?" Nathaniel's voice demanded a response.

Salome stood and shrugged when he spotted her.

"What are you doing here?" he asked.

"Don't be mad," she said. "I needed to get away from the house and thought I would look at your plants."

He held up an unplanted cutting. "What do you think?"

"What do I think?"

"About the vines."

She pointed toward her feet. "I found one that isn't doing so well."

A frown creased his face. "Let me take a look at it."

The sun moved quickly across the sky as the trio examined the budding vines, added stakes, fertilized, removed diseased plants, and even pruned where necessary. Hannah chattered like a squirrel. The positive relationship this girl had with her father, compared to Zebedee's relationship with his children, created a strange attraction in Salome's heart for her friend.

Is this the kind of love that Yeshua knew with his Abba?

Upon completion of their tasks, Salome bid farewell and scurried home. Walking into her empty home, she realized that no one had even missed her. The realization brought both a relief and a sense of regret.

The senior rabbi had taken on an assistant and at least he was friendly. One day, at the village well while she was drawing water, he happened by. Salome dared to speak to him. "Rabbi . . ."

He hesitated, knowing rabbis didn't usually talk with women—especially married ones.

"Rabbi, please. A moment for a question."

The rabbi looked around and then stood with his head down, turned away, as if contemplating. "Speak quickly!"

Salome played along by sitting on the edge of the well with her back to him. "Rabbi, how does a simple woman gain the pleasure and favor of Ha'Shem?"

The lengthy pause almost convinced her that the rabbi had walked on but before she turned her head the response came. "My child, such deep questions from a fisherman's wife. Only do these things. Walk humbly with Ha'Shem, please your husband, teach your children the fear of Ha'Shem, serve those who call on you for help or hospitality, speak what is true, attend the synagogue and obey the teachings you hear, give generously to the poor, stay pure in your marriage vows, pray for the coming of Messiah. Such things will win the favor of Ha'Shem."

Salome soaked in the list. "Thank you, rabbi. Such are the practices of the righteous ones. Shalom." She waited, watching a pup at play chasing a butterfly. No further instruction was given.

A light footstep nearby prompted her to quickly add another question. "Rabbi, how do I gain the favor of my sister?"

The footstep halted and Salome spun around. Mariam stood six feet away. The heat rushed up her neck and cheeks.

Salome followed Mariam's gaze toward the retreating rabbi already entering the synagogue compound a hundred steps away. "Ah, I was trying to ask the rabbi a question," she said.

"I heard," Mariam replied. "Perhaps I can answer that question for him."

Salome lowered her gaze. "I am sorry. I can't seem to do anything right anymore. Everywhere I turn I end up ruining the relationships I value most."

"Salome, look at me."

Mariam's face was gracious and compassionate. She held out a sling.

"How did you find that?" Salome asked as she accepted it.

"John was using it to shoot our chickens." Mariam smiled, then shrugged. "It looks like we're having one for dinner. I have a suggestion."

"I'm sorry about the chicken," Salome interrupted. "I'll repay you. Please don't tell Zebedee. He'll be so angry I wasn't watching after the children better."

"Ha'Shem decided that we will have enough meat for our families to share dinner. You can help me prepare later. First, we need to go for a walk."

"Where are we going?" Salome asked.

"To a tree."

"A tree?"

"Yes, follow me." It didn't take long before she could see which tree. Her target tree.

"How did you know?"

"I've seen you here at least twice," Mariam said. "I didn't ask but I know this sling belonged to our brother before he died. Abba thought it was lost forever. Why are you shooting at this tree?"

Salome sighed and sat down with her back against the trunk. "Nathaniel and I once climbed this tree. I've tried so hard to be good all my life but this is the tree he fell from. I should have been watching him better."

"So, why do you shoot it with all those rocks?"

"I think Abba always wished I was a boy who could do the things boys could do. I promised myself that one day I would make him proud even if I was a girl. With every rock I say a prayer to Ha'Shem for him to make me good enough."

"Why does he need to make you good enough?"

Salome turned to Mariam. "How else will I be loved? I am the good daughter but it feels I can never be good enough. Oh, Mariam, I have been so bitter in my heart towards you for gaining love I thought you didn't deserve. Please forgive me."

Tears poured down Mariam's cheeks as she reached out to hug Salome. The two women cried away the wasted years until Salome patted her sister's back and pulled away. "We've got a supper to prepare. I hope that one day we can rebuild what we should have had."

"Ha'Shem's specialty," Mariam said. "The years the locusts have eaten."

"What are you talking about?" Salome asked.

"The prophet speaks about how Ha'Shem will restore the years the locusts have eaten and I believe that even now he can restore the years that have slipped away. Let's walk—there's still time for supper preparations. I know there are many things you question about my life. We'll talk when you're ready."

Salome shuffled toward the familiar forest paths. "The one person I would like to speak with is Ha'Shem. How can you deal with someone you can't see? Someone who is so far away from his sinful creation that they can't ever hope to make things right again? If only Ha'Shem would come and walk with us and talk with us."

"Perhaps he has."

"What are you saying? And don't start talking to me about angels and Messiahs and prophets."

Mariam stopped on the trail until Salome halted and spun to face her. "That pretty well wipes out everything now, doesn't it?"

"I don't want you acting like you're some kind of rabbi who knows everything."

"Okay. Did you know Yuseph finished building the extra room on our house? He's going to add an extra room on your place in case Ha'Shem chooses to bless you again."

Salome took a step and increased her pace toward home. "Tell him not to bother. Zebedee and I have finished our family. I can't handle the boys as it is. Leah won't listen to me. I don't want another child."

"Surely, if Ha'Shem chooses to bless you."

"Stop. Mariam, I know you don't think you have to have relationships between a man and a woman to have babies but in my world we still do. And that's not happening."

"I didn't know," Mariam said, extending her arms toward Salome. "That must be so hard."

"It's what happens when you age. Say, remember where we used to get those berries when we were young. Wasn't that in a ravine near here? I think my children would love some with that chicken dinner."

Mariam stopped and slowly turned in a circle. "Yes, I think we used that tree and that hill to the right of Mount Hermon as our guiding posts. Take it easy now, there's another little one on the way and I'm not as young as I used to be. Yuseph insists on doing things the old-fashioned way."

The ravine wasn't hard to find but the creek bed they used to wade across as children was now a small rushing river. Two logs had been felled and placed across the water to form a bridge. Salome didn't hesitate to step up and walk.

"Wait!" Mariam stood with one foot on the log before stepping back.

"What?" Salome stopped half-way across.

"I'm not sure I can make it." She stepped away from the makeshift bridge.

"Come on." Salome took a few more steps. "It's solid."

Mariam continued to back away. "I don't want to risk falling and hurting the baby."

"Okay, wait where you are." Salome finished the trek across the log bridge. "The berries should be right next to the small hill. I'll pick as many as I can carry."

"Hurry, they'll be waiting for dinner back home," Mariam said. "We're already going to be late."

Salome hurried up the trail, across a small meadow and focused on the tree to the right of the hill. She had entered a patch of brush when she heard voices. Men. Arguing.

Baby-stepping forward she slid into the bushes off to the side of the trail. Memory traces of a cave ahead prompted her to remember an encounter here with the Zealot, Thaddeus.

It was the first time Thaddeus had brought her to the local hideaway for the young Zealots. Most of the meetings had been empty talks of bravado and vague plans of revenge on the Romans. Three of the youth had connected with a group of Parthians wanting to forge a trail of smuggled goods through the area without being caught by the Romans.

Thaddeus was an emerging leader who insisted that everyone had to have secret names. Without hesitation, after a vague oath of secrecy had been taken, he had announced the animal epitaphs. "Wolf, lion, ox, warhorse, leopard . . ." He had hesitated when coming to her before finally announcing . . . "Sparrow."

"No," Salome had objected. "Everyone else has a strong name. A sparrow is too fragile, too weak."

Thaddeus had smiled before putting his hand up and caressing her cheek. "A sparrow is cunning and able to nest in places where few suspect she hides. I need you on the inside."

Within a few months Thaddeus had paid the price for his Zealot enthusiasm. Salome had never returned to the group—suspecting that one of them had been a traitor. Ox had been the only one to track her down and recruit her for more missions. He had confirmed her name in this same place.

The voices grew heated so she turned and walked back. As she turned a corner, she came face to face with a tall, broad-shouldered man whose beard hung half-way down his chest. His hood hung down over his forehead and his brown tunic reached to the ground. The dagger in his hand glinted in the setting sun.

One look into his eyes and she knew. "Wolf?"

The man glared as he stepped forward with his dagger raised. "How do you know me?" Then the dagger lowered. "Sparrow?"

"What are you doing here? Who is that arguing?"

"The question is what are you doing here? Come, let's take a walk." He motioned for her to turn around and head up the trail toward the cave.

There were four men near the cave entrance. One was facedown, hands tied behind his back. One stood with his foot resting firmly on the small of the man's back. Two others knelt with daggers drawn—waggling them threateningly in front of the man's face. The group turned as one when Salome stumbled into view.

"Who have we here?" asked the leader who had been standing with his foot on the prisoner's back. Warhorse?

"Remember Sparrow?" Wolf announced.

The leader removed his foot from the back of the prostrate victim and walked quickly toward Salome. "Well, well, well. And we thought that Leopard was working alone all this time. It looks like we'll have two throats to cut."

The bearded faces all came into focus. Bear, Lion, Warhorse . . . and Leopard on the ground. Salome stepped back quickly and nearly impaled herself on the dagger held by Wolf. "Whoa, No. I'm not involved. I'm here picking berries with my sister."

"And where's your sister?" Warhorse asked.

"She's pregnant so she waited on the other side of the stream so she didn't have to cross the logs."

"Go check it out," Warhorse directed Wolf. Wolf left. Warhorse grabbed hold of Salome and had her sit cross-legged in the dirt near Leopard. "And here, I thought you were working with us."

"I am," Salome stammered. "You saw me. I was. I've got a family."

"You haven't answered the call of the feather in over a year," Warhorse growled. He was larger than Ox but not as muscular as Wolf. "Ox told us we could count on you. We've never seen you and Leopard together so how did you communicate?" The Zealot took a step closer. "Where do you keep the stolen girls?"

"We're not together," Salome declared. "Warhorse, you know me. I'm a mother, married to a fisherman in Capernaum. I'm visiting my sister in Nazareth. I've helped Ox when he called."

Warhorse knelt on Leopard's back. "She says she's not with you. Tell us where the centurion takes the stolen girls."

"I'm a simple mason trying to earn a living for my children," Leopard croaked. "I'm telling you that it was a coincidence the Roman infiltrator worked on my group of tradesmen. When Thaddeus died, I was too afraid to stay involved. I know nothing about where the stolen girls go."

"Cowards talk," Lion said. "Now that these two know we're still fighting against the Romans there is no option but to slit their throats and to bury them in the cave with the others." He pulled out his dagger again and placed it against Leopard's throat.

Footsteps sounded and Wolf burst into the clearing. "The sister has crossed the logs and is coming. We can't afford to kill them here. I say let's swear Sparrow to secrecy and leave her out of this. We need to move and finish this somewhere else."

Lion shoved a rag into Leopard's mouth and hoisted him to his feet. "One noise and we gut you right where you are. This trial isn't done."

The men pushed off down the trail and Salome collapsed to her knees, shaking, head to the ground. It was there that Mariam found her.

CHAPTER TWENTY-FOUR

Nazareth – The Cave

"Salome! What's wrong? I thought you were getting the berries and coming right back."

Salome wobbled to her feet and threw her arms around her sister, sobbing. "We need to get home. Now! Hurry! We need to get home."

Mariam braced her sister by the shoulders with both hands. "But what happened?"

Salome pulled away and headed for the path. "I can't tell you and even if I did you wouldn't believe me."

"I think I know that feeling," Mariam said.

The two women walked as quickly as Mariam could manage until they came to the logs. Salome stepped up and was halfway across when Mariam shouted, "Salome, wolf!"

Salome looked up quickly and misstepped. Her ankle twisted as she hurtled off the side of the makeshift bridge. The wolf, the four-footed kind, examined her, head cocked, fangs bared, snarling. Deliberately it moved toward the water.

Both girls screamed. Reflexively, Salome bent down and reached into the riverbed. She grasped a single smooth stone and rose. From the fold in her tunic, she pulled out her sling and fit the stone in place. The projectile caught the wolf hard on the ear and it jolted to a stop, snarling louder. Salome reached down and picked up another stone, slinging it quickly. This stone caught the wolf on the snout and it yelped, turned, and bolted back into the brush.

Mariam crouched by the river, urging her sister out of the cool water. Salome slowly backed out, limping.

"Wow, two out of two. You never missed." She wrapped her arms around her sister's waist and pulled. "How did you do that?"

"Ha'Shem was merciful. He heard my prayer."

The Zealots were behind. The wolf was ahead. A swelling ankle meant she was going nowhere despite how badly two families sat at home waiting for their chicken dinner while the sun disappeared behind the hills.

"I should have told someone where we were going," Mariam said as she knelt examining her sister's swollen ankle.

"It's my fault," Salome responded, wincing at the prodding and twisting. "I'm the one who wanted the berries."

"What are we going to do?" Mariam stood and scanned the forest around them. "You're not able to walk far and I don't want to face that wolf again. Especially after you hit it."

"It's getting dark quickly." The path back could mean shelter. "Help me back to the cave where you found me. I'm not sure what might be in there but at least we'll be safe from the wolf."

Using Mariam's shoulders for support, Salome hopped and hobbled up the slope until they reached the clearing. Mariam stepped into the cave and rushed out screaming, clutching at her hair. "Get it off, get it off."

Salome rolled back on the ground laughing. "It's a bat, girl. Brush it off. There are probably hundreds more inside."

Encouraging each other, the two women crept into the cave—one crouching and one crawling on hands and knees. The acrid smell of ash and bat guano was strong. "Check the firepit for coals," Salome coaxed. "Someone may have used this place recently."

Mariam rummaged through the firepit and found a still-warm bit of charcoaled wood. Gathering dried grasses, twigs, and the hem of her tunic she cupped her hands around the emblem of hope and gently blew on it. The tiniest spark of red glowed.

The sisters set up a new firepit by the entrance to the cave and took turns feeding the flickering flame. With Salome injured, Mariam sang her psalms and made quick forages into the woods nearby, dragging branches and sticks.

There was no sleep and slowly time unsealed the years of memories shared by two sisters.

Mariam probed her sister first. "Shoshanna met me in the market the other day as Nathaniel walked by. She told me he's the one you were meant to marry. I know there's a story behind that so if you were meant to marry him what happened?"

The rocky ground grew uncomfortable under Salome. The cave walls got closer. A hot flush settled in her cheeks and her shoulders grew tight. She cleared her throat and wiped her wrist above her lips, then dabbed at her eye with her fingers. When she'd stalled long enough, she said quickly. "Guess some things aren't meant to be."

Mariam persisted. "Didn't you tell Abba? Surely, he would have spoken for you."

Salome's chin rested on her chest. "He did ask. I told him no."

"But why?" Mariam plunked down beside her sister. "He's turned out to be one of the best men in our village."

Salome looked away. "I couldn't marry him when I almost killed him."

"What? Since when did you almost kill him?"

"When we were younger, I taunted him to climb that tree I was in." She stroked her throat repeatedly, pulling at the skin. "He climbed it and then fell and broke his foot. He still limps. I couldn't let him remind me of that wicked act every time we were together."

"Surely, he doesn't hold that over you?" Mariam said. "He is better bred than that."

"Yes," Salome acknowledged, "now I know, but it's too late. I was too worried about being seen as the good sister." She pushed another log into the fire and settled back on her hands. "Okay, enough about me. It's your turn for true confessions and I want straight answers."

Salome listened to Mariam's stories of the angelic pronouncement regarding Yeshua's birth, about their journey to Bethlehem, about the boy's circumcision and the prophesies shared at the temple. She soaked in details of the visit from the Magi and the trip to Egypt. While her mind raced to find holes in the stories, her heart soaked in the comfort of knowing that Ha'Shem had not forgotten even the humblest of his people. She needed that kind of God now more than ever. Especially, if there were dead bodies in this cave like Warhorse had said.

Mariam provided that comforting sense of presence as she sang the psalms of their ancestor David. One song especially stood out for Salome:

"Do not fret because of those who are evil or be envious of those who do wrong; for like the grass they will soon wither, like green plants they will soon die away. Trust in the LORD and do good; dwell in the land and enjoy safe pasture. Take delight in the LORD, and he will give you the desires of your heart. Commit your way to the LORD; trust in him and he will do this: He will make your righteous reward shine like the dawn, your vindication like the noonday sun. Be still before the LORD and wait patiently for him; do not fret when people succeed in their ways, when they carry out their wicked schemes."[4]

Salome imagined David out at night in a place like this as he looked toward the stars and sang. Whatever scheme her former Zealot friends had planned she would rest and be still in this refuge provided by Ha'Shem.

"Too bad you're not left-handed," Mariam said as she tossed a handful of twigs into the flames. "Abba once told me about seven hundred left-handed slingers from the tribe of Benjamin who could sling stones at a hair and not miss. At least you can hit a wolf."

Salome examined the sling and tried it with her left hand. The stone was out before a dozen rotations. "Not a chance," she said. "I'm with the tribe of Judah for sure."

"How did you ever learn to use a sling?" Mariam asked. "I mean why would you even want to?"

"Do you remember David?" Salome responded. "He taught me."

Mariam rubbed her arms up and down to warm herself as she shifted closer to the fire. "Didn't he run off to join one of those Zealot freedom fighters?"

"Yes, he wanted to make a difference in our land."

"I'm sure glad they don't let women take such crazy risks." Mariam stood and kicked a few coals back closer to the flames. "Can you imagine getting yourself killed and leaving your children without their mother?"

"That wouldn't be very good, would it?" Salome said.

~ ~ ~

Nathaniel poked baby Deborah in the belly as she giggled and flung her arms and legs around. "Nothing like a happy baby," he called out to Sarah as she set out loaves of freshly baked bread on the counter. "Where's Hannah?"

"She's out in the yard with the dog," Sarah answered. "Don't worry, I'm not letting that girl out of my sight. I should call her in. It's getting late and we need to light the lamps." A moment later she spoke up again. "It looks like we've got company and it looks like this company is not too happy."

Nathaniel opened the door at the same moment that Zebedee swung his fist and caught him in the jaw. He stumbled backward as the fisherman reached for him again. "Where's my wife?" the attacker yelled. "What have you done with her?"

Sarah reached for a broom and swung it at Zebedee. "Get your hands off my husband and get out of my house."

Nathaniel put out his arm to block the broom and pushed Zebedee toward the door. "I have no idea where your wife is. If you'd treat her like a decent woman then maybe she'd be around when you need her."

Zebedee stood his ground in the doorway. "If you'd keep your hands off of her then maybe she'd want to stay home with me."

"What are you accusing my husband of?" Sarah yelled. "It's your wife who has been throwing herself at him. Maybe she's off chasing someone else for once."

"Ima!" It was Hannah standing outside. "Ima, what's happening?"

Nathaniel stepped past Zebedee and took his daughter into his arms. "It's a misunderstanding, Hannah. This man can't find his wife. We're going to go and look for her."

Zebedee stood quietly. "If you've seen Mariam, I think the two of them are together."

Nathaniel turned around, hand on Hannah's back. "How long have they been missing?"

"James says he hasn't seen her since this morning," Zebedee answered. "I got home from work and there was no dinner and the children were upset. I didn't know where else to look."

Nathaniel lit two lamps and gave one to Zebedee. "We'll go house to house. Someone will have seen the two of them. I'll start with my father who is the gatekeeper to see if he saw them go to the city."

The next two hours of knocking, calling, and searching yielded nothing. Darkness covered the land like a blanket and the night sounds were in full swing. A howl sounded near the ravine. "We'll have to get started in the morning again," Nathaniel said. "I hope they're not in the forest. I hear there's a wolf prowling around. I saw the remains of a deer yesterday when I was out with the sheep."

Zebedee handed over his lamp. "I'm going to get Yuseph and Yeshua. We'll go over to Sepphoris. Someone has to have seen her somewhere."

CHAPTER TWENTY-FIVE

Nazareth / Sepphoris – The Rescue

Early the next morning, Mariam agreed that she would hike out to find help. Salome would stay in the cave and wait until someone arrived. Both of the women prayed hard that the wolf had gone hunting somewhere else.

Mariam had been gone only a few minutes when Ox poked his head into the cave. "Don't worry Sparrow. I've been here all night. Warhorse is trailing your sister to make sure she's okay. We always look after our own."

Salome struggled to her feet, crouching low as she hobbled out of the cave. "What happened to Leopard?"

Ox scanned the surrounding bush. "We recruited him in exchange for his life."

Salome scanned the bushes. "Is that what you're planning to do with me?"

The big man slowly wagged his head back and forth. "We know you have children. Maybe you could watch out for anything happening in Capernaum and maybe you could provide a little hospitality for a friend or two of ours who might drop in."

"Do you mean Parthians?"

Ox put up both hands as if warding off an attacker. "You know we don't like to use names." He handed a chest-high notched stick to Salome.

She took it and found her balance with it, tucking it under her armpit. "How do I get you messages if something does happen?"

"Same as before. Stuff it into the bread and our messengers will get it to where it needs to go. Keep it all hidden until someone sees you." He moved close, holding out a vine. "Let me tie this to that stick. It will give you somewhere to put your hands when you walk."

The fix seemed quick and she twisted the vine around her wrist, the stick, and then onto the crotch of the pole. "You know I'm not a Zealot."

"None of us like to use names," Ox said. "We're sons and daughters of the homeland trying to be free."

"I heard you talk about the stolen girls." Salome tried a few steps but still found the contraption awkward. "What can you tell me about Anthony's role with them?"

"Anthony? You mean the centurion? He has five or six men who help him capture girls from villages to service his men." He checked over his shoulder. "Since you killed Suetonius, Anthony has had to find his own girls. Lion's sister and cousin disappeared last month and we think that the centurion is behind it."

Salome winced. "There's an Egyptian named Hamurti who used to work with the stolen girls in the fortress. She still lives in Sepphoris and can tell you where they might be kept. Hide! Someone's coming."

Ox was out of sight when Nathaniel burst into the clearing and swept her up into his arms. Her crutch fell away. "Salome, are you okay? Everyone is out searching for you. I couldn't believe it when I found Mariam on the trail. What did you two think you were doing way out here on your own?"

Salome rested in Nathaniel's arms and then put her index finger to the end of his nose. "I was sitting here waiting for a hero to come and rescue me. I guess you win the prize."

Nathaniel chuckled. "I haven't been up here since we were young looking for berries. Remember that time I tried to carry you across the creek and we both fell in? Looks like I'm going to have to try and get it right this time."

"What about your leg?"

"It's your leg I'm concerned about. Stay still and relax."

Salome squirmed as he took the first wobbly steps. "Nathaniel, there's no way you're going to be able to carry me all the way home. I'm not a child anymore. Let me rest on your arm and I can hop."

Nathaniel adjusted his grip and set to walking. "If you haven't noticed, I'm not a child either. Why don't we take it a step at a time? You can hobble when the ground is a little more level."

Salome laid her head against Nathaniel's shoulder and settled in for the ride. She clenched her jaw tight while he shuffled across the logs and tried to distract both of them with mindless chatter.

A few minutes after crossing the bridge, running footsteps pounded on the trail ahead. Nathaniel was setting her down when Zebedee, Yuseph, and James rushed into view. "Salome, thank Ha'Shem you're okay," Zebedee said. "Nathaniel, what are you doing with my wife?"

Nathaniel stepped back with his hands raised. "She twisted her ankle and couldn't walk. I was helping her get home."

"Well, I'm here now." Zebedee marched up and possessively put his arm on her shoulder. "I'll get her back to Nazareth. You can go ahead and tell the others that she'll be back to make the supper they missed last night." He turned abruptly. "Yuseph, why don't you stand on the other side and she can lean on us as we walk home?"

And so, Nathaniel was dismissed. He backed away, gave her a nod of understanding, and turned to take the trail home alone. Getting back wasn't easy but at least with Yuseph and James there, Zebedee held his tongue. His quick staccato questions were met with equally brief answers. Yuseph filled in the gaps with stories on Sepphoris and Nazareth. Salome turned her mind to prayers of thankfulness to Ha'Shem for Ox, Warhorse, Wolf, and Leopard. Quickly, she tagged on one more name. Nathaniel.

Despite feeling unwashed, in significant pain from her throbbing ankle, and exhausted from a sleepless night guarding her sister, Salome hobbled into Nazareth, accepted the mobbing of the children, family and neighbors, and started to set about preparing dinner. Rachel clung to her until Zebedee ordered her outside with the other children.

Mariam wasn't too much better, as far as mental alertness, but she had washed up and now she ordered Salome to care for herself while Mariam prepared the chicken dinner. It felt good to strip down and wash with a basin of clean, cool water. She relished the privacy of being alone and soaked in the pleasure of having no demands for a few minutes.

It didn't last. She was reaching for her fresh underclothes when Rachel arrived outside the curtain to her room. "Ima, I dreamed of scary wolves howling last night and I cried but Abba wouldn't let me sleep with him. Can I sleep with you tonight?"

"Yes, little one. I'm sure you can sleep with me tonight. Please see if you can help Auntie Mariam with the dinner."

She was reaching for her fresh tunic when Leah arrived. "Ima, Abba says you were irresponsible for not letting us know where you were and now he says I'm not allowed to hike on the trails with James and John. I don't think that's fair. Can you talk with him?"

"Yes, I'll talk with him. He's right. I should have told someone. Would you please make sure everyone is called for dinner?"

She was reaching for her hair brush when Zebedee arrived. He flung the curtain open without announcing himself and she winced. "What are you telling your daughter?" he yelled. "I told her she was not to go hiking with her brothers and I mean it. What is taking you so long? Your sister is having to prepare the supper all on her own?"

Salome glared hard at him. She stepped into her sandals and limped toward her sister's outdoor kitchen. As she walked, she brushed her damp hair. Over her shoulder she said, "I think it's time for us to get back to Capernaum."

~ ~ ~

Anthony, seated on a log, was waiting for Nathaniel when he arrived home. He wasted no time. "Your daughter is looking better every day," he said. "I hear there are Zealots active in the area and yet I hear nothing from you. What am I supposed to think?"

The surge in blood pressure almost unleashed his tongue to the point of regret. Instead, a vision of the dungeon flashed and he took three deep breaths before sitting on a large boulder near his gate. "Were these Zealots in the village?" he asked.

Anthony smiled. "We're getting closer to breaking this ring. Since I'm not hearing anything from you, I have to assume that our lesson meant nothing and that when the rest go down that you will be going down with them. If I was the father of a daughter like yours, I would be much more careful about finding ways to protect her."

"I will do my best to protect her, sir."

The centurion rose from his seat and whistled. His stallion stepped out from behind a shed and walked up to him. "Shepherd!" Anthony said, as he climbed onto his mount. "I'm looking for a woman we call the Shadow.

She's young, mesmerizing. She was the face for the mosaic." He looked toward Sepphoris. "She betrayed me before and she's done it again. I was sure she came from Nazareth but one of my informants said they've seen her in Capernaum. I will give you the chance to choose whether I take the Shadow or your daughter." He galloped away.

Nathaniel spun, walked through his door, and hugged Hannah hard. "Sarah," he called. "You, Hannah, and Deborah need to get back to Cana. We can't stay here anymore. I have got to do something to stop this insanity before we're all destroyed."

~ ~ ~

Within a week, the fisher family from Capernaum were on their way. Zebedee refused to allow Rachel's duck to go with them and the tears from leaving were mingled with a deep-hearted grief that would not be quenched. Rachel gave the duckling to a neighbor girl who was holding it as they started the journey. The duckling flapped its wings hard and frightened the girl who released it. Before the bird landed, the village dog pounced and grabbed it by the neck. Rachel screeched as her Abba held her in place and urged the donkey forward.

The donkey cart swayed so much on the rough road that Salome, despite her limp, found it easier to walk with Leah and Rachel. *Is this how Nathaniel felt?* Rachel consoled herself with psalms and no one objected. The trip back to the lake seemed shorter than the first time Salome had taken. There was so much she hadn't noticed along the way—even if her mother had tried to point it all out.

This time they stopped overnight at a caravansary where a cage full of gladiators and Zealots were resting. The Romans worked to repair a wheel on the wagon while ignoring the screams and pleas of the men behind the bars. Six of the eleven were barely more than boys.

Zebedee was restless—pacing and looking at the captured men. "Why do they have to parade them past all our women and children? Why can't they kill them where they find them and get it over with?"

Salome was drawn toward the terror-filled faces. She snatched an apple, some grapes, and a few rye rolls out of her bag and hid them in the folds of her tunic. With an eye more on Zebedee than on the Romans, she made her way to the men. With a quick toss she flipped the food through the bars.

The reaction of the men shocked her as they jumped on the food and beat each other to get what they could. The cage rocked violently and the Romans pulled out whips and rods to lash at the men. "Get away from there," yelled the centurion as Salome scurried away, limping as best she could.

"What was that all about?" Zebedee questioned as she arrived back at her own campfire. "You need to stay here before those criminals all escape and kill you."

"They're hardly more than boys," she answered. "James could easily be among them if we weren't careful."

"Then keep your eye on that boy," Zebedee said. "If the Romans do get him, we both know who is going to be responsible."

The Romans pulled out before dawn and took their screaming carnival act with them. It was a mercy as no one had been sleeping.

Zebedee left several hours later walking with James and John so the journey for Salome was peaceful as the sun slowly rose in the sky. A deer and her fawn didn't even run as they passed.

As the women walked beside the cart Rachel sang,

"You have searched me, LORD, and you know me. You know when I sit and when I rise; you perceive my thoughts from afar. You discern my going out and my lying down; you are familiar with all my ways. Before a word is on my tongue you, LORD, know it completely. You hem me in behind and before, and you lay your hand upon me. Such knowledge is too wonderful for me, too lofty for me to attain."[5]

Salome soaked in the song, awed by the message. "Rachel, where did you learn that song, turtle dove."

Rachel beamed. "Aunt Mariam taught it to me. It's a song of our ancestor David. He was a great king you know."

Salome nodded. "Yes, I know. There's more to that song isn't there?"

"Yes. I only know some of it. Do you want me to sing it for you?"

"Yes. Please, sing me what you know."

"It's something about me being in your tummy."

"Really? Was Aunt Mariam talking to you about how babies are born?"

Rachel shook her head. "No, she was singing a song."

"Try hard to remember."

The little girl knit her eyebrows together, pursed her lips and then broke into a smile. "Now I remember."

And she sang in a lilting chorus that definitely sounded like Mariam.

"For you created my inmost being; you knit me together in my mother's womb. I praise you because I am fearfully and wonderfully made; your works are wonderful; I know that full well. My frame was not hidden from you when I was made in the secret place, when I was woven together in the depths of the earth. Your eyes saw my unformed body; all the days ordained for me were written in your book before one of them came to be. How precious to me are your thoughts, God! How vast is the sum of them. Were I to count them, they would outnumber the grains of sand—when I awake, I am still with you."[6]

"That is marvelous," Salome praised. "You're such a good girl for remembering these songs. You're going to be like your Aunt Mariam when you grow up."

"But I want to be like you," Rachel said.

Salome bent down and gave her daughter a huge hug. "Nothing would make me happier," she said. "You've been good enough to be loved like you are. Don't change anything."

"I don't think anyone can be good enough to be loved," Leah said. "There's got to be another way."

"How about if I love you just because you are," Salome said.

"I don't think you really believe that's possible," Leah said. "If you can show me how to live that way I might still believe."

Salome reached out and stroked her daughter's hair. "Maybe if you'd been singing the psalm like your little sister than maybe you might change your thinking."

I could have sung that," Leah chimed in.

"Why don't you sing me a different song that you know."

And so, they finished the next leg of the journey singing.

The sun glistened off the lake surface as they crested the hill and turned toward Capernaum. Dozens of fishing vessels bobbed lazily as the men plied their craft—calling across the water to each other on the success of their catch. Gulls and kingfishers dove into the thrashing flashes of silver as tilapia and other fish were netted and brought to the surface. Strangely, it felt more like home than Nazareth.

They were still quite some distance from the house when Diana came rushing up the hill to greet them, engulfing them with bear hugs. "The fish are back. I'm going to have a baby. I cleaned your house. Guess what we're having for dinner?"

Leah didn't hesitate. "Fish Stew."

Diana looked disappointed. "How did you know?"

~ ~ ~

From his perch above the pool, overlooking the valley, Nathaniel had watched the dust from Salome's cart filter away in the breeze just as he'd watched Sarah's horse-drawn carriage disappear the day before. Hannah's quivering lip and tears, a result of Sarah's anxious warnings for him to be careful, tore at him. He hadn't bid farewell to Salome.

Plans had been set. Five of them would shoot flaming arrows into the Roman barns and swoop in during the panic to burn the carts used to ferry the children to the coast. The Almighty could not condone the perversions of the occupiers and his daughter would not be targeted because of him.

All day, as the sun slid across the heavens, he sat watching. Two of the shepherd boys arrived before dusk to take the sheep to the pens and still he watched. The Romans moved like clockwork. At each three-hour watch they streamed out of the city and charged down the road in both directions stopping whomever they met. Within the hour they were back in the city walls.

The last ride happened shortly before the sun slid toward the horizon. His limp hardly slowed his gait as he raced across the road and the valley floor, into the forested hills below Sepphoris. The other four waited in place and handed him his weapon. A clay jar of pitch provided the coating for each arrow. A small rag wrapped around each shaft, coated with another layer of pitch. Nothing was said. The plans had been made. The Zealots had burned Sepphoris to the ground before and they could do it again.

The sentries along the wall made their pass, carrying small olive-oil lamps as they marched along the perimeter. There would be a very short gap when no one was close enough to see. The arrows were dipped, wrapped, and dipped again. A small lamp hidden in a canister provided the flame. They would have to be fast.

Nathaniel's hand shook as the first two Zealots lit their first arrows and notched them to their bow. He was third and performed the task as he had practiced. Five arrows sped over the wall and into the barn. They were dipping their third arrows before the shouts grew loud enough to create attention. Horses neighed, stable boys yelled, and sentries raced in their battle shoes toward the fire.

A shout at the gate when they released their fourth arrows betrayed their discovery. One of the Zealots used a rope to hoist a clay amphora with the bows and lamp into a tree, tied it off, and then the five split into five different directions. Nathaniel's limp was a significant problem.

Other Zealots, hidden outside the gate, with their own bows would attempt to slow the military response from the legionnaires and sentries. The horses wouldn't be able to navigate the forest trails they took. Nathaniel had carefully dug himself a refuge under the roots of a large cedar and he found it, moved aside the small bush he used to cover the entrance, nestled in, and pulled in the bush against the base of the tree.

Within minutes, dozens of feet pounded by. It wouldn't be long before Zealot arrows rained down from the other side of the city.

CHAPTER TWENTY-SIX

Capernaum – The Eloper

The first Parthian visitor came by a month later. He was dressed as a potter, complete with his wares. Zebedee was out fishing with James and John while Leah stood alongside Salome trying to skip stones, across the lake surface, like her mother.

"You skip good," the Parthian said in rough Aramaic.

"Practice," Salome responded.

"Looking for bird," he continued.

"What kind of bird?"

"Sparrow."

Leah stepped closer to him. "There are all kinds of birds. What does it matter which kind you find?"

The potter caught Salome's look. "Only want sparrow. Need to nest for night."

Salome nodded. "We have room. Come stay and we will see if the sparrow is near."

Leah fell into step with her mom as the trader pulled his donkey cart over the stony beach behind them. "Ima, you don't even know this man," she whispered. "Abba is not going to be happy. Why is he looking for sparrows?"

Salome looked over her shoulder and picked up the pace. "Ha'Shem calls us to be hospitable to everyone. Your Abba will understand."

Leah reluctantly took the man's donkey to the stable where she watered and fed it. Since Rachel trailed her, she picked up a brush and handed it to her little sister. "You're a big girl now. You brush the donkey. Brush him slow."

Salome left the two girls and rushed back to the kitchen where the Parthian sat. She poured a bowl of water and unstrapped his sandals. "Let me wash your feet," she said. "It is our custom. You have been on a long journey. Soak your feet for a minute and then I'll dry them."

"I bring message for Sparrow," the man said. "You give Ox. Many problems. Chinese silk. Romans."

"Give me the message but then sell me a bowl or something," Salome urged. "This is not a good time to be bringing trouble into my house."

Salome heard a stone dislodge right outside the kitchen door. Leah may have overheard. What would she be thinking? It was clear from the look on the man's face as he snatched out his dagger that he had heard it to. She motioned for him to put the knife away.

"Sell me something," she mouthed.

The man nodded and pulled at his woven basket filled with pottery. "Good piece, good price," he said to her while looking toward the door. "You take one."

Salome took the piece he held out to her. "This could be good for a sparrow's house. I get the message. I would love to wrap it up in Chinese silk and give it to someone special. Right now, I only need a soup pot."

The Parthian potter held out two.

She chose a large ceramic piece into which she could pour Zebedee's favorite fish stew. The stew bubbled in a copper pot hanging over the fire and five new loaves of barley bread baked against the sides of the oven. The aroma even made her stomach gurgle in anticipation. Looking at her nervous guest, she knew. She really was a long way from Nazareth. It was so hard to be good.

When she casually made her way out the door there was no one in sight. A freshly dislodged stone betrayed the fact that someone had been listening. When she reached the stables, Leah stood brushing the donkey with Rachel. Neither of them looked back at her.

By the time Zebedee walked through the door demanding his supper, the guest was already settled on a fresh bed of hay in the stables. Salome's secret stash of messages was concealed within a woven basket set aside for her menstrual cloths. Leah and Rachel washed up the bowls and sat on stools quietly in the corner.

Zebedee hardly listened to her explanation of the potter who had stopped by to offer his wares and to take advantage of their hospitality. He was too preoccupied with James in discussing another fishing boat they wanted to purchase. Salome finally sent the girls to bed and crawled onto her own sleeping mat.

Before the first rooster crow, she slipped out of the house. A small clay lamp flickered in her hand. She retrieved five eggs and stepped into the stables where she lit a larger lamp.

A lone figure slid out from the shadows. "He's gone."

"Leah, what are you doing here?" The eggs nestled easily into a basket.

"I should ask you the same thing." The girl picked a feather off of an egg shell. "What are you doing having secret meetings with men you don't even know? Abba would be furious."

Salome looked over her shoulder and stepped closer to her daughter. "The man wanted me to pass on a message to someone I know in Nazareth. He's a Parthian and he couldn't be seen because the Romans who come around here would crucify him for being who he is."

Leah moved toward the house before turning. "Is he like a Zealot?"

Salome threw a handful of grain toward the scratching chickens. "Maybe a friend of the Zealots but that's enough to get him in trouble. You must keep this to yourself."

Leah nodded. "How long have you been passing messages on for these strangers?" She picked up a broom and slowly swept.

Salome locked eyes with her, hesitating. "This is the first man who has stopped by our house with a message like this." A bucket of water was poured into the donkey's trough. "I didn't know he was coming. I don't want to get Abba involved so that if the Romans come, he can honestly say he knows nothing. Others have come before but only to pass on news for someone else."

The sweeping continued. It provided enough noise to cover their whispers. "The Romans could crucify you and us for helping the Parthians."

Salome gave a pat to the donkey and scooped up the basket of eggs. "That's why it is important that you and I look like we are good women doing what good women do."

"Ima, I'm scared." Her eyes backed her words.

"I know." She wrapped an arm around her daughter's shoulders. "I am too. Please say nothing to anyone."

"Okay, Ima. As long as you let me help you, I will say nothing. I need you to tell me what good women are supposed to be doing when bad men come to visit."

~ ~ ~

It had been five weeks since the raid on the fortress at Sepphoris. Nathaniel sheltered in Cana, rarely walking the streets of the town. His father-in-law accused him of laziness for refusing to tend his vines. Sarah urged him to get out and walk to keep his body healthy. Hannah lavished the attention he gave her through stories, teachings, and games. He focused his other time on tanning hides and stuffing the animals Uncle Zeke had dropped off to him.

Soldiers pillaged village and town alike in their pursuit of the Zealots. Somehow, Ox and his close-knit crew evaded betrayal through their network of spies and informers. The sons of Judas had withdrawn to the southern desert. Barabbas had moved his base camp across the Jordan and spent more time in Egypt, training new recruits. Anthony frequently dropped by Nazareth, pressuring anyone connected with Nathaniel. Four times, the centurion had visited Cana.

The effort with the four men had provided temporary relief of his desire for revenge but the emptiness inside quickly grew again. What else could he do?

Once, on a quick trip back to Nazareth, Aaron found Nathaniel standing at the edge of the precipice looking down into the pond. "Nathaniel, I think you're too close to the edge," he said.

He dropped his cane by his side. "Have you ever wondered what it would be like to step off the edge and fly down into that water like the geese?"

Aaron stood at a distance, waiting. "You're scaring me, Nathaniel. Your wife and daughters need you to be strong right now. The Romans don't know what you've done for us."

A flock of pelicans flew by and headed for the Great Sea. "There are some things even the Romans can't change," he said. "If our own people could have worked together for peace then things would be so different right now. I wouldn't have to worry about my girls growing up in a land where they could be snatched at any moment. I wouldn't have to worry about young men like you or Nahum being killed by our own freedom fighters." He shuffled back a half-step. "Life is so strange sometimes. I was standing right here that day I saw Salome run down into the woods. I followed her, took her dare, fell, and my whole life has been different since then." He turned and grimaced. "I'm not sure if what happened that day has turned out for the best and I'm not sure if I would follow her again if I had the chance. I have a good life and I don't want to give up anything I have. Aaron, if you have the chance, chase what you know Ha'Shem calls you to and chase it with all your heart." He picked up his cane. "Live without regrets as much as you can." He ruffled the hair on Aaron's head and moved toward the flock grazing nearby.

"I'll be here for you," Aaron said. "Live for what you love."

$$\sim \sim \sim$$

Parthians continued to drop in with their messages and soon Leah was caught up in the encounters. Salome exchanged their stay for work on a project she was constructing in the forest. One particular Parthian dropped by more often and Leah would disappear for hours at a time when he was near. One day, as Salome and Leah walked along the shore, Leah asked her mother about marriage, but Salome laughed and said she was too young to be thinking of such things.

Salome saved up some shekels from the weaving she had been selling at the market and purchased a small brass ring for Leah. "For all the secrets you will have to keep," she said.

"Thank you," Leah said. "As long as I wear this ring, I will share whatever secrets are needed to protect the men and the messages we guard."

Occasionally, the centurion Claudius, or one of his men, would walk through the homes—"checking for Parthians or Zealots"—and that always added a surge of adrenaline to their efforts at hospitality.

Sometimes, it all seemed a childish game like the ones she had played with Ox, Warhorse, Lion, Leopard, and Wolf so long ago. Or like the games she had played with Nathaniel and the other village children. The bigger world seemed so far away.

Then, Salome caught her daughter and the Parthian in the stable late one night, whispering. Only a single clay lamp lit the enclosure. "What do you think you're doing out here this late?" she asked.

Leah jumped and stepped away from the man, lowering her head. "Darius and I were planning how to pass on the next messages if things got more dangerous."

Salome glared at the Parthian before gently tugging at her daughter's elbow. "You can save the planning for the daylight. You should be in bed."

Leah stood her ground. "But Darius has to leave before the first light."

Salome stepped back. "Then we can talk the next time he comes." She waited a moment as the two youth exchanged glances. "This is not the kind of work I had hoped for you to be involved in. Come inside and we'll talk about this tomorrow."

Leah followed her mother reluctantly and crawled onto her mat without saying goodnight.

At the first rooster crow, Salome turned over lazily as Zebedee left to fish. James and John rummaged around the larder and took provisions for their morning's work. At first light, Salome heard Rachel getting up to feed the chickens and to pick up the eggs.

A minute later, Rachel stood over her.

"Ima, where's Leah?"

Salome propped herself up on an elbow. "Perhaps she is using the latrine—did you notice if she took any of her menses cloths? Maybe it's her time of month."

"No, Ima. She was finished two weeks ago." Rachel's fists were planted firmly on her little hips. "She was gone before Abba. She took her blanket."

Salome shuddered but stilled the fear that raced up her back like a line of pinching ants. "Perhaps, she's feeding the donkey."

"I already checked."

Salome slipped on her sandals and walked quickly out the door. The latrine was empty. She stepped quickly toward the lakeshore and prayed that a single silhouette may be somewhere within view. A few fishermen, some traders, and a mother washing her clothing in the lake were all she could see.

"Rachel, go to the edge of the forest and call for her." The throb in her neck was impossible to ignore. Her temples hurt. "Perhaps, she's with the other cousins. Check there. I'll ask if anyone else has seen her."

Neither the fishermen nor the washing woman had seen Leah walk past them. Images raced in her mind. She looked to the hills for flickering light but there was nothing to give her peace or hope.

"Ima, she's not there." Rachel hadn't put the pieces together. Leah was somewhere out of sight. But Salome knew. Her daughter had eloped.

She raced to the stable where the Parthian kept his horse. It was gone. The only thing left was a small leather pouch with a brass ring in it. Leah's ring.

Zebedee's fury and fists left her withered and hurting for days but nothing compared to the loss of her daughter. She took her own blanket and curled up in the cave Diana had shown her so long before. And she wept a lake full of tears. She would never be good enough now.

~ ~ ~

Aaron's words swam through Nathaniel's mind like netted herring. They struggled to be free but lay bound. "Live for what you love." He hadn't meant to scare the shepherd boy, just as he'd never meant to jump off the cliff. He was testing his ability to overcome his fear of heights. If he ever had to face Salome in a tree again, he could do it now without giving in to the inner quivering that had unbalanced him the first time.

Sarah shook him by the shoulder as he tossed and turned on his mat. "Nathaniel, wake up! What are you mumbling about?"

He opened one eye reluctantly and tried to focus on the blurry image of his wife in the first light of dawn. "What do you want?" he asked.

"Why are you muttering about living for what you love?" she asked. "I hate it when you thrash around with those nightmares. It seems that you're constantly dreaming about being caught by Romans or Zealots or lions. Maybe we need to move from this place so that you aren't under so much pressure." She tossed off her blanket and put on her robe. "What are you dreaming about this time? It better not be Salome again."

Nathaniel lay back with his fingers interlocked behind his head. "Aaron told me to 'live for what I love' yesterday when he saw me standing near the edge of the cliff. He thought I might be depressed and want to jump."

"What in the world would make you put your life at risk so that you scare a boy like that?"

"I used to be afraid of heights," he said. "That's why I fell from the tree and broke my foot. I wanted to prove that if I ever got up high like that again then I'd be okay."

Salome stood over him. "So, this is about Salome, after all. Is she really the one you love and live for?"

Nathaniel sat up and wrapped his arms around Sarah's thighs. "No, little deer. You are my love and the reason for my life—you and the girls."

Sarah ran her fingers through his hair and gently massaged his shoulders. "That's good because this is your last chance to get things right. I can live with the fears you have about Romans and Zealots and even lions. It's just that woman I can't compete with."

Nathaniel struggled to his feet and embraced her, laying her head on his chest. "From now on, it's you, the girls, the sheep, the grapes, and the olives," he said, chuckling.

She punched him gently in the side. "You do know how to win a woman's heart, don't you? Live for what you love. As long as I'm the one you love I can let you live."

CHAPTER TWENTY-SEVEN

Capernaum – Searching For Good

The hills vibrated again with shimmering waves of red, purple, blue, yellow, and white as anemones, cyclamen, lupine, and marigolds fought for space and sunlight. The abundance of new growth on cedar, olive, oak, and brush once again added to the artist's palette. Nearby, poppies, buttercups, tulips, sage, and thyme made their presence known. In the crook of Salome's arm nestled a handful of jasmine. This time there was no Parthian arrow to make her dive for the dust. She pulled out a dagger and dug out the barbed head of the missile that had snagged her cloak ten years before.

Diana had her own basket of flowers. She pointed across the lake toward the distant basalt hills. "One day I'd like to cross this lake and see what other people live like. I can't imagine my whole life lived within the boundaries of what I could see when I was ten. What are you hoping for while you live?"

Setting her basket down, Salome stretched for the sky and yawned. "I am hoping to live long enough to see my children's children grow up. I'm hoping to see peace in this land and no more children stolen for the perverse hungers of men. I'm hoping that I will finally learn to be a good wife."

Diana smiled. "That's so important to you, isn't it? I think you and Zebedee have your own pattern going. Tell me all the ways you've tried to be a good wife."

Salome held up her fists and raised her right thumb. "One, I've had Zebedee's children and haven't run away even when things were bad." She raised her right index finger. "Two, I've learned to make every kind of fish stew he likes and have fed him well even when we faced drought. Three, I've learned to be kind to his sisters and to help at their weddings and special events." She scrunched up her face. "I guess the most important thing is that I've gotten past my feelings of being trapped. I used to feel that I was forced to be married to your brother, that I was forced to have his children, and that I had to act like his slave. Now, I think that every day is a choice in which I can act to make a difference with whomever I am with—even with my husband."

"Those sound like significant things for any wife," Diana said. "I hope I can do half as well as you with Simon. Anything else you think I should add to my quiver of things to do?"

Salome raised her ring finger to join the others. "Four, I've tried to keep his house clean and provide hospitality to all he brings for dinner. Five, I've tried to overcome my fear of water so I don't lecture him every time he wants to take the boys out fishing." She raised her other hand. "Six, I've tried to support him in the expansion of our home and his business. Seven, well, that one is none of your business but I've got a few children because of it."

Diana chuckled. "What would you advise me to know about things a good wife shouldn't accept in her relationship."

Salome sat and sighed. "Do all you can to keep him from hitting and hurting you. Do all you can to keep him from humiliating you in front of the children. Do all you can so he doesn't take you for granted and treat you like a slave." She picked up her basket. "Take an interest in his world. Take time to talk and go for walks. Involve him with your children as soon as you can."

"I know things haven't always gone well for you," Diana said. "I wonder some days how you put up with so much. I know that Ox and Simon taught you how to fight and yet you never fight back. Do you think a wife always has to put up with her husband's temper?"

"A good wife will do what she can to protect herself and her children—whatever that may mean. In my training with the Zealots, I've learned the importance of controlling my thoughts, my emotions, and my reactions. What I do with them I am learning to do at home."

Diana snapped off a long stem of grass and held it to her teeth. "Do you think Simon will come back for me? Do you think he'll end up like Zebedee?"

Salome set a hand on Diana's wrist. "Every man is different and every relationship is different. Don't try to compare yourself with anyone else."

She squeezed lightly. "Ask Ha'Shem to give you strength, wisdom, hope, and gentleness. Learn to talk with your husband about the things he loves. Look after your own heart and find things you enjoy to add resiliency and endurance to your mind and body."

"Do you think the Messiah will come in our time?" Diana asked.

"From what I hear, he's already here," Salome replied. "I'm not sure what he may ask of me one day but for today I believe that being a good wife is a start."

ENDNOTES

1   *Psalm 144:1 NLT (Tyndale: Carol Stream, Ill.) 2015.*

2   *Psalm 37:39-40 NLT*

3   *Deuteronomy 32:39*

4   *Psalm 37:1-7 NIV 2011*

5   *Psalm 139:1-6 NIV 2011*

6   *Psalm 139:13-18*

Printed in Canada